PRAISE FOR PATRIARCH RUN

PRAISE FOR STORYTELLING

"Truly marvelous. *Patriarch Run* is a breathless thrille   erary meditation clutching a straight razor behind its back.   page-by-page, this is one of the most assured debuts I've eve.   ;."
  — MARCUS SAKEY, BESTSELLING AUTHOR OF THE BRILLIANCE TRILOGY

"*Patriarch Run* accomplishes something few thrillers have achieved: it gets the guns right, and it gets the psychology of the gunfight right. Benjamin Dancer writes with a realism seldom seen in fiction."
  — LT. COL. DAVE GROSSMAN, AUTHOR OF *ON KILLING: THE PSYCHOLOGICAL COST OF LEARNING TO KILL IN WAR AND SOCIETY*

"Unsparing, violent and cinematic, *Patriarch Run* starts with a bang and doesn't let up. Benjamin Dancer is an immensely talented writer; his assured, lean prose and stark realism will appeal to fans of Cormac McCarthy and Don Winslow."
  — A. J. BANNER, INTERNATIONAL BESTSELLING AUTHOR OF *THE GOOD NEIGHBOR*

"Benjamin Dancer tells a story that moves at breakneck speed and draws you into the mind of a madman. The story is packed with realistic gunfights, and the bad guy presents an apocalyptic vision that haunts us because of how easily his nightmare can become our reality."
  — SCOTT PRATT, AUTHOR OF THE BESTSELLING JOE DILLARD SERIES

"*Patriarch Run* is a hard-shooting kick of a thriller. The first time through, I read it in a rush, my head on fire. But it's also a novel shot through with intelligence and humanity. So the second time, I put the fires out and forced myself to read slow and cold, taking in Dancer's every insightful word. This is a spectacular book, and I can't recommend it more."
  — BENJAMIN WHITMER, AUTHOR OF *PIKE* AND *CRY FATHER*

"From the first page, *Patriarch Run* will hook you, reel you in, pull you out of the pond, and leave you gasping for breath at the bottom of the rowboat!"
  — GREGORY HILL, AWARD-WINNING AUTHOR OF *THE LONESOME TRIALS OF JOHNNY RILES*

"Written with heart and guts, Benjamin Dancer's action-packed debut is as exciting as it gets."
  — ERIKA KROUSE, AUTHOR OF *CONTENDERS*

"*Patriarch Run* is a great novel. Fast-paced, frighteningly realistic, and on par with some of the best thrillers in the genre."
  — ISAAC HOOKE, USA TODAY BESTSELLING AUTHOR OF *THE ATLAS SERIES*

"Full of action and realistic gunfights, *Patriarch Run* is one heck of a ride. It takes off and keeps going, right up to the apocalypse!"
  — G. MICHAEL HOPF, AUTHOR OF *THE NEW WORLD SERIES*

"In this story of lives colliding, Dancer walks the line between action and emotion, weaving the two with a careful hand. Dancer's characters are as finely chiseled as the land where they make their home."
— RACHEL WEAVER, AUTHOR OF *POINT OF DIRECTION*

"*Patriarch Run* is a thriller with a soul. At first glance, it's a realistic spy novel, vetted and endorsed by national security experts. It's also a coming-of-age story that captures in intimate detail the universal longing for a father. And behind the heart-pounding plot and the rich characters, readers will find a thought provoking narrative that informs the way they see both themselves and the world around them."
— MAURA WEILER, AUTHOR OF *CONTRITION*

"*Patriarch Run* is, in its heart, an old-school western set in modern-day Colorado. Dancer's swift, efficient chapters come at you like machine-gun fire until the final bullet gives them all some peace. Just my kind of story."
— MICHAEL MADIGAN, AWARD-WINNING AUTHOR OF *DOUBLE DARE*

"*Patriarch Run* is fast-paced, artful thriller set amid a Rocky Mountain backdrop. Dancer writes, with precisely-described action and convincing detail, of gunfights, daring escapes, and harrowing rescues, as well as the love that keeps a mother and son seeking each other long after less indomitable souls would have given up."
— JENNY SHANK, AUTHOR OF *THE RINGER*, HIGH PLAINS BOOK AWARD WINNER

"Gripping thriller from the very first page! One of those rare novels where the story and characters are equally riveting."
— STEVE RICHER, AUTHOR OF *THE PRESIDENT KILLED HIS WIFE*

"*Patriarch Run* is a page–turner that also gives pause. Benjamin Dancer takes readers to a small town where buffalo still roam to set spy versus spy and to ask big questions: is it more important to protect our children, to prepare them for life's cruel realities, or to make a better world for us all? Dancer suggests it's not only whether we survive that matters, but how we live."
— CARA LOPEZ LEE, AUTHOR OF *THEY ONLY EAT THEIR HUSBANDS*

PRAISE FOR REALISM

"The description of the vulnerabilities of our infrastructures, especially that of the often neglected-to-mention vulnerability of our food supply system due to its dependency on the long term availability of electricity, seems to me both accurate and thought provoking. "
— DR. MICHAEL J. FRANKEL, FORMER EXECUTIVE DIRECTOR OF THE EMP COMMISSION; FORMER ASSOCIATE DIRECTOR FOR ADVANCED ENERGETICS AND NUCLEAR WEAPONS

"*Patriarch Run* captures the vulnerability of our nation's critical infrastructure. In this case the fiction is as frightening as the reality. A seemingly futuristic story about a new way of warfare, played out against a seemingly futuristic background of disillusioned patriotism, divided personal loyalties, and identity crisis—except Dancer understands that the future is now!"
— DR. PETER VINCENT PRY, AUTHOR OF *BLACKOUT WARS*, EXECUTIVE DIRECTOR OF THE EMP TASK FORCE ON NATIONAL AND HOMELAND SECURITY, SERVED IN THE CIA

"My friend Tom Clancy taught us how fiction can illustrate important truths—if we are willing to pay attention. This book captures the extent of the vulnerability of our nation's critical electric infrastructure to EMP and cyberattack."

— PETER HUESSY, PRESIDENT, GEOSTRATEGIC ANALYSIS; SENIOR DEFENSE CONSULTANT, AIR FORCE ASSOCIATION; VISITING PROFESSOR, US NAVAL ACADEMY

"Not only is *Patriarch Run* an entertaining read filled with intrigue and human drama, it captures, in realistic detail, the existential threat hanging over our nation. Benjamin Dancer has done his homework. He gets the facts right about the vulnerability of the power grid. That part of the story isn't fiction."

— DREXEL L. SMITH, FOUNDER OF DREXEL CONSULTING GROUP, EXPERT IN TEST AND EVALUATION OF CRITICAL EQUIPMENT FOR AEROSPACE, DEFENSE, AND ENERGY

PRAISE FOR COMING-OF-AGE THEME

"In *Patriarch Run* we have a first-rate novel, full of intrigue, excitement and gorgeous prose, as well as a gripping exploration of our gendered culture and the poignant moments and difficult decisions entailed in coming of age. Without being heavy-handed about the right choices, Dancer provokes our much needed questioning of the rules by which we live."

— TERRY A. KUPERS, M.D., PROFESSOR AT THE WRIGHT INSTITUTE, AUTHOR OF *REVISIONING MEN'S LIVES* AND *PRISON MADNESS*

"*Patriarch Run* is a compelling coming-of-age story that explores the universal longing for a father."

— DAVE STALLS, CO-FOUNDER OF STREET FRATERNITY

"This thoughtful thriller invites readers to consider both motherhood and fatherhood on multiple levels—emotional, psychological, even practical. A gripping coming of age story, *Patriarch Run* demonstrates the real meaning of mature self-acceptance in the face of terror, trauma and abandonment."

— GLORIA DEGAETANO, FOUNDER AND CEO, PARENT COACHING INSTITUTE

"*Patriarch Run* is an extraordinary literary achievement packed with intrigue, suspense, and soul. At its heart, this is a story about boys and fatherhood; about coming-of-age and self-acceptance. This is a perfect read for young men who are questioning what type of man they want to be."

— CAROLINE HELDMAN, SOCIAL JUSTICE PROFESSOR, ACTIVIST, AND AUTHOR

PRAISE FOR SUSTAINABILITY THEME

"Benjamin Dancer has illustrated that our greatest villain is overpopulation. Can the global community confront this most daunting adversary—too many people on a limited planet?"

— PAUL R. EHRLICH, BING PROFESSOR OF POPULATION STUDIES EMERITUS; PRESIDENT, CENTER FOR CONSERVATION BIOLOGY

"*Patriarch Run* reminds us that progressive, human-rights enhancing initiatives that help women and men plan their families are the best option for slowing down and eventually halting global population growth."

— WILLIAM RYERSON, PRESIDENT OF POPULATION MEDIA CENTER, CEO OF POPULATION INSTITUTE

PATRIARCH RUN

PATRIARCH RUN

A Novel

BENJAMIN DANCER

A Division of Samizdat Publishing Group

CONUNDRUM PRESS: A Division of Samizdat Publishing Group.
PO Box 1353, Golden, Colorado 80402

Originally self-published in 2014 as a paperback with the same title.

For more information, email info@conundrum-press.com.

Conundrum Press online: conundrum-press.com

print ISBN: 978-1-942280-22-4

epub ISBN: 978-1-942280-32-3

mobi ISBN: 978-1-942280-33-0

Library of Congress control number: 2016939808

Conundrum Press is distributed by Independent Book Group: IPGBOOK.COM

To fathers and mothers and sons and daughters
who are trying to figure out who it is they want to be.

WASHINGTON, D.C.
A FEW WEEKS AGO

He staggered past burning vehicles. An old woman sat rocking on the curb, hugging her chest. Her cheek was covered in blood. A sedan was upside down, on top of another. He moved past emergency crews delivering aid to the burned and bleeding, past ambulances and fire trucks, and turned down the first street he came to.

Dizzy, he stopped to catch his balance and saw his reflection in the glass door of a storefront. It was a man he did not recognize. His green parka and beard were splattered with blood. His shoulders were gray with ash.

He looked at himself again. He had no idea who he was. All he could remember was feeling nauseous.

As he searched his pockets for an ID, he saw a man round the corner, black mask pulled over his face, drawing a submachine gun from his leather jacket.

He opened the glass door before him and stepped into a bank. Then he noticed the cameras and regretted his choice. That the gunman was tailing him suggested he had been the target of the bombing. What else did he know?

There were no customers inside the bank, and the employees were standing opened-mouthed at the street windows, staring at him.

He stumbled through the lobby looking for another exit.

A woman in a red blouse said, "He's been hurt."

He tried to go further back in his memory, further back than the nausea. He remembered vomiting. He could still taste the bile. At the time, he had been handcuffed in the backseat of a leather-trimmed SUV. Was that before or after the blast? He couldn't remember.

He felt warm steel against the crest of his hipbone and remembered the Colt Commander in his waistband. The heat meant the weapon had been recently fired.

He pushed a sticky palm to his temple, bringing him back to his present situation. If he killed the masked gunman, he might have time to take the bank's CPU with the camera footage, but he wasn't sure that would help: the bank employees could ID him. He could kill the employees, but that didn't seem prudent. He didn't know for whom he was working, which meant he didn't know the rules of engagement.

He passed the open vault, saw the green sign identifying the emergency exit, and bolted down the corridor.

He heard shouting in the lobby and knew the gunman had entered the bank. He slammed his palm into the bar on the exit and felt as if his skull might splinter from the force of the alarm. He was in an alley and coerced his legs to sprint for the nearest street corner.

Bullets ricocheted off the brick around him, but he did not look back. He turned the corner, crossed to the far lane of traffic, and broke the driver's window of a red 1968 Ford Mustang with the grip of his pistol. He opened the door, pulled out the driver, and commanded him at gunpoint, "Lie down! Now!"

He slid in and gripped the wheel.

The rear window shattered. Bullets pierced the sheet metal of the Fastback. Without shutting the door, he jammed the accelerator to the floorboard and skidded around the corner.

PRESENT

Billy sat the horse with his binoculars and glassed Keigwin's pasture. It was empty but for the windmill. He glassed the dirt road separating the two properties then turned the mare. Patriarch Peak was white above timberline. He rode the fence until he came to where it had been trampled by Moses. The steel post was slanted like grass in the wind.

The fact that the herd wasn't in Keigwin's pasture bled the urgency from the morning's work, but not the exasperation. The fence wasn't adequate for sheep, let alone bison. And there was no capital to do anything about it.

When Billy heard his mom's voice, he turned the mustang and rode toward the house.

He saw her holding his boots, standing beside the flagpole he had erected a few years after his father disappeared.

He rode past the east water tank, which was covered with a thin layer of ice, and raised his binoculars to search the pasture on the other side of the highway. He saw cattle feeding on the steep mountainside. There was a belt of timber above the pasture, and jutting high above the trees was the tallest of three snow-dusted, craggy peaks known as the Matriarchs. All three towers of granite rose well over 13,000 feet. Rock walls and steep talus fields made the mountains to the east impenetrable to bison.

His mother's 4,000-acre ranch, Patriarch Run, was situated at the base of Patriarch Peak, which formed an even more formidable barrier to the west. It was the second highest summit in the Rocky Mountains. The ranch took its name from the avalanche chute that buried the original town of Patriarch on a Sunday morning.

The nearest pass over either mountain range was seven miles down stream, toward town. Which meant that the only practical migratory route available to a herd of American bison followed the north-south course of the valley.

It was Billy's habit, when Moses led the herd over the fence, to rule out the worst-case scenario: that the herd might head into town. He glassed as far as he could see in that direction. Then he turned the horse and searched the shoulders of the two-lane highway that accompanied the serpentine path of the Patriarch River along the valley bottom. He found the dirt road he was looking for in the binoculars and followed it up to the entrance of the ranch.

A black SUV was parked outside the gate.

Billy looked back toward his mom then glassed the SUV. Despite the darkened windows, the rising sun flooded the cab with light.

The driver was glassing him back.

SHE HANDED HIM THE COFFEE FIRST. BILLY DRANK IT IN A GULP. SHE TOOK the cup and gave him a hot burrito wrapped in tinfoil. He put it in his coat pocket.

"They weren't in Keigwin's pasture."

"What about the aspens?"

"Nope."

She nodded.

"I'm gonna check the willows next."

"You're gonna go to school."

Billy sat bareback on the buckskin mare, listening to the flag above him whip in the wind.

"From now until the end of May, you're gonna go to school. Graduate and you can do as you please." She held up his boots and socks. "It can't be more than thirty degrees, Billy."

Billy turned his head, and she followed his gaze to the stone house. The sheriff was standing on the porch buttoning his uniform.

Billy was twelve before he understood that the sheriff's visits to Patriarch Run contained more significance than his concern for the new calves or the condition of the fence. He had always hoped the sheriff and his mom would marry, but they never did. He never heard them speak of it either.

Billy lifted his chin. "Sheriff." It had become a term of affection.

Regan shook his head at the sight of the bare feet and smiled. "Mornin', Billy."

Billy took the white socks from his mom and, without getting off the mare, pulled them on. Then he took the boots and pulled them over the cotton socks.

"You're gonna be late for school." She slapped the mare's flank and the mare stepped forward. "We'll take Moses to the butcher this afternoon."

Billy turned the horse, rode past his mom, and said, "The black SUV is back."

MAIDEN TOOK THE TRAIL THROUGH THE BUDDING ASPENS, AND BILLY DID nothing to change the horse's mind. The path was deeply troughed, and the shaded aspects were covered in frozen mud and snow.

The trail crossed the namesake of his mother's ranch, the Patriarch Run. The avalanche chute was created in 1886 by a mining operation that triggered a rockslide near the top of the mountain. That rockslide removed the only barrier between the original townsite of Patriarch, Colorado, and the estimated 200,000 tons of rock and snow that would, the following winter, bury the headquarters of the mine and all but one of the town's 198 inhabitants. The only survivor, Antoinette Brown, was the whore-turned-prophet who warned the people of Patriarch that God would use not only their avarice, but their ignorance of his laws as a means to their destruction.

Billy was nine years old the last time he saw his father, fourteen the day he joined the JROTC. Before he and Sally got together, college seemed like a fool's errand. It was his intention to graduate high school, join the United States Marine Corps, and apply as a candidate to the Navy SEALs.

That was until January. He had no idea what he would study, but if Sally had her mind set on the university in Gunnison, he wasn't about to go somewhere else and lose her to a more ambitious suitor. It took him about a week to figure that out. The Monday after she sent in her college application, he downloaded the paperwork and followed her application with his own.

Billy stopped the horse in the ponderosas across the parking lot from the high school where the mare liked the forage. He slipped off the horsehair rope he used for reins and bridle as he dismounted and hobbled her, all in one motion. The five-gallon water bucket was spilt in the grass. He picked it up and walked down the hill to the Patriarch River.

When he crested the hill, he saw Sally shut the door to her steel blue 2007 Jeep Wrangler and start toward the ponderosas. Billy put down the bucket of water and stroked the mare along the withers.

"Hey, Maiden." The horse turned her head to Sally, who fed her a carrot. "There's a bonfire up at Miner's Creek Saturday night."

"Yeah."

"Wanna go?"

"Sure."

They held hands as they walked through the new cars in the parking lot, then through an assortment of older, well-maintained Subarus in the staff designated spaces.

"The herd got out again," Billy told her.

"I know. Your mom texted me."

"Texted you?"

"She told me to tell you they were over by the beaver ponds. She thought they were spooked."

Billy didn't tell Sally about the SUV.

Sally opened her phone and read the display. "She's herdin' them with the truck now."

"If Moses wasn't such a perfect stud . . . "

"What are you gonna do with him?"

A McDonald's bag blew past their feet onto the patio and stopped against the flagpole. Billy picked it up then looked at the flag.

"I expect we'll barbecue a few pounds of him at Miner's Creek Saturday night."

Billy opened the door for Sally and followed her into the school. Some of the boys walked in a wide, impractical, and shuffling gait. They wore the crotches of their jeans at their knees. Their round asses, in brightly colored boxer shorts, hung out over the tops of their belts. Besides his boots and white, cotton socks, Billy wore tight, bootcut Wranglers and a leather belt. He tucked his denim shirt into his jeans, wore a Cabela's baseball hat and an unzipped, brown Carhartt coat. Some of the boys wore lipstick and mascara. They dyed their hair unnatural colors and wore their bangs in their faces. Billy wrestled, swam, ran track, played baseball, basketball, and football. He was friends with them all, but understood none of them, least of all the punks and anarchists.

Sally had a level head and avoided the drama of what so-and-so was wearing. She didn't forward dirty pictures of other kids on her phone or worry about who was sleeping with whom. Sally had good grades, good friends, and ambition. From the eleven months Billy had been with her, he had learned everything he liked in a woman.

The human traffic was flowing to first period. Kids were texting while they walked, while they talked, while they drank out of Starbucks cups. The boys waddled like geese, one hand on their belt buckles to hold up their jeans.

Dan and Eric occupied the Senior Bench. Eric reeked of weed. His face was barely visible beneath a hoodie.

"Some guy was looking for you." Dan spat tobacco juice into a Mountain Dew can.

Billy dropped the McDonald's bag in the trash. "Who?"

"He had an accent."

The five-minute bell rang.

Billy pulled on Sally's hand. "Come on."

Sally opened her phone. "Your mom wants to know what time you can be home."

"Three o'clock if I miss practice."

She texted the response and hugged Billy outside her physics class. "See you at lunch."

He kissed her on the lips and turned down the hall.

ENGLISH WASN'T A SUBJECT BILLY EVER CARED FOR, NOT UNTIL HIS SENIOR year. Nobody knew how old Mr. Stathopoulos was. He looked seventy, maybe eighty. The old man had worn the same pair of wool slacks every day since September.

Billy stepped through the doorway as the tardy bell rang and sat in the front of the classroom next to the window, where he could see Maiden in the trees.

Mr. Stathopoulos opened the lesson by reading from the Bible, "So God said to Noah, 'I am going to put an end to all people.'" Without reading any more of the text, the old man looked up and asked, "Why? What for?"

Billy was still searching his homework for the line. Nobody answered the question.

Mr. Stathopoulos shut his book.

A girl sitting in the middle of the room offered, "It says they were corrupt."

Mr. Stathopoulos nodded. He shuffled in his slow, unsteady gait to her desk and tapped his knobby index finger on her text. "And full of violence."

Someone offered, "The flood was a punishment."

"Or was it?" The teacher stood in the center of his classroom, holding the book to his chest. "How can we be sure?"

"We just read it."

"But . . . " Mr. Stathopoulos' eyes lit up.

"But what?" someone asked.

He shuffled to the back of the room and searched his bookshelves. Students twisted in their desks to look at the eccentric old man. He never gave grades, never took attendance, but he assigned more reading, more papers than any teacher anybody had ever heard of.

"But what do the other myths say?" He pulled out a leather-bound collection of ancient Mesopotamian texts. "There is always another story."

Billy's face wrinkled.

Mr. Stathopoulos spoke softly, almost to himself, as he shuffled to the front of the classroom. He kept his balance by putting his hand on the shoulders of the male students. "The Epic of Atrahasis was written in the seventeenth century BCE, which means it predates the text we read for homework."

Every eye in the room followed him.

"According to the older account, the flood wasn't a divine response to human iniquity. The flood was a response to something much simpler, much more profound." He paused in front of the whiteboard for effect. "There were too many people."

The old man crossed to the window. It was as if he had lost his train of thought. Billy followed his gaze. A bearded man was moving toward Maiden in the trees.

As Billy walked across the parking lot, he focused his attention on the mare. Her head and tail were raised, her ears forward. She walked toward the man, who was no more than three or four yards from her.

The man seemed bewildered. He wore a green parka and muddy shoes.

Billy stepped over the curb, into the ponderosas, and saw that Maiden's nostrils and eyes were relaxed. Although he couldn't yet hear the man's voice, he saw the beard bounce beneath his chin and knew he had said something to the horse.

"Is there somethin' I can do for you?" Billy's tone offered no threat, but it contained an authority that made the man look at the ground and fidget with his hands. Billy closed all but seven yards between them. "She's a good horse by any measure I concern myself with."

The mare lowered her neck, and the man stroked her forehead.

Billy looked back, saw Dan and Eric come out of the high school, and felt emboldened. "But she's never been known to take so well to strangers."

The man stepped back from the horse and studied Billy from the corners of his eyes. His clothes were badly stained. They looked and smelled as if they'd been on his body a long time.

The mare followed the man and nuzzled his chest.

"Now if there's somethin' I can do for you, mister, I'd be happy to hear about it." It bothered Billy to see his horse acting so familiar.

The man raised his hands to keep them off the animal, but Maiden nickered and pushed him on his heels.

He said, "I apologize for any trespass."

When Billy heard the man's voice, he felt dizzy and thought his legs would fold. It felt like cracking helmets with a 245-pound fullback in the third quarter of the Homecoming game. His vision tapered. He balled his fists.

"I've had memory spells lately, and to be frank . . . " the man said.

Billy was too overwhelmed to hear the words. His mind was reeling, trying to comprehend what his body already understood, that this man was his father.

The bell rang.

Dan and Eric were holding their pants up with their hands and running across the parking lot. A few other students came out of the main entrance.

"She reminds me of a horse . . . " the man continued. "Maiden. Her name was Maiden, a buckskin mustang foaled in a spring snowstorm. We had to shovel our way to the barn in the dark."

Billy was just beginning to form the word dad with his mouth when the man asked, "Do you know where I might find a library?"

The question was as senseless as the rest of it. The shock Billy felt would have been no different if a stone had raised itself in the forest and begun to prophesy.

He heard the click of cars unlocking behind him and knew he was out of time, but for what? He had to avoid being seen with his dad. He didn't know why, but he had to avoid being seen.

Dan called his name. He and Eric were winded.

Billy's mind began to form another conclusion. His father did not know who he was. Billy had seen the condition in other vagabonds. For all his charm, the man standing before him was witless.

A black Town Car turned into the parking lot.

"I can take you to the library." Billy was surprised by his own voice. He unhobbled the horse and led his father down the hill into the trees.

He looked back. Dan and Eric didn't have the stamina to pursue him.

BILLY WANTED TO KEEP TO THE TRAIL, BUT TO GET TO THE HOUSE THEY HAD to cross Main Street. It'd be better to do that out on the highway. If they walked up the Patriarch River for a few miles, they might be able to cross the road outside city limits without being seen.

His father inquired about the names of the surrounding mountains. Billy gave him the answers. It was like humoring a child.

It wasn't until he was waist deep in the river that Billy asked himself what he was doing. He thought about turning around and taking his father to the sheriff. But he needed time. He needed to know why his dad had returned. He needed to know where he had been. What Billy needed was time to think. Then he realized the sheriff likely knew something already: Dan and Eric would have used their phones. Billy decided he'd call the sheriff once he got to the house.

Billy led the mare to the stony river bank and climbed toward the highway. His father followed. They crouched in the spruce trees, waiting for a window in the traffic.

When a northbound Ford F-150 disappeared around a wooded hill to their left, Billy said, "This is as good as it's gonna get." He stood and ran up the hill.

Maiden followed. His father was on the other side of the horse.

Billy had just climbed up to the gravel shoulder of the highway and wasn't yet to the asphalt when he heard a vehicle approaching from the south. It was too late to stop. He fought against the weight of his soaked jeans and the water in his boots as he pumped his legs for the woods on the other side of the road. He was in the near lane when he turned his head to look.

The black Town Car barreled down on them. All eight cylinders roared.

Maiden galloped up the steep hill. Billy sprinted past the first trees and began to climb. Then he tripped and was on all fours.

Billy's father held him down. Dirt and pine needles leapt up from the forest floor. Although Billy heard the buzzing of the incoming bullets, he didn't make the connection between the noise and the tiny eruptions appearing on the ground. Unaware of the gunfire, he flipped over and tried to kick his father off.

That's when he noticed that the man's whole demeanor was transformed.

Billy went limp. There was a presence about his father Billy remembered from when he was a child. It communicated authority—a self-assurance born of competence—something Billy had not seen in anybody else but the sheriff.

His father was on his belly, covering Billy's torso with own. "Stay down."

There was smoke coming from the parked wheels of the Town Car. Both the driver and passenger doors were open.

His father flipped over and drew a stainless-steel Colt Commander from a shoulder holster.

The driver of the Lincoln was firing a semi-automatic pistol.

Billy saw the muzzle leap in his father's hands, heard him fire two shots that sounded like one long shot, then a third. All three ejected cases were simultaneously in the air.

The Town Car's passenger was crouched and shooting a pistol over the black, polished hood.

Billy saw the Colt's muzzle leap again in his father's hands, two shots. His ears were ringing when his brain finally put it together: they were in a gunfight. Billy started crawling for a tree.

"Let's go," his father said.

Billy looked back at the highway, stunned by the sudden silence. The driver was slumped on the asphalt under the door. The passenger was no longer visible. Billy knew most gunfights were decided quickly, but he hadn't even had a chance to move.

Through the spruce trees, he saw a black SUV slowing to a stop.

"Come on." His father was climbing the hill above him.

He didn't think the gunmen would've come up the hill, and he certainly wouldn't have killed them if it weren't for the terror-stricken kid running up the longest shooting lane in the trees. The kid was fast, and if he hadn't caught him, it would've been an ugly scene.

He still could not remember anything from before the bombing and little since. He didn't know where he was or why he had come to these mountains. Worst of all, he didn't know what the consequences of the two corpses on the highway might be.

What did he remember? That it was important not to kill the gunman in the bank. He must have made a mistake: how else did they find him?

He had been shot and needed to treat his wounds.

He put a fresh magazine in the Colt. Then he secured the weapon in the holster with only his left hand, which was an awkward movement. He let the parka slip off his shoulders and down his arms to the grass. Both sleeves of his brown shirt were stained black with dried blood.

He heard the kid, out of breath, before he saw him. Then the kid came over the top of the hill and stooped, both hands on his knees.

He would have to get him to safety before things got worse.

He tore off his right shirtsleeve and twisted his arm to examine the wounds in his triceps. Then he unbuttoned his shirt.

Y<small>OU DON'T KNOW WHO</small> I <small>AM, DO YOU?"</small> B<small>ILLY ASKED.</small>

"Nope."

Billy looked at his father's wounds. One of the bullets had gone through his arm and into his rib cage. "What about those two guys on the highway?"

His father didn't answer.

Whatever Billy's life was before he looked out that classroom window, it wasn't that anymore. Any ideas he had about his past, his father, his future were gone with nothing to replace them. Billy opened his pocket knife, cut the sundered shirtsleeve into a bandage, and helped tie it around his father's torso.

Maiden was nowhere to be seen.

Rachel pushed the accelerator to the floorboard, and the two-tone, tan and buckskin 1978 Chevy Scottsdale leapt forward and swallowed a three-foot sagebrush under the front bumper.

Moses trotted for the aspens beneath the beaver ponds.

"Oh, no you don't!"

Grass slapped the chromed grille. Rachel bounced on the bench seat, cranked the steering wheel, and ran over willow shrubs and an aspen sapling. Then she smashed her foot into the brake pedal.

The pickup barred Moses's path.

Next to the bull, the vehicle seemed small. Moses was taller than the cab. From nose to tail, he was several feet longer than the bed of the truck. He grunted, swung his massive head, and trotted to get around the pickup.

Rachel threw the transmission into reverse. She watched Moses through the driver's-side mirror, playing the accelerator and the brake to keep the truck between the two-thousand-pound animal and the trees. She turned Moses in a semicircle.

He broke into a bounding gait.

Through the side mirror, Rachel saw the back end of the truck smash through a shrub of wax currant. The wheel jumped, the cab rocked, and her head nearly hit the triangular vent window.

She stopped, put the transmission in drive, and turned the truck so she could better steer the terrain.

Dust obscured her view of the other forty-three bison following Moses at a bound toward the south gate. She kept her distance, bouncing over badger holes.

Rachel was eight years old when her father was routed from the house by a fusillade of words. She hadn't had time to unwrap her present:

a wooden doll house, empty and about as tall as she was in 1975.

When she was twelve, she knew she'd have to leave like he did. She got a job as a waitress and moved into her own apartment when she was sixteen. She graduated from high school early then spent the next five years trying to survive.

She had paid cash for the Scottsdale on her twenty-first birthday, a present to her from her, the only gift she had received since 1975. As she drove the truck home from the dealer's lot, it occurred to her that nobody else was going to give her anything.

MOSES SAW THE OPEN GATE AND AVOIDED IT. HE WAS TROTTING PARALLEL TO the fence. The herd followed.

She gunned the V8 engine and smashed into an antelope brittlebush. The front end of the truck popped up. She rocked over sage and junipers and had to brace herself with the steering wheel in order to keep her skull from breaking the back window. Then she cranked the wheel, skidded to a stop, and cut the animal off.

Moses pawed the ground. Dust rose and drifted through his hind legs. He raised his head, opened his mouth, and bellowed. His tail stood erect. Then he lowered his head and charged.

Rachel moved away from the door.

The bull bounded, three or four feet between him and the earth, and landed on all four hooves, his sharp horns inches from the sheet metal. He looked Rachel in the eye and snorted.

Rachel aimed Billy's .44 Magnum at Moses's head and cocked the hammer. "You put a scratch on that door, and I'll put this bullet in your brain."

Moses grunted, nostrils flaring. His wooly face was huge between his brown eyes.

She could smell the grass on his breath. "Now git!"

Moses blinked, swung his mountainous neck, and trotted back toward the herd. He charged the first bull he saw—Hippie's Son. Their craniums collided with a crack Rachel heard from the truck.

Moses was pushing the younger bull steadily backwards when Rachel drove around them and pushed the herd through the south gate.

RACHEL UNLOADED THE REVOLVER AND PUT IT AWAY IN BILLY'S ROOM. SHE took off her denim coat, pulled the phone from her pocket, and called the butcher as she walked the hall to the front of the house.

"Todd, it's Rachel." She stopped at the living room window to look across the field at Moses. He was fighting another bull. "Can I bring Moses over this afternoon?" Rachel walked to the kitchen, laid her coat over the back of a wooden chair, added water to a saucepan, and set it on the stove. "Thanks, Todd."

She set a pot of beans on another burner and lit the stove. Then she pulled cornmeal from the pantry, set a package of ground bison in the sink to thaw, and cored a dozen Roma tomatoes.

By then, the water was boiling in the saucepan.

She blanched the tomatoes, pulled off their skins, quartered them into wedges on the cutting board, and pushed out the seeds with her thumbs. Her hands were trembling.

"Goddammit." She wiped her eyes with her knuckles. Rachel turned around, looked across the empty house, and began to cry.

She pressed her tomato-stained palms together around her nose, pulled her shoulders back, and flung off the tears. "Shit!"

SHE AND JACK USED TO MAKE GREEN CHILI WHEN THEY WERE LIVING IN THE yurt. Each night the chili froze, and each afternoon they put the huge pot back on the wood-burning stove.

By spring, she was pregnant. She was twenty-three years old and had never known anybody like Jack.

The day he vanished, taking nothing but the clothes on his back, two government men pulled up to the house in a black SUV. They asked her questions about events she knew nothing about. Then they searched her house and told her that Jack was a threat to her and Billy's safety.

RACHEL DREW A BATH. SHE PUT HER CELLPHONE ON THE COUNTER AND SAT on the toilet to take off her boots and socks. She would load Moses in the trailer once Billy came home. She folded her jeans and t-shirt and stacked them on the ceramic tile floor.

She had colored the clay to look like water. Then she rolled the tiles on her kitchen table. She fired them and laid the ocean in her bathroom on her fortieth birthday. When she turned forty-one, she installed a bronze bust of herself beneath the bathroom window.

Rachel tied up her hair and slipped into the steaming water. Like the charcoal sketches in the studio, the bust embarrassed Billy. He wouldn't enter her bathroom on account of it. Rachel never felt the need to defend or explain it. With each passing year, she was more and more generous with herself.

She heard car doors shutting. Rachel reached for a towel and stepped into the hall to look out the window. Two men were approaching the front door.

Her jeans stuck to her wet thighs. She hopped to yank them up, threw on her t-shirt, and looked in the mirror. She could see the color of her skin where the wet cotton clung to the tops of her breasts.

Rachel opened her phone as she stepped, barefoot, into the hall. She had received a text message. There was a Mercedes outside and men on the porch. She turned into the kitchen and grabbed her denim coat.

Billy heard sirens before he opened the backdoor to the house. He smelled smoke and ran to the living room. Through the open front door, he could see the bison by the water tank. Two patrol cars were coming up the road.

He turned into the kitchen. Thick smoke jetted from the saucepan on the stove. The counter tops were covered with food: sacks of corn meal and flour, tomatoes on the cutting board, a paring knife. He crossed the kitchen to turn off the gas on the stove, then froze.

His mom's cellphone lay open on the parquet floor.

Billy forgot about the gas burner and picked up the phone. He coughed as he called for her. He walked back through the house and saw his father standing at the back door. He was holding his side and looked to be in pain.

Billy followed him into the master bathroom.

There was a puddle of water on the tile, boots and underwear on the floor. His father put his hand in the bathwater.

Billy was still coughing. He crouched beneath the smoke and looked in her studio.

She wasn't home.

His father was looking out of his bedroom window. "There's nothing they can do for her."

The statement confused Billy until he saw the two patrol cars parked at the gate. He was relieved to see the sheriff get out and open it.

Billy turned from the window and saw his father going through the ammunition on his reloading bench. The sheriff had helped Billy build the bench, along with the shelving to organize his powders and tools. His father read the load data penciled onto a box of .30-30 Winchester cartridges. Then he lifted a Model 1894 rifle out of the wooden gun rack on the opposite wall. Billy watched him load the magazine and put the box with the remainder of the .30-30 cartridges in his parka.

Without saying a word about what he intended to do with the rifle, his father stepped out of the room.

Everything was wrong. Everything. He had no idea what had happened to his mom. He needed to talk to the sheriff.

Billy looked into the empty hallway after his father and bit his lip. Whatever it was that was happening, his father was at the heart of it. He knew it in his gut: if he lost him, he might never see his mom again.

He turned back to the window. The sheriff's patrol car led the deputy's. As they skidded around the corner and raced up the winding drive, a wake of dust billowed higher than the trees.

Billy was paralyzed by indecision. "Fuck it," he said as if to catalyze an action. Any action.

There were six hand-loaded .44 Magnum cartridges on the bench: hard cast, 300 grain wide-flat-nose bullets. He had cast them himself and knew that at 1,200 feet per second they would punch a gaping hole through just about anything. He swept them up and slipped his Super Blackhawk revolver into his interior coat pocket.

Billy found the burrito wrapped in tinfoil when he dropped the six cartridges in his right-hand pocket. He heard car doors shutting out front and remembered he hadn't turned off the burner on the stove.

The back door to the house was still open from his father's exit. Billy considered waiting for the sheriff again, but decided to stick with his dad. He stepped outside then thought better of keeping his mom's cellphone on his person. He checked the last number dialed: 9-1-1. One minute before that, she had received a text from Sally.

Billy dropped the phone and sprinted after his father into the aspens behind the house.

Rachel was wearing a hood over her head, and it was hard to breathe. Her hands were bound. When she slid across the carpet in the trunk, her head struck the wheel well. She heard the transition from asphalt to gravel under the tires and could feel the Mercedes accelerating out of the turn.

She found the escape latch with her foot and waited. They had taken her clothes at the house. She knew she couldn't get away. So she hoped to make a scene, to create witnesses. When she felt the car slow down again, she popped the trunk.

The light, even through the hood, was piercing. She heard the tires skidding over the gravel, and her body slammed into the seat backs.

Before she could sit up, she felt hands pressing on her. Her nose was jammed into the carpet. Someone bound her ankles and wrenched her arms nearly out of their sockets.

Then the lid of the trunk slammed and the light was extinguished.

The tear in the muscles of her shoulder and the carpet burns on her flesh were already forgotten. It was the silence that occupied her thoughts. The wordless efficiency with which the men had just hog-tied her quelled any hope she had of escape.

What Rachel couldn't understand was the why of it. She thought through the players Regan had crossed over the years. He had always performed his law enforcement duties for everyone in the county, not just those with influence. That idealism more than riled the power brokers of the business class.

Although Regan talked to her about the risks involved in his career, she had never worried about her own safety. She had worried every day for Regan's, and sometimes for Billy's, but never for her own.

She no longer heard the gravel under the tires and realized the car had stopped. They hadn't been driving long, so she figured they were somewhere in town. She heard voices, Mexican accented Spanish. The Mercedes rocked on its suspension. One of the doors shut. She could see light again through the fabric of the hood. Then a pair of arms pulled her through the pass-through into the backseat. The friction reopened her rug burns.

That they didn't take her out through the trunk meant they didn't want to arouse suspicion, which meant there might be people around.

She lay on her stomach while they cut the restraints off her legs. The hood was removed from her head and someone covered her eyes with a hand. She was wrapped in a blanket, yanked from the backseat, and made to stand barefoot in the snow.

With her eyes covered, they carried her through a carpeted room. She hardly touched the ground. Then she heard a door latch behind her.

The hand came away from her eyes, and Rachel saw that she was in a dimly lit room with the man who undressed her at the house.

There was a queen bed with a rose duvet. A print of one of Vincent Van Gogh's oil paintings, *A Pair of Leather Clogs*, hung on the opposite wall. There was a stainless-steel nightstand, an armoire. Thick white curtains were drawn across the window. The bathroom door was open. So was the door to the empty walk-in closet.

It must have been a hundred degrees in the room.

A second man entered the room without looking at Rachel and dropped a knee-length skirt and wool sweater on the tile in the bathroom. He unsheathed a fighting knife and cut the plastic restraint off her wrists.

"Please," he said, pointing at the clothes with an open hand.

Rachel stepped into the bathroom. It was stifling. Someone shut the door behind her. The bathroom was lit by a row of glass block just under the ceiling. She dropped the blanket, pulled the crinkled skirt up to her waist, and examined the bleeding carpet burn on her elbow. Then she raised the thick sweater, let it drop over her head, and pulled it down. The high neck of the sweater squeezed her throat.

The fact that no underwear was provided did not go unnoticed. Rachel knew the men had taken her clothes to make her feel dependency.

They wanted her to know that they would decide when and where she was afforded privacy. They were trying to get inside her head.

There were no towels or toilet paper in the bathroom. There was no soap. She opened the medicine cabinet and found it empty. She searched the tin cabinet under the sink. Nothing. She looked around for something she could use to escape. There wasn't even a roller on the toilet paper dispenser.

She pulled at the neck of the sweater and stepped out of the bathroom.

The man who brought her the clothes was waiting for her. He cuffed her ankles then her wrists in front of her body.

Bᴵᴸᴸʏ ᴡᴀꜱ ʀᴜɴɴɪɴɢ ᴛʜʀᴏᴜɢʜ ᴛʜᴇ ᴀꜱᴘᴇɴꜱ ʙᴇʜɪɴᴅ ᴛʜᴇ ʜᴏᴜꜱᴇ ᴡʜᴇɴ ʜᴇ heard more sirens echoing through the valley. By now, the sheriff would be aware of both crime scenes, the one at the house and the gunfight on Highway 132.

He saw his father on the trail a hundred yards ahead and caught up to him.

His dad was holding his side, clearly in agony. "We need better cover," he said and stepped off the trail to climb into the dense lodgepoles above.

"Wait!" Billy was out of breath.

His father turned around, communicating his annoyance with compressed lips and lowered brows.

Billy met his glare. "I know you don't remember me, but I'm your son."

There was no recognition on his father's face.

"That house we just left," Billy told him, "you built it with my mom."

His father's mouth slackened, and his brows came together in confusion.

"You left when I was nine." Billy saw the question forming in his mind. "You're Jack Erikson."

The poise that had marked his dad since the gunfight was gone.

Billy reminded him, "We need better cover." Then he climbed off the trail.

Wʜᴇɴ ᴛʜᴇ ꜱʟᴏᴘᴇ ᴄʜᴀɴɢᴇᴅ, Bɪʟʟʏ ᴄᴏᴜʟᴅ ꜱᴇᴇ ᴛʜᴇ Tᴏᴡɴ Cᴀʀ ᴏɴ ᴛʜᴇ ʜɪɢʜ- way below. Its front doors were still open, and it was surrounded by fire trucks, two ambulances, and a half-dozen patrol cars. Traffic was backed up in both directions. Billy could see men in black suits climbing through the trees.

Jack spoke in whispers. "We need a hide site."

"A what?"

"A safe place to watch and wait until dark."

"There's a cave," Billy turned to point, "just beneath that outcrop."

"It needs to be closer to town, or they'll pick us up when we move."

"In the dark?"

Jack seemed impatient. "Yes."

Billy did not like his tone of voice. He did not like the idea of hiding, especially from the law. Everything was wrong.

"Who are they?" he asked.

"I don't know."

"What did you do?" Billy spat the question like an accusation.

Jack's mouth moved, but it took several seconds for him to finally articulate a response, "I don't know."

The Doppler sound of approaching rotor blades brought Billy's attention to a treelined ridge a few miles to the south. He watched the ridge until a black helicopter came over the treetops and banked east toward the highway.

RACHEL WAS ALONE IN THE BEDROOM. SHE WORRIED BILLY WOULD COME home from school to find the front door open, her clothes in the driveway.

She didn't know what kind of trouble Regan was in. But whatever it was, it was bad. And the last thing he needed right now was another worry on top of everything else. She knew him. Worrying about her would only cloud his judgment.

She looked at the window above the bed then back at the bedroom door, which was shut. She listened for a full minute.

When she didn't hear anybody outside the room, she sat down on the bed. Her wrists and feet were bound, so she had to roll onto her side and kneel on the bed before she could stand on it. She opened the curtains. The window was covered on the outside with black plastic sheeting. Rachel thought she might faint from the heat. She unlocked the window and attempted to slide it open, but the window sash was screwed to the side jam with three black drywall screws.

Shit.

Her eyes welled. She felt like she couldn't breathe and pulled at the sweater's neck. She needed a screwdriver. Something. A dime would do. Rachel slid off the bed and hopped across the room. She opened the armoire and searched the drawers. She lay on her stomach to look under the furniture and saw the shoe molding. That was something they didn't think of.

Rachel wiggled over the almond colored carpet like a worm. She used her sleeve to wipe the sweat from her eyes and shut herself in the bathroom where she began to pry off the floor trim behind the toilet.

If she broke the window with the trim piece, she could use the blanket to protect herself from the glass. But how could she do it quietly? She didn't know the answer to that question.

She'd start by pulling the nails from the trim. Rachel pushed the points of the finishing nails through the blanket, which she used as padding against the tile floor. Then she centered her bound hands on the piece of trim and pressed with the weight of her body. The wood lurched unevenly down the pair of nails until it quietly stopped against the blanket.

She heard the bedroom door brushing against the carpet. Someone had entered the room.

Did they hear her?

Rachel pulled both of the nails with her teeth and hid them in the waistband of her skirt. She flushed the toilet to make noise. Then she got on her side between the toilet and the wall and wedged the trim back into place.

She looked in the mirror. Her face was flushed. Beads of sweat ran from her brow. She mopped the perspiration with the sweater then opened the bathroom door.

A man she hadn't seen before invited her to sit on the bed. He wore black, military-style cargo pants.

Rachel hobbled out of the bathroom.

"I apologize for the circumstances in which we find ourselves, Ms. Erikson." His skin was white and his Mexican accent was of the aristocratic class.

The statement pissed Rachel off. "You mean you apologize for coming into my home, taking my clothes, and stuffing me in a trunk?"

The man looked up at the window curtains.

She cursed herself for leaving them open.

He turned and walked to the bathroom. The man looked back at Rachel and the open curtains then he kicked at the blanket on the floor.

"I accept your apology." Rachel hobbled toward the bedroom door. "I'll let myself out."

The man intercepted her and escorted her by the arm to the bed. "Please." He pointed his manicured fingers toward the duvet.

Rachel sat down. Sweat stung her eyes. "I can't see that it'd hurt much to turn down the heat."

He was trying to figure out what she had been up to in the bathroom. He picked the blanket off the floor. "Yes, it is warm."

"A wool sweater?" She pulled on the throat of the turtleneck. "You mean to tell me this is all you could find?"

He came out of the bathroom and opened the bedroom door. "I'll have an opportunity to look into the problem of the heat, Ms. Erikson, after we've talked. When you're in a more cooperative mood." He carried the blanket past a thin man with graying hair.

"Anything cotton would do," she said.

The thin man in the hall looked at her without expression then shut the door.

COLORADO
2002

Rachel never rode over the summit of the mountain because of the treacherous nature of the trail. It was against all rational judgment that she found herself on that trail now. At tree line, the horse stepped out of the spruce forest and onto the packed scree that made up the trail from there to the tundra. The mountainside below them gave way to granite cliffs.

The trail snaked along the top.

At the highest point among the cliffs, with nearly 1,000 feet of empty space beneath Old Sam's hooves, Rachel spotted two figures several hundred yards in the distance. She talked to the horse. Said she couldn't be sure, but it looked to be a man and a bristlecone pine.

The horse walked on. As they closed the distance, Rachel recognized the man and saw that he was untying a rope from the gnarled tree.

"You couldn't have picked a better view," she said.

Regan had looked at her once when he first heard the hooves on the scree, then he went back to his rope. Now he looked up at her face. He looked the horse over. Then he studied her eyes. She had divined his purpose.

He looked away. "Yeah, it'll do."

The two knew each other, but rarely had cause to speak.

"I don't mean to meddle, but it seems to me that the rope is ill-conceived."

Regan retied the rope to the tree, tested the knot, and asked, "How so?"

"Too much length and the wind, along with your own momentum, will lacerate your flesh against the rock."

He looked over the edge. "I thought of that as you were coming up. I shortened the rope."

"Not enough length, and it'll be slow and painful."

He studied the coil of parachute cord on the ground and said with very little inflection, "It looks about right to me." Then he walked over to a granite boulder.

"Seems you've thought it through,"

Regan sat down and pulled off his right boot. "We'll see."

Rachel reached behind her and took out a water bottle, drank some, then offered the bottle to Regan with a gesture.

He put out his lower lip and shook his head almost imperceptibly.

She capped the bottle and put it back. "Mind if I ask you a question?"

"Go ahead." He pulled off the other boot.

"Why the rope and the cliff?"

"Coyotes."

"I don't follow."

"When I was a kid, coyotes killed my dog. I heard the fight, but by the time I found her in the dark, they were already feeding on her guts." He took off both socks and stood up. "They pulled her insides out through her anus." He stepped over to the precipice and surveyed the valley.

"How old were you?"

"Six."

Rachel nodded her head, which he didn't see.

"With only the rope or only the cliff, I'd be left for the coyotes."

"But this way it's only insects and birds."

He spun to face her, his widened eyes betraying surprise or maybe alarm.

"Birds always eat the eyeballs first," she continued. "Must be a delicacy to them. The insects just want a womb for their maggots. A nutrient-rich source to give their young a good start."

Regan fidgeted with the socks in his hands.

"You could've picked a high branch."

He looked distracted, as if he was still digesting the other image. "I thought of that." He walked over to his boots, unbuttoning his silk shirt.

"Yeah?"

"A bear could cut the rope."

"It seems you've thought it through."

31

He took off his shirt, folded it, and set it on a rock. "We'll see."

Rachel looked back over the trail. "Well, I best be goin'."

"Okay."

She turned Old Sam and said, "Those are some fancy clothes."

"Yeah." He took off his belt. "The boots alone cost me eleven hundred dollars, and that was before tax."

"I suppose it's fitting."

"It seemed that way to me, too, down at the house. But after being up here, I don't think so." He looked out at the expanse beyond the lip of the cliff. "I think I'll be more comfortable without them."

"What are you going to do with those eleven-hundred dollar boots?"

Regan carried the clothes over to the bristlecone pine tree. He put the boots on top of the folded shirt, the socks inside the boots, and the belt around the boots. "Come back and get 'em if you like."

"Well, I best be gettin' along."

"Okay."

"You know my place?"

"I know it."

"We'll be sittin' down to supper around six. Sirloin and potatoes. If you have a mind to, you're welcome to stop by."

He picked up the loose end of the parachute cord and started tying a hangman's noose. "I appreciate that."

PRESENT

It was hard to breathe. Rachel wiped the sweat from her eyes.

The filtered sunlight in the bathroom was her only means of telling time. She thought through it again. There hadn't been any stairs. She was on the ground floor. If she broke the window above the bed, she could likely get out. She just had to plan it right.

What bothered her most at the moment was that she had to take a shit. She'd been putting it off since she saw the submachine gun on her front porch. But the moment was becoming unavoidable.

It's the little things.

Then Rachel realized she wouldn't be able to get anywhere if she broke the window. Not with the restraints on her ankles and wrists. She felt deflated. That she had failed to consider a handicap so obvious was disturbing. How long had she been in here?

She was dehydrated, she explained to herself. Her brain lacked blood and, therefore, oxygen. If she was losing her ability to think properly, what else was she failing to consider?

She turned the cold water tap in the sink. Nothing happened. She turned the hot water tap all the way over. Same result. She hopped over to the tub and opened both faucets. Nothing.

The only water in the toilet was in the trap at the bottom. The bowl hadn't refilled after she'd flushed it. She told herself that she was stupid for wasting the water.

She looked in the tin cabinet under the sink and felt the supply valves. They were both open. So was the supply behind the toilet.

For the hell of it, she flipped the light switch. There were no bulbs in the sockets.

That's it, isn't it? They're fucking with me.

Rachel hobbled into the bedroom, stood in front of the door, and listened. She turned the knob and was surprised when the door opened. The cool air felt like an open window.

The expressionless man studied her from his chair.

"Could I get a glass of water?"

He stood and shut the door in her face.

Colorado
2002

A<small>T SIX O'CLOCK, EXACTLY, THERE WAS A KNOCK AT THE DOOR.</small>

"Billy, can you get that?"

Billy came out of his room and saw the extra setting on the table. "Are we expecting company?"

"It's the sheriff."

Truth was, the idea had always been alluring to Rachel. She toyed with it, even courted it—but prior to the confrontation on the mountain that afternoon the idea had only been an abstraction. A strategic exit Rachel held in reserve. Seeing the rope in Regan's hand, the vertical space on the other side of that ancient tree, changed that.

It must have been the meticulous precision with which Regan prepared his single step into the eternal void that gave form to the abstraction. Old Sam was still descending through the spruce forest when a notion she had been digesting for decades suddenly crystalized in her mind. No one was given a choice about their birth—not the location, the circumstances, nor the time. Everyone, however, was given a choice about their death. One could either hold out until life was snatched away or decide for oneself that it was time to leave.

Rachel knew how she intended to play that card. To her, the choice was sacred. It was comforting, the knowledge that she had an exit.

Billy opened the door, "Hi, Sheriff."

They shook.

"Hey, Billy."

"Come on in."

"Sure smells good in here."

Rachel came out of the kitchen holding a knife in one hand and an onion in the other. "Make yourself at home. Billy, get him a beer."

"No thanks, Rachel. I don't drink."

"Get him a glass of water then. You eat steak, right?"

"Yes, I do."

Billy brought him the glass, and he emptied it. Billy filled it again and brought it back.

"Did you arrest anyone today?"

"No, I have the week off."

"Is that why you're not wearing your uniform."

"Yep."

"Those real alligator?"

"You mean my boots? Yeah, they're real alligator."

"You want to see my guns? I got a Winchester lever action in .30-30." Billy led the sheriff to his room. "But all my mom lets me shoot are the .22s."

Regan could tell by the bottles in the trash outside, by the color of her skin, that Rachel had been drinking. He knew about Jack and figured the drinking started after he left, sometime in the last six months. Whereas, Regan recently quit, as recently as six o'clock. He also knew she had taken to solitude. Whereas, he had taken to chasing women. Besides all that, he was at least ten years older than she was.

But he'd be a fool not to recognize it. Not to recognize that Rachel didn't like the road she was on, that she saw in him what he saw in her, an opportunity for redemption. Not that he viewed his vices through a prism of morality. He simply didn't like how it felt, didn't like what he saw coming. Up until today, he could only see one exit. Rachel was offering an opportunity to turn. There was no question in his mind—he was going to take it.

"When I'm eleven, my mom'll let me hunt animals bigger than a turkey. But I told her I'm ready now."

Rachel passed the butter.

Regan took a slice, which melted into his cleaved potato. Then he passed the butter dish to Billy, winked at Rachel, and asked, "What'd she say to that?"

"She said she believes me, and that I can get a big game license when I'm eleven."

"Sounds like that settles it then."

Billy hung his head.

After the butter came sour cream, then chives from the garden. Billy put a heaping spoonful of sour cream on his potato. Then a second.

"You aim to use that .30-30 on big game?"

Billy was excited again. "Sure do."

Regan looked at Rachel, "I could load it down for him. Take the bite out of the cartridge. Then we could work up the load slowly so that when he turns eleven, he'll be ready."

She played it stern. "I don't know. What do you think, Billy?"

"I think it's a great idea!"

"I suppose if the sheriff thinks it's alright, it'll be okay."

A timer sounded.

"That's the pie." She got up to tend to the oven.

"Rachel, this steak is as tender as the butter."

"That's kind of you to say."

Billy cleared the supper plates and Rachel brought the pie.

"How good are you with that 39A?" he asked Billy.

"Inside of thirty yards," Billy said from the kitchen sink, "if I can see it, I can hit it."

"I'll tell you what then. As soon as you can shoot a soda can off the fence four times out of five at fifty yards, I'll bring over some handloads for that .30-30 Winchester."

AT SIXTEEN, RACHEL UNDERSTOOD THAT THE DEFAULT SETTING OF HER LIFE was to age and become a copy of her mother. That the only way to alter that destiny was to be intentional about who she wanted to be, to make conscious choices.

The first choice she made was to move out. Before she did, she wrote a letter to herself in which she penned the line: "I want to be a strong woman so that I can be a good mother." She dated the letter to be opened on the day she turned thirty-six, in the hope that by then she would know what the words meant.

Rachel stayed away from parties. Paid her bills on time. She worked her way through college. She sought mentors among the faculty, in the literature she read. She consciously assembled from the characters in her life—both real and imagined—a collage, a vision of the woman she wanted to be.

It wasn't that she was eager to become a mother. It was that she wanted to prepare herself so that when the time came, she would be ready. In that sense, Billy had always been her motivation to grow, to live. That desire, to be good for him, guided her through nearly two decades of her life.

But it wasn't working anymore. She hadn't yet opened the letter she wrote, but she already knew that Billy wasn't enough. What she had lived for up until now simply wasn't enough.

It wasn't just that Jack was gone. That was a blow, no doubt. But the blow of his betrayal was magnified catastrophically by the identity she had chosen for herself. It was simply inadequate. She recognized that now. Life was so much more difficult than she thought, at sixteen, it would be.

THE THREE OF THEM TALKED AT THE TABLE FOR TWO HOURS AFTER THE leftover potatoes were cold.

"It's late," Regan said. "It was kind of you to have me." He stood up and shook Billy's hand.

Billy walked him to the living room. Rachel followed.

Regan gave them both a nod then opened the door.

"See ya, Sheriff."

"See ya, Billy." He stepped onto the porch and looked back at Rachel. "After you left, I realized I hadn't thought it through."

"Would you like a ride home?"

"I think I'd just like to walk. Think about how I'm going to spend my vacation."

"It's a good thing you kept those boots."

He was off the porch when he turned around again. No one had switched on the light, and in the darkness, Billy couldn't see the tears flowing over the sheriff's cheeks. "Thank you."

He was well down the driveway when she called, "You're welcome to supper tomorrow."

PRESENT

H̲ER HEAD HURT. SHE WAS AGITATED MOST BY HER OWN HELPLESSNESS. SHE needed to sit down. No, not on the bed. Rachel hobbled into the bathroom and sat on the toilet lid.

What time was it? Where was Billy?

AFTER WHAT SHE THOUGHT WAS AN HOUR, SHE MOVED AND SAT ON THE RIM of the tub. Rachel looked behind her and saw the mouth of the faucet. She stared at the faucet for several minutes before it occurred to her to use the chrome plated edge. She got on her knees inside the tub and tried to saw through the plastic restraints on her wrists.

Colorado
2005

Rachel met Ivelis Vizcaino on the shoulder of Highway 132. Ivelis was pacing alongside a Buick Electra. The hood was open, and she held a baby wrapped in a pleated coat.

Ivelis was slow to accept Rachel's offer of a ride into town. She looked at Rachel's truck, at Rachel's callused hands. She studied her eyes. They stood no more than a foot apart. Then Ivelis passed the baby to Rachel and asked for a moment to gather her things. She took a paper bag out of the backseat.

The baby had a flattened face and slanted eyes. Down syndrome, Rachel thought, and hoped Ivelis wasn't trying to raise him without a father. But she knew she was.

By the time Rachel parked the truck at the service entrance behind the Holiday Inn, she knew the baby's name—Agapito. She knew about the other children. They were three and four and deemed old enough to be left at home in the care of their six-year-old sister.

"Do you want me to call a tow truck?" Rachel asked.

"No. With some things, it's best to let them go."

It was the third time she had been late to work that week.

Rachel contemplated stepping through the steel door with Ivelis. She wanted to say something on her behalf, but knew she would only make it worse.

She asked, "What time are you done?"

Ivelis was looking at the hotel door. "*Será tarde.*"

"*¿A qué hora?*"

Ivelis finally accepted the offer, "*A las nueve.*"

Rachel came back twelve hours later and drove her home.

The next week she found Ivelis a better paying position as a domestic servant at the Tisch residence.

Rachel didn't keep a lot of friends. Ivelis was one of the few women she would call on the phone. At first, it was to practice her Spanish. Then she invited Ivelis and her four children to the ranch. She taught them to ride horses. She'd put Agapito on Old Sam and walk horse and rider around the pasture.

They came over on the last Saturday of every month until it turned cold. Then they started again the following spring.

To be truthful, there weren't a lot of women Rachel liked. She trusted fewer. The two would cook together. They stayed up the night before Billy's thirteenth birthday making tamales. They'd sit on the porch, Ivelis nursing Agapito, and they'd talk into the darkness while the older kids were out with Billy doing god-knows-what on the mountainside.

Present

THE METAL EDGE OF THE FAUCET WASN'T GOING TO CUT THROUGH THE restraints, not before she passed out. Rachel couldn't concentrate. She could barely sit up.

Her breath was raspy, her tongue swollen. She waited for her vision to stop spinning. Then she looked in the mirror: her face was flushed and clammy, but there was no more sweat. A rash was spreading up her neck.

She tried to remember what she knew about heatstroke. It wasn't much. She needed water.

The dizziness didn't quit.

She felt as if she were being choked by the wool sweater. She grabbed at the neck with both hands and tore the fabric to relieve the pressure. Then she turned and saw the guard spinning with the bathroom doorway. Rachel put her hands on the counter and waited for the dizziness to pass.

The sweater was torn down to her chest, and the guard was grinning and nodding his head.

Rachel narrowed her eyes and squared her shoulders to face him.

He looked at his feet and went back to the hall.

COLORADO
2007

IVELIS DISAPPEARED TWO MONTHS AFTER AGAPITO'S THIRD BIRTHDAY. Stephan Tisch was spreading the rumor that she was in Mexico with a new lover. That Ivelis would abandon her four children, leave without talking to anyone—it didn't make sense.

Rachel brought the children into her home. A week went by. Then a honeymooning couple from Rhode Island put the rumors to rest. They were pedaling a tandem bicycle on the path that connected Main Street to the resort when they swerved to avoid the mongrel dog that was dragging Ivelis's remains out of the forest.

REGAN FOUND RACHEL THAT EVENING IN THE BARN BRUSHING OLD SAM. HE stood in the doorway, his left hand on the timber frame. He was still wearing his sheriff's uniform.

"What is it?" her voice was flat.

Regan stepped into the barn and took the brush from Rachel's hand. "What?"

"The coroner reported the cause of death as undetermined."

"But how . . . "

"I don't know. He claimed decay, loss of body parts . . . other justifications."

"Regan, somebody . . . " the words were too awful to say.

He nodded.

"Somebody sawed . . . " Rachel bit her lower lip.

Regan heard a skein of honking geese and turned, out of habit, to scan the sky. The silhouette was beneath the silver clouds. "There are a lot of people who want this to go away."

Ivelis wasn't an American citizen, she didn't have documents to work in the United States. And Stephan Tisch was the president of the Chamber of Commerce.

Regan looked at the barn floor.

"Can they really do that?"

Tourism was the lifeblood of the county's economy, and mutilated bodies were bad for business.

"Only if I allow it."

Rachel didn't know if Regan's unwillingness to calculate the politics of an interaction was his greatest asset or his greatest liability. If the Sheriff's Office arrested Stephan Tisch, it would tear the county apart.

She took his hand.

"He'll take it out on me in the election. It won't go further than that."

"You need to move prudently. Gather support . . ." There wasn't a politician, a business owner, or a newspaper in the county who would stand with Regan against Tisch, not unless he uncovered more evidence.

"I'm not worried about myself."

"You can't do this alone."

"I'm not worried about me."

She stepped outside, finally comprehending.

He followed and put his arms around her.

"What can they do to me?" she asked.

"I don't know." He pulled her into his chest. "I'm afraid that if I do this, we are going to find out."

PRESENT

THE TOWN OF PATRIARCH WAS DIVIDED INTO TWO RESIDENTIAL NEIGHBOR-hoods, one on the east side of Main Street and the other on the west. The eastern side of town was laid out in a conventional grid. Whereas, the larger, western development sprawled along the low shoulders of the Patriarch Range. The smallest of these lots were on an acre of forested land.

The pastels of the afterglow had just faded from the evening sky when Jack led Billy out of a small playhouse at the back of one of these unfenced yards.

They crossed the dirt street and a wide beam of light swung through the trees. Jack pulled Billy to the ground where they lay prone behind a juniper shrub. A car slowed and nearly came to a stop in front of them. Then it turned into a driveway Jack had not seen. He heard a garage door motor groan. Then he watched as the car pulled inside.

The smell of exhaust hung in the cold air.

He listened to the flight pattern of the helicopter then had the kid lead him up the lampless street.

A NEW GUARD LOOKED INTO THE BATHROOM TO CHECK ON RACHEL. THERE had been three.

Her tongue was sticky and filled her mouth. She heard her pulse pounding in her brain and worried about what might happen to Billy if she lost consciousness.

Rachel felt heavy. She slid off the rim of the tub and landed on her hands and knees. The heated tile floor beneath her felt like a hot mug of coffee. She threw up. Then she looked at her bile on the floor and tried to think of a way to recover the moisture.

COLORADO
2008

IN AN HONEST EXAM, NOT EVEN THE EXTENSIVE LOSS OF ORGANS, TISSUE, AND limbs to scavengers could conceal the fact that Ivelis's head had been sawn off. The DA had no choice but to investigate the case as a homicide. There was a trial, but no conviction.

The Chamber put out a statement claiming that the prosecution was politically motivated. Its members smeared the sheriff as an alcoholic and a man of violent temper. They spread rumors of cocaine, illegitimate children.

As far as the slander went, it was all true. Or had been at one time.

"I'M SORRY," SHE TOLD HIM.

They sat side-by-side on the porch. After the sun went down, the emblazoned clouds formed an outline in the sky where, minutes earlier, the granite towers of the three Matriarchs had been visible.

"It's okay. It'll give me a chance to try something different."

The campaign against him was devastating. Friends no longer returned his calls. People he had known all his life no longer greeted him in the grocery store. Women on the street either avoided eye contact or stared him down. He'd come home from work to find his windows broken, manure in his living room.

"I'm sorry," she said again.

"Me too. For Ivelis."

The sky slid from gray to black. It was cold.

He said, "Maybe we can go down to Mexico."

"What they did to you." Her teeth were clenched.

"Let it go."

They sat in the darkness for minutes before she asked, "Is there any chance you could win?"

"Rachel, I consider all this a bonus." He was referring to everything since the day she rode up to him on Old Sam. "It's best just to let this one go."

REGAN COULDN'T BRING HIMSELF TO ADDRESS THE ALLEGATIONS. TO DIGNIFY them. The only public statement he made about the scandal was to a local reporter after a town meeting.

The reporter asked, good-naturedly, if the sheriff would like an opportunity to address the accusations before the election.

"Oh, come off it, Jeremy. How long have you known me?"

"All my life."

"Have I ever made a pretense of righteousness?"

THE POLITICAL STRATEGY OF ADVERTISING THE SHERIFF'S PERSONAL TRANS-gressions most certainly would have led to his electoral defeat if the public's love for scandal was not bested by mortal fear. Two months before the election the body of another decapitated female was discovered in the forest.

The first homicide—the victim being an undocumented, domestic servant—precipitated more gossip than alarm. There hadn't been a murder in the county for a dozen years, and there were still households that, on principle, never locked their doors.

The second homicide, however, incited a terror just shy of panic. Liz Keach, the victim, was a high school student, the youngest daughter of the Baptist preacher. Parents kept their teenaged children at home, the movie theater temporarily closed, and both of the town's pulpits delivered sermons on God's justice.

The fact that the sheriff had already made an arrest, and at great personal cost, was not lost on people. It was the jury that freed the accused. Now there were rumors of bribes, and the jurors were receiving hate mail.

When the Sentinel published the transcript of his trial in a special edition, Stephan Tisch and his family decided to vacation out of state.

JEREMY WAS SURPRISED WHEN THE SHERIFF GRANTED HIM AN EXCLUSIVE interview. The reporter brought nine pages of hand-written notes. He sat down in the sheriff's office, flipped through his legal pad, and effusively thanked the sheriff for his time.

The sheriff ignored the flattery. "Why is it your paper is suddenly being so friendly in its coverage?"

"It's the natural lifecycle of a scandal." Jeremy held his index finger on the first question in his legal pad. "I have twelve prepared questions, and if it's okay with . . . "

"Lifecycle," Regan said it with contempt. "Now I want you to understand something about all this. I used to be a real son-of-a-bitch, I don't deny it. Booze, women. You name it. As for the cocaine your paper's so fond of mentioning, that was when I was a kid. I can't think of a man my age born in this county that didn't experiment with the same things back then. But that's not the point."

Jeremy's finger was still poised over the question in his notes.

"The point is this—and I don't give a shit whether or not you believe what I'm about to tell you—five years ago I was fixin' to step into eternity when an angel on a white horse rode out of the forest and convinced me otherwise. I ain't had a drink since. As for womanizing, I'm satisfied with what I got."

Jeremy fumbled with the digital recorder.

"I'm proud of the man I've been for the past five years. I only tell you this because your daddy, God rest his soul, was a good friend."

The sheriff stood, walked out from behind his desk and took the recorder. "Besides, your aunt was my high school sweetheart. Now I did lie to you about one thing. This ain't an interview. You print a word of what I said, and I'll skin you alive."

He opened the office door.

"Now get out of here."

In the end, the vote was counted twice. Regan was reelected by four percentage points.

That Thursday, Rachel came into town with Regan in the patrol car. The errand wasn't pressing, but the loss of Ivelis had taught them to look for excuses to be together. They were coming up on the Safeway at the north end of town when a call came over the radio.

The sheriff answered it and hung up the microphone.

"Maybe I can drop you off."

"You don't have time for that," she told him. "Just do your job."

"Are you sure? It sounds grisly."

Rachel dismissed his concern, "Why do you think he picked the Sheriff's Office?"

"I don't know." It took about a minute to drive the length of Main Street. "Maybe it's some kind of statement."

He pulled into the parking lot. Rachel got out of the patrol car. She could smell the blood. Charlie, one of Regan's deputies, had already taped off Stephan Tisch's Corvette. It was parked askew, blocking the main entrance to the building. The rear window was shot out. Brains were smeared over the bumper and asphalt. The Corvette's roof was perforated by two pellets of buckshot. A note in a Ziploc bag was pinned under the windshield wipers.

Regan pulled on a pair of gloves and opened the driver's door. Denis Tisch, Stephan Tisch's eldest son, was dead. There was a short-barreled shotgun in his lap.

Regan looked over the top of the Corvette at Rachel. She had both hands covering her nose and mouth. Then he read the confession in the suicide note.

Present

Rachel felt for the toilet in the dark. She was lying on her belly and disoriented. She pulled herself over the heated bathroom tile. When she finally found the toilet, she wrapped her arms around its base.

God, it's warm. She lay panting.

Then she got to her knees and rested her torso on the lid. With so much of her weight on the lid of the toilet, it took awhile for her to figure out how to open it. Because her arms were bound, she couldn't reach the little pool of water at the bottom of the bowl.

Rachel lifted the wooden seat and put her cheek on the porcelain rim. She caught her breath. Then she twisted her forearms together and writhed, ignoring the pain, until her fingertips were submerged. She flicked the water upward. But it did not reach her tongue.

She was dizzy, and she kept thinking her eyes were closed, but no matter how hard she tried, she couldn't get them to open. She couldn't concentrate. Couldn't think.

She sucked the moisture off her fingertips. She felt like she was running out of time, like she was spinning. A drum pounded in her ears. Then she felt the toilet bowl whirl as it rose from the floor to meet her.

THE PORCH LIGHT CAME ON, AND BILLY HEARD THE DEADBOLT RETRACT. He was holding the rifle.

"Billy?" Rob had on a pair of jeans, as if he slept in the nude and hadn't bothered to find more to wear. He was almost as tall as the door, and his hair had an electrified look. Rob stared at the other man. "Jack? Jesus Christ!" He switched off the porch light.

Billy locked the door behind them. "He's shot up."

Rob led them to the exam room on the side of the house, turning off lights as he went. "Everybody's worried about you, Billy. They're talkin' about you on the news." Rob lowered the bamboo blinds, then switched on the florescent ceiling lights. There was a stainless-steel examination table in the center of the room. A complement of bamboo cabinets hung above the stainless-steel countertop along the wall. "I got kids in the house. Put that down."

"Everything's gone to shit." Billy stood the rifle in the corner of the room. "He told me to take him to a vet. I didn't know of another place to go."

"It's alright." Rob shook Billy's hand then reached for his godfather's. "It's good to see you, Jack."

Jack had dried blood on his wrist and palm.

"He doesn't remember me either."

Rob lifted his lab coat off a hook and put it on. "Take off your coat, Jack. Let me see what it is."

When Jack took off his parka, Rob saw that the right sleeve of his shirt was missing, that it had been used to bandage his arm.

Jack slipped off the holster rig and laid it on the stainless-steel table.

Rob took his pulse and looked at the cocked 1911 in the holster, the two spare magazines. "Where's Rachel?"

"The front door was open. Mom wasn't home."

Jack unbuttoned his shirt, revealing another bandage on his torso.

Rob stretched a pair of exam gloves over his hands, took a pair of scissors from a drawer, and cut the bandage off Jack's arm. He found two holes plugged with wads of fabric and a corresponding pair of stellate wounds on the other side of the arm.

"Let's take some X-Rays and see what we got." He positioned the X-Ray tube and motioned for Billy to stand behind the shield. "We got news anchors here from Denver. They interviewed the sheriff." Rob took the image and repositioned the capture arm. "He called it a kidnapping. He thinks you're with her."

Rob studied the images and told Jack, "Apart from the broken rib, the wound in the torso looks superficial."

He plucked out the fabric plugs in Jack's arms and found two oval holes, each encircled by a thin abrasion, black in color. The halos of abrasion were caused by the spinning of the bullets and were thickest where the bullets had the longest contact with the skin. He had seen it in dogs and cattle. From the oval shapes of the entrance wounds and the lopsided thickness of the halos, Rob knew the bullets had penetrated the lateral and long heads of the right triceps brachii muscle at an angle.

The bullet holes started to bleed and Rob repacked them. "I had to keep the kids out of the room because of the bloody pictures on the TV."

Billy's eyes moved to the holstered weapon on the stainless-steel table.

Rob followed his gaze. Then he looked at Jack incredulously. "Was that you?"

Jack was perspiring and gave no indication that he heard the question.

Billy unzipped his Carhartt.

"You can put your coat on the counter," Rob offered. "Have you talked to Regan?"

"No, not yet." Billy didn't want to take off his coat. He didn't trust his father, he didn't know who had his mother, and he didn't want to be separated from the revolver in his pocket.

"If you don't call him, I will."

Billy wrung his hands. He stepped across the examination room, looked out through the blinds then came back. "Did the news say anything else about Mom?"

Rob made eye contact with Billy, shook his head slowly, then peeled the brown shirtsleeve from Jack's torso. Underneath the bandage, he found red, ragged tissue.

"You should make that call," Jack said. His voice was void of emotion.

It took Billy several seconds to process what he had been told. "But that'll lead them here."

"I'll worry about that." Jack didn't look at Billy when he spoke. "There's nothing you are going to be able to do for her on your own."

The statement felt like a chasm expanding between them.

Rob asked, "Who took her, Jack? Who's after you?"

"I don't know."

The knotted spheres of Billy's jaw muscles were twitching. He heard the words on your own and discerned from them what his father did not say. It was clear now that the man was not interested in him, was not interested in his mom. The hope that Billy had placed in his father's reappearance now seemed childish.

"What do you know?" Billy's question came out like a snarl.

Jack wiped the spittle from his eye. "One of the men from the highway chased me through a bank after the Washington bombing."

"What were you doing there?"

Jack didn't answer.

"This is going to hurt, Jack, but I need you to take a deep breath, as deep as you can."

As Jack's chest expanded, his broken rib popped. He grunted involuntarily. The outline of the fractured bone was visible through the muscle wall.

"Charlie told me the driver of that Lincoln had two bullet holes in his heart." Rob opened one of the cabinets and found a bottle of isotonic saline. He looked at Billy then pointed with his eyes, "Put that over there."

Billy picked the shoulder rig off the exam table and put it on the counter. "Who were they?"

"He didn't say." Rob took two vials from another cabinet. "Jack, I'm going to give you some cephalosporin and a tetanus booster."

He administered the shots then prepared a stainless-steel tray of medical instruments.

"Neither bullet hit anything that won't heal in your arm. I'm going to clean the wounds and do a more thorough exploration. You need to take off your pants if you don't want them to get wet." He opened a sterile package and took out an irrigation syringe. "Jack, I need you to sit down."

Naked, Jack winced as he climbed onto the stainless-steel table.

"This is going to make gettin' shot feel like a love pat. Just hold still." Rob filled the syringe with isotonic saline and irrigated one of the holes in Jack's arm.

There were yellow tufts of insulation embedded in the wound. The insulation was packed into the hollow point of the bullet as it passed through the parka. Then it was released into Jack's arm upon the bullet's expansion. Rob took a pair of forceps from the stainless-steel instrument tray and picked out the tufts of insulation.

Billy said, "I got to pee."

AFTER HIS FATHER DISAPPEARED, BILLY HAD HEARD THE GOVERNMENT INVES-tigators use the word *collaborator*. At the time, he hadn't been sure what it meant. He was nine years old. It had been one of many things that didn't make sense back then.

He had known his father was a wanted man. That he had stolen something. Secrets.

Billy switched on the bathroom light and looked at himself in the mirror. He knew it now and stated the fact to himself: My father is a traitor. Against America. Against my family. Against Mom.

"YOU'RE LUCKY THE BULLET THAT FRACTURED YOUR RIB DIDN'T PENETRATE deeper."

Jack looked through the open doorway and checked for Billy in the empty hall. "What was it I did?"

"You mean for a livin'? Hold still." Rob was excising the blackened tissue.

Jack clenched his teeth. "Yes, for a living."

"You were an independent contractor for the Federal Government. You never said more than that." He refilled the syringe then irrigated the wound again.

"Which agency?"

"I don't know. You traveled a lot. Nine years ago just about everybody with a badge wanted to talk to you."

"What year is it now?"

"2010."

Billy was drinking milk from a cereal bowl when Rob led Jack to the kitchen. There was a box of Captain Crunch and a phone beside Billy on the table.

He hadn't yet made the call.

"You want somethin' to eat?" The shape of the rifle barrel was visible through the nylon gym bag Rob set on the counter. He opened the fridge. "We got lasagna I can heat."

Jack was wearing one of Rob's shirts and the Colt in the shoulder rig. His right arm was in a sling. He found a picture of himself with Billy and Rob on a Skeeter fishing boat. He took the picture off the refrigerator and turned it over. Someone had written, "August 2001."

"That was at Lake Powell."

Rob looked about eighteen. The striper Billy held by the gills measured from his ankles to his nine-year-old chest. The pride on Billy's face was matched by Jack's own expression. He was standing behind his son.

Jack paced the kitchen and chewed his lower lip. Although the blackouts were becoming less frequent, he had little memory of the day. He could remember the gunfight, the house, and Billy. That was about it. He ran his index finger back and forth along his mustache. He didn't know who he was or what he had done, but he knew with a resonating certainty that Billy was his son.

Jack needed Billy in order to remember who he was. He put the picture in his pocket. But he couldn't keep Billy with him. That much was clear. His son wasn't safe, not as long as he was with him.

Rob put a plate of lasagna in the microwave.

Billy heard an engine outside, went to the window, and pulled back the edge of the seersucker curtain. There was an SUV parked on the street.

"Shit."

Jack looked at the kitchen door then at Rob. "Tell them I held you at gunpoint."

Rob was trying to make sense of the statement when Jack's left fist broke his nasal bone.

Billy heard the crack from across the room, turned, and saw Rob stooped, holding his face. Blood gushed from his hands.

"Jesus Christ!" Billy ran to him.

"Let it bleed." Jack turned the deadbolt on the kitchen door. "Get as much blood on you as you can." He opened the door and was gone.

Billy stood paralyzed.

A shotgun blast brought his hands to his head and his chin to his chest. He heard a second blast and saw pieces of wood ricocheting off the tile floor in the entry way.

If Billy lost his father, he might never find his mom.

The front door was open. Some type of grenade was rolling across the floor. He grabbed the gym bag on the kitchen counter and heard the explosion as he careened into the dark.

Billy tried to put as many lodgepoles as he could between himself and the light that spilled from Rob's kitchen door. The revolver in his breast pocket bounced and slammed into his collarbone as he ran. When he did not hear the expected burst of gunfire, he looked over his shoulder and saw a man in a black suit giving chase.

He pressed his left hand against his coat to control the bouncing revolver and looked over his shoulder again: the man in the suit was a hundred yards back. Billy felt certain he could outrun him.

He crossed Marion Street in three strides and turned uphill toward the National Forest.

He triggered a set of motion-detecting floodlights on a neighbor's house and veered behind the structure in an attempt to cut off his pursuer's line of sight.

Billy lost his hat. He had his left hand pinned to his chest. The gym bag he carried in his right hand was lurching wildly. The imbalance slowed his gait, and he could hear his coach's voice, "Eye socket to hip pocket." Billy reached inside his Carhartt, pulled out the revolver, and held it by the rosewood grips. With the gun in his hand, he was able to swing both arms in synch with his hips.

He looked back. The man in the suit was closing. Billy considered dropping the gym bag.

He jumped the creek and willow branches slapped his cheek. He leapt over a raised garden and saw the outline of the Girard place–a four story, stone castle. It was the last house on the mountainside.

His quadriceps were on fire.

He saw the Rottweiler after he heard it snarl, a dark, galloping body, no more than ten yards in front of him. The Rottweiler leapt. Billy knew the dog. He swung the gym bag and struck Senator across the jaw with the barrel of the rifle. He heard the animal yelp.

Billy stumbled. He lost his grip on the gym bag, and the rifle was gone.

He thought if he kept running uphill, his pursuer would get winded and quit. He looked over his shoulder and saw the silhouette of a carbine in the man's hand. He was fifty yards back.

Billy's stride was wide. Only the balls of his feet made contact with the steep mountainside as he lunged upward in a side-to-side gait.

He was two hundred vertical feet above the last house and gasping. His legs could keep driving, but his lungs were finished.

The ground beneath him was loose scree. Billy scrambled up it on all fours until he was stopped by a wall of granite. He pulled himself up the rock face, rolled over the top, and lay on the forest floor sucking oxygen—unable to get up. It felt like he was suffocating.

Billy saw the hands and shirtsleeves first. Then the reflection of starlight in the man's eyes as he pulled his upper body over the granite outcrop.

Billy got to his feet and kicked the man in the chin. He saw him fall, turned around, and jogged up the mountainside. He made it about three paces.

"Shit."

Billy walked back, squatted on top of the outcrop, and saw the man in the suit twisted on the scree below. He put one hand on the granite by his feet and dropped down.

He pulled the hammer back on the revolver. Then he cleared the sweat running into his eyes with his coat sleeve. Billy circled the man and chewed his thumb knuckle. Then he prodded him with the toe of his boot. "Hey."

The man in the suit didn't move.

Billy wanted to run. Everything in him wanted to run. But that wouldn't help his mom.

He put his boot under the man's shoulder and turned him over. In the starlight, the man's teeth were black. His eyes were closed. Billy kicked the M4 away from his hands. Then he knelt in the scree and patted the man's waist.

What he found made him flinch. "Jesus Christ, mister."

Billy pulled a six-inch knife from the sheath on the man's belt and tossed it toward the M4. He found an armored vest under the suit jacket.

He wiped the sweat from his eyes with the back of his hand. If there had been any doubt before, it was gone now. He was on the wrong side of the law. How did he get here?

In the vest's nylon pouches were two thirty-round magazines, a half-dozen flex-cuffs, and a radio. Billy followed the radio cable to a PTT button and found an in-ear headset in the left ear.

He felt cold.

He stepped back and was squeezing his own head, the blued-steel cylinder of the revolver pressed against his ear. "Shit! Shit!"

Billy sat down with his back against a tree. "You've done what you've done," he reasoned. "How would it benefit her to run away now?"

Billy put his revolver in his coat pocket, picked up the M4, and switched on the rail-mounted light.

"Who are you?"

He shone the light on the man's face and saw the red gash in his chin. The teeth were broken and made more ghastly by a bloody drool.

"Jesus . . . " He averted his eyes.

He searched the vest again and found a Wilson Combat CQB (Close Quarters Combat) .45 caliber pistol and spare magazine. He threw the pistol into the trees then patted the man's thighs.

He pulled on the cable of the in-ear headset, unclipped the PTT switch, and threaded the piece out of the bloody collar. Then he wiped the back of his hand across his mouth.

Billy took the Motorola digital radio out of the man's vest and put the headset in his own ear.

". . . is out of contact."

"The TOC has sent a bird to those coordinates."

"Roger that."

Billy looked into the orange glow hanging over the valley, heard the helicopter, and turned off the rail-mounted light on the M4 carbine.

"You are a giant jackass. A stupid, giant jackass."

The volume of the approaching machine swelled.

Pine needles swirled in the rotor wash. Billy had dirt in his mouth, eyes, and nostrils. He bounded down the mountain, breaking unseen branches. He dropped the M4 and radio and held up his arms to protect his face. He was worried about getting shot and had the presence of mind to reach into his pocket and drop the revolver. Billy stumbled. Using his momentum to recover, he kept running.

By the time the slope of the mountain relaxed, the sound of the rotors was in the distance. Billy could see headlights through the trees.

His thigh thudded into what felt like a large animal. Billy was upside down. His shoulder hit the earth and he tumbled, landed on his feet, and started to run. Billy felt a crack against his skull, and everything went white.

When he came to, he was in the backseat of an SUV. His wrists were cuffed behind his back. The driver wore a black suit. So did the man sitting beside him.

THE SNIPERS WERE SCREENED BY THE MOUNTAIN MAHOGANY. THEY HAD command of the long driveway, most of the pasture, and the house.

The moon was rising.

Jack withdrew down the backside of the ridge, crossed the willow marsh, climbed over 1,000 feet in elevation, then angled down through the aspens to approach the house from the other side.

The key was under a pot beneath the bathroom window. He also found a cellphone near the back porch. He put it in his pocket and unlocked the door.

JACK SAT ON BILLY'S BED IN THE DARK. HE TRIED TO REMEMBER EVERYTHING his son had told him since they met. Which wasn't easy. He picked slowly through what he could recall and was not encouraged.

The assault team was improvising, otherwise they would have sealed off the neighborhood around the clinic. Improvising off of what information? What mistakes was he making? Jack couldn't sort it out.

He went to the mirror over the dresser and looked at his moonlit reflection. The answers were in his past. He needed to know what he had done.

HE WAITED IN BILLY'S BEDROOM UNTIL IT WAS LIGHT ENOUGH TO SEE. THEN he slid his arm out of the sling and moved on his belly. There was an open trapdoor in the hall, along with several open Bankers Boxes. He crawled over tax papers, mortgage statements, insurance documents, bills, invoices, and photographs—inches thick on the carpet.

The sun had not yet risen above the horizon.

The house was being watched, and he was conscious of every window, of every line of sight. He crawled to the master bedroom and searched the walk-in closet. He searched the studio, living room, and kitchen.

Then he crawled back to the open trapdoor and let himself down.

The dirt floor of the crawl space was covered by a plastic moisture barrier, and there were boxes labeled JACKS CLOTHES spilt on the sheeting.

He picked out a Merino wool sweater and smelled it. He found a pair of blue jeans, a pair of Merrell shoes, and a black leather jacket. He laid the clothes on the mess of papers in the hallway.

Then he took the cellphone out of his pocket and pressed the power button. On the cracked display was a picture of Billy on the buckskin mustang.

He closed the phone and undressed. Apart from the bandages and the Colt in the shoulder rig, Jack stood naked in the trapdoor opening. He picked up a photograph of himself and a woman. There was another photograph of her breastfeeding an infant. Jack was in the next photograph with Billy. There was crumpled wrapping paper in the background, along with a box of space Legos, a BB gun, a Christmas tree. Billy looked to be five or six.

There was another photograph of the woman. She was in the driver's seat of a Chevy pickup looking out the open window, laughing. Her eyes were sparkling.

Jack found a photograph of himself in his early twenties standing beside an old man who appeared to be an Asian military commander. The man was armed with a Chinese pistol in a leather holster. There was a camp in the background. They were Cambodians: soldiers, women, and children. He turned the photo over—*1970 Colonel Um Savuth*.

What was he doing in Cambodia?

He lifted himself up to the floor of the hallway and crawled to the master bathroom.

There were orange evidence cones on the blue ceramic tile. He searched the cabinet and found a pair of shears. Jack cut his beard over the toilet. Then he took the razor from the whirlpool tub, lathered his face with hand soap, and shaved.

Jack opened the shower door and hung the holster rig on the door frame. Then he wet a towel and cleaned his skin without dampening the bandages.

He brushed his hair and pulled on the blue jeans. They fit.

The only explanation he could come up with for his presence in Cambodia was a task force named SOG (Studies and Observation Group). Jack could recount episodes from its secret history, but, apart from the faces in the photograph, not his role in the unit.

He needed to know who he was.

He crawled into the studio where he found charcoal sketches pinned to the brightly painted drywall. There were ceramics on a steel cart and stacks of canvases leaning against a taboret. At the back of the room, he found an embroidered bison skin on a drying rack.

He looked closer at the charcoal sketches. They were all of the same woman—the woman in the photographs.

Jack backed out of the studio and took a pillow from the bed. He held it to his face and inhaled. He could hear the woman's voice. He could smell wood smoke. He inhaled again and saw her shoveling the deck of a deerskin yurt. The yurt was surrounded by a ponderosa forest and six feet of untracked snow.

JACK HEARD A VEHICLE APPROACHING ON THE GRAVEL DRIVEWAY. HE HAD TO get out of the house. As he crawled to the back bathroom, the cellphone received a text. He opened the frosted window, climbed out, and read the display on the phone: *owl creek trail visitor registration.*

JACK CUT THROUGH A FOREST OF LODGEPOLE PINES. THE PAIN IN HIS SIDE HAD him doubled over.

He didn't know how he understood the meaning of the text. He just did. It was a dead drop. And he knew the trail. Someone had contacted him, someone with the wherewithal to use Rachel's phone. He felt encouraged.

He crouched in the raspberries and watched. His fractured rib made it excruciating to breathe. Maybe twelve minutes had passed since he received the text. He was looking at the back of a wilderness boundary sign. The visitor registration station was a few meters further down the trail.

Jack found an area map and a wooden, padlocked box at the registration station. He studied the map for a message. Then he saw the stack of blank permits in a Plexiglas tray.

Under NAME on the first permit, someone penciled CB and under DESTINATION, *27 3rd Street. Noon.*

The only car in the parking lot was a dark cherry Honda Pilot. The owner, a petite woman dressed in running tights, was standing outside the vehicle. There was a chocolate Labrador retriever on the driver's seat.

The woman gasped when Jack opened the passenger door. She had been trying to untangle the dog's leash. The Lab wagged his tail, put both paws on the center console, and slobbered on the slide of Jack's gun.

Jack was out of breath. "I need you to sit down inside the vehicle."

"Just take the car," her hands were vibrating with fear. "Let me take my dog and you can take the car."

Jack put the muzzle of the gun into the dog's mouth. "Get back into the vehicle."

The woman pushed the dog out of the driver's seat and sat down with her head bowed.

"Start it." Jack got in and pushed the Lab into the back.

She couldn't control her hands, so Jack helped guide the key into the ignition.

"Drive out to the highway and turn right."

He opened the glove compartment and read the address on the vehicle registration.

She put the Honda in reverse and looked him in the eye for the first time. "Are you the man from the news?"

He found the digital clock on the dashboard. It was 9:17. He had until noon.

Who was CB? He knew they were initials, but for what? For whom? It was like searching for a specific word, a word he had used without trouble all his life, but could not now recall.

The Honda was approaching the first curve when they heard the screeching of the tires. Then they saw the oncoming SUV. The vehicle was going much too fast for the curve and swung into their lane.

"Jesus!" She braked, almost to a stop.

He threw his head in her lap. "Drive the speed limit and keep your eyes on the road."

She accelerated again and set the cruise control.

She had the seat so far forward his chin was against the steering wheel. His sweat ran onto her black tights, through which he could feel her racing pulse.

Then the muscles stiffened in her leg. The dog slammed into the back of the seat. "Jesus Christ!" She swerved onto the gravel shoulder. "How many of these guys are after you?"

He heard the engine roar past and looked over the dash.

You're doing great. Now take a left on 10th."

Her eyes fell to the glove compartment. She hesitated before she turned the wheel. "Where are we going?"

"I need to leave you in a safe place."

He pressed the button and opened the garage door. She pulled forward reluctantly, and he shut the door behind them.

Jack holstered the pistol and let the dog out of the Honda. There was an oil stain on the slab in the empty bay. He took a roll of duct tape from the workbench and opened the door to the house. The Lab, its tail smacking him in the legs, ran inside.

She waited on the far side of the Honda.

"I'm not going to hurt you."

He heard the Lab drinking from a toilet, followed the animal into the house, and shut the bathroom door.

When he turned around in the hall, he met her blue eyes. She was standing at the threshold. Her skin was pale and smooth, and her dark hair was pulled into a tight ponytail.

He led her wordlessly to the stairs.

"Put your arms through the banister."

She wove her arms so the uprights were in the crooks of her elbows.

He sat on the stairs and held her hands together. She was unbelievably beautiful. "What time will he be home?"

She didn't answer.

"He'll untie you then." He taped her wrists. "After that, you can call whoever you need to call. Tell them whatever you need to tell them. I won't come back."

Jack moved behind her, unzipped the pocket on the CamelBak, and took her phone. "I'm sorry."

He brought a chair to her from the dining room table and went out the front door.

RACHEL SLOWLY BECAME AWARE OF A MAN STANDING OVER THE BED. THE pillow under her head was damp. It troubled her that she could not explain why it was damp.

She sat up and noticed that her skirt was bunched around her waist. She pulled it down. The fabric was wet. So was the sweater she was wearing. So was the bedding. She felt her wet hair with her bound hands.

"We were worried about you," the man said.

Through the open door, she saw the guard in the hall.

Her lower lip felt swollen. She licked it and tasted blood.

A brown fiber was pasted on her knee. She scratched it off with her fingernail. The fiber was also smeared along her thigh.

She didn't want to look at the man. She didn't want to have to process anymore information, not until she could sort out why she was drenched and how she had gotten to the bed.

Rachel felt the filth in the bedding and realized that she had shat herself. She didn't want to, but she blushed.

"If you're feeling better, maybe you would like to clean yourself up."

Rachel still couldn't bring herself to make eye contact. She pulled the duvet over her legs.

"I need to ask you a few questions, Ms. Erikson. Then I can leave you to attend to your needs."

She was furious at herself for feeling shame. Be careful. He's still fucking with you. Only it's more dangerous now.

Rachel threw off the bedding. Then she swung her bound legs off the bed and stood up.

The man stepped back in surprise.

The stain on her white skirt was much worse than she thought. Clumps of shit thudded on the carpet.

"You're going to leave whenever it is you choose to leave. Neither of us believe I have any say in that. Meanwhile, I'm going to clean myself off."

She hobbled into the bathroom. The tile was wet. So was the porcelain inside the tub. Which meant someone had turned on the water. She tried to turn the faucet, but it was already open.

She couldn't bring herself to look at him.

There was dried blood on the toilet. She looked at her busted lip in the mirror and decided they had placed her in the bed after she collapsed. But how long had it been?

Rachel stood in the bathroom doorway for a moment to prepare herself. Then she met his eyes.

"Perhaps we could finish our conversation. That would free me to look into the problem with the water."

"What is it you'd like to know?"

"Your husband has created a determined set of enemies. Are you aware of his line of work?"

She exhaled a two syllable laugh. "Regan being re-elected sheriff is no secret in this county. But we're not married."

He looked as if he didn't know what she was talking about.

"Jesus Christ," she hobbled toward him, "you boys are a bunch of amateurs."

The man's eyes hardened. He pressed his lips together and turned his head to the side. Then he raised his arm and backhanded Rachel in the jaw.

She lay on the carpet, bleeding from the mouth.

Billy was wearing his boots and coat when the driver woke him and let him out of the room. Billy's legs were so stiff it was difficult to walk. His head throbbed behind his right ear. He saw Regan in the parking lot and recognized the hotel he had spent the night in as the Cedar Lodge.

"Don't ever let him get up to speed." The driver's eye was bruised and swollen. "He's a son-of-a-bitch to stop."

The sheriff led Billy over to the patrol car and opened the passenger door.

Each step hurt.

Billy's hat and revolver were on the front seat, along with a baggie of cartridges. The rifle was on the floorboard.

Billy held onto the roof and eased himself into the passenger seat.

The sheriff walked around the front of the patrol car, took off his hat, and got in. It was about ten o'clock in the morning.

Billy pulled his hat from under his thigh and put it on. Then he opened the loading gate on the revolver and spun the cylinder. It was empty. He picked the .44 caliber cartridges out of the baggie and loaded the gun. Then he dropped the revolver into his breast pocket.

There was a Loaf 'N Jug on the north end of town and a Valero on the south end. The half mile of Main Street between the two gas stations was lined with historic buildings. Patriarch preserved its Victorian mining-town charm by containing most of the valley's development to the ski resort.

The sheriff parked the car three blocks from the lodge. "There's laws against concealing a weapon, Billy."

Billy drew the revolver from his Carhartt and placed it on the floor.

The sheriff opened the driver's door and put out a leg. "How you feelin'?"

"I don't know. Like I got thrown from a bull a couple times, got up, and did it again."

"You hungry?"

"I guess."

They walked across the street to the Moose Jaw. While they stood at the podium waiting for the hostess, the conversations in the dining room stopped. An elderly man suspended his fork midway to his mouth, leaving potato salad on the tines. The woman across from him turned around to look at Billy.

"Come on, let's get out of here." The sheriff went out the door.

They got in the patrol car, and the sheriff took him to the drive-through at McDonald's. He ordered a cup of coffee for himself and two double quarter pounders with cheese, fries, and a coke for Billy.

They drove past the black SUVs in the parking lot of the Cedar Lodge, and a block later the sheriff parked on the street.

"Be right back. Nancy needs me to deposit this."

BILLY, AT TEN YEARS OLD, WANTED TO SHOOT THAT WINCHESTER 1894 MORE than he wanted anything else in the world. He set five Coke cans on five fence posts a full hour before the sheriff was due back. He paced off fifty yards, marked the distance with a line in the dirt drawn by his boot heel, and waited on the porch until the sheriff's car finally came up the long drive.

Regan saw the lever-action rifle in Billy's hand before he got out of his vehicle. "I take it you want to show me some shootin'."

Billy loaded five cartridges into the magazine of the .22. "You reckon that's fifty yards?"

The sheriff thought it was closer to sixty. "Looks like it to me."

Billy shouldered the rifle and shot the first can off the fence. He levered in another round and did it again. After the fifth shot, all five cans were perforated and lying on the ground.

The sheriff put his hand on Billy's shoulder. "I'd say that settles it."

The next day he brought him a thousand .30-30 handloads. "This is a starter load. Shoot four cans out of five at seventy-five yards and I'll heat it up a little."

A month later, Billy shot another five cans off the fence.

The sheriff had always been cautious with his praise, but Billy had never heard a word of criticism from him either. When the sheriff did compliment Billy, he focused on his effort. He talked about the boy's grit.

They walked over to the fence together. Billy picked up one of the Coke cans and showed the sheriff the hole he shot through it.

Regan nodded his head and smiled. "You think you're ready for squirrels?"

"If you think so."

The sheriff gave him another thousand handloads. "This is a good load for squirrels. Just keep it away from the house. And it's probably best not to talk about it with your mother."

"Alright."

"And you leave an Abert's squirrel alone. He has a right to do as he pleases. Shoot the fox squirrels."

They walked together behind the house.

"You'll find, as you get older, people aren't all that different than squirrels. There are those who sustain their habitat and those whose sole purpose is to destroy it."

Billy had no idea what the sheriff meant by that, but he remembered the words.

By the time the boy harvested his first mule deer, he was shooting paper plates at a hundred and fifty yards with iron sights. The sheriff would watch his trigger pull. He'd watch for movement in the boy's jaw muscles, for signs of flinching in the muscles of his eyes.

"That's it. Nice and smooth."

Billy'd hit the plate with every round in the magazine. And the sheriff would pat him on the shoulder and say it again, "That's the evidence of a disciplined mind." Then he'd draw his service revolver, take Billy's place on the bench, and empty a few cylinders into the same paper plate.

"YOU WANT SOME?" BILLY SUCKED THE KETCHUP OFF HIS FINGERS AND HELD out a carton of fries.

The sheriff started the car. "No thanks."

Both cheeseburgers were devoured before they got out of town.

"Why'd they let me go?"

"What reason did they have to keep you?"

About half the drivers in the oncoming lane lifted a hand from the steering wheel as they passed. The sheriff said each of their names as he waved back.

Billy put the empty carton of fries in the McDonald's bag with twelve or thirteen empty ketchup packets, the unused napkins, and the two sandwich wrappers. "I think I hurt one of 'em."

"You certainly got their attention." The sheriff set the cruise control and placed his coffee in the cup holder. "And the way I heard it, won more than a little respect."

Billy wiped his hands on his jeans, rolled down the top of the bag, and put the trash on the floor. He could see the Patriarch River through the trees. There were bicyclists and joggers on the bike path.

They drove by the high school, and Billy sat with his head hung.

"You haven't done anything wrong, Billy. You and your mother have been caught in a mess you did nothing to create."

Billy didn't look up.

"Listen to me, Billy. You don't have to answer for what someone else has done."

"What is it he did?"

The sheriff sipped his coffee, moved his arm to return the cup to the holder, then brought it back and held the coffee below his lips.

"They talk about him like he's some sort of psychopath."

A Mexican man was looking under the hood of a two-tone, wood-paneled Plymouth Voyager parked on the shoulder of the oncoming lane.

The sheriff slowed.

It looked to Billy like the vehicle had been manufactured during the eighties. Frisbee-sized chips were missing from the paint and much of the wood paneling was shorn off. The tires were bald.

The sheriff flipped on his lights, turned around, and parked behind the Voyager.

"You speak better Spanish than I ever will. Give me a hand with this."

Billy could not disguise his rigid gait. He peered in through the glass on the passenger side and counted six children. The eldest looked to be about thirteen. The woman in the front seat couldn't have been more than thirty. Billy saw the pair of infants breastfeeding in her lap, looked

74

away, and felt his face heat up.

The man met them on the passenger side of the engine compartment. He was wearing boots, jeans, a western-style shirt, and a baseball cap.

The sheriff shook his hand, "I'm Sheriff Dowell."

The man's eyes jumped to the woman on the other side of the window. "Mucho gusto."

The couple was terrified.

"And this is Billy."

Billy shook the man's hand.

The Mexican looked down and didn't offer his name.

Curious drivers slowed in both directions. Some of them waved.

The sheriff gestured with a small movement of his head for Billy to say something.

Billy lifted his hat and ran a hand through his hair. "*¿Tiene usted un problema?*"

"*Sí.*" The man stepped around to the front of the van.

Pieces of the shredded serpentine belt were scattered throughout the rusty engine compartment.

The sheriff said to Billy, "It looks to me like they can't afford decent tires, let alone a tow into town."

"He needs a new serpentine belt. If we give him a ride to Auto Zone, he can be on his way again for about fifty bucks."

The sheriff looked at the mess and nodded his head. "Ask him if he has any tools."

"*¿Usted tiene herramientas?*"

"*¿Herramientas?*" The man smiled and nodded his head. "*Sí.*"

"Tell him what we're doing so we don't terrorize that poor woman."

Billy thought through the sentence. "*Nos dirigiremos al* Auto Zone," he pointed to the sheriff, himself, the Mexican, then the patrol car, "*y usted puede comprar la parte.*"

The man smiled, nodded his head, and shook both of their hands. He spoke to the woman in the Voyager then got in the backseat of the patrol car.

On their way into town, Billy learned that the man's name was Javier. That he wasn't married to the woman as Billy had thought. Her name was Lola, and she was his sister-in-law.

The sheriff parked in the Auto Zone parking lot, and he and Billy waited for Javier in the car.

"Isn't it supposed to snow tonight?"

"I haven't been watching the weather."

The sheriff picked up the microphone and pressed the PTT button. "Nancy, is it supposed to snow tonight?"

Her voice was full of static on the radio, "They're calling for four inches."

Javier came out with a serpentine belt and two quarts of oil.

The sheriff passed the van and turned the patrol car around so Javier wouldn't have to cross the highway.

"Tell him the sheriff in the next county will arrest him if he doesn't put better tires on that vehicle."

Billy looked confused.

"They won't make it in the coming weather. Just tell him it's the law."

Javier and Lola, both infants in her arms, and a line of kids, the two eldest holding a toddler apiece, stood waving on the side of the road when the sheriff drove off.

"You ever been to Mexico, Billy?"

"No, sir."

"You see any children's car seats in that vehicle?"

"No, sir."

"You think they wear seat belts in Mexico?"

"I don't know." Billy chewed his thumb nail.

"Neither do I, but I doubt they sue somebody when their kid falls off the swing set."

Billy didn't follow.

"No amount of precaution can alter the fact that life is precarious. When the inevitable happens, you can accept the damage or look for someone to blame. I think that Mexicans are more accepting."

"I wouldn't know."

"You know what I think?"

"No."

"Caution itself can erode a culture. Once people start believing they can be safe, they start to believe they should be safe."

Billy spat a fingernail on the floor.

The sheriff looked in his rearview mirror. "You think I should've asked Javier for the license, registration, and proof of insurance he didn't have?"

Billy didn't answer. He didn't have to. The sheriff knew his mind. To Billy's way of thinking it was about fairness. What's right and what's wrong. There was a long line of hard working people willing to risk everything to get a shot at a life in this great country. It didn't matter to him what color they were or what language they spoke. Make it fair. Give them all the same chance of making that life. It sickened him to see those who had cheated and broken the law rewarded.

"Those folks might find a way of making a living, but they're gonna lose somethin' more."

"There's still a law."

"Yes, there is."

"You're paid to enforce that law."

"Yes, I am."

"I see a contradiction."

The sheriff pursed his lips. He started to say something. Thought better of it. Then he said it anyway, "You think Ivelis had any papers?"

They passed the road to Billy's driveway.

"Where we goin'?"

"To the airport."

"I'm not leavin'."

The sheriff nodded his head. "I'm afraid you don't have a choice in it, Billy."

"Put me on any plane you want. I'll come back."

"They didn't release you to me because they thought they needed your help. I convinced them I had a safe place to put you. You're going to stay with my brother."

"No, sir."

"There's not a thing you can do for her but get in the way. They got professional manhunters on this. Serious men."

A voice came over the radio, "Hey, Regan?"

He picked up the microphone. "I already made the deposit, Nancy."

"Thank you."

"Every resource I have is being brought to bear on this." He glanced at Billy. "You know your mother better than I do. She'd skin my hide if I didn't make sure you were safe from whatever this is."

They came around a corner and the glare on the snow-dusted peaks made the sheriff squint. It didn't matter how many times he drove this stretch of highway, the granite towers of the Matriarch Range were stunning to see. The thick timber growing on the tallest of the three peaks stopped abruptly at the base of its spire, which projected another 2,000 vertical feet above the valley.

"What'd they have to say to you?"

"Nothing. Asked a bunch of questions. Who were they?"

"The good guys. Did you tell 'em the truth?"

Billy's eyes were watering. "Yes, sir."

The sheriff looked in the side mirror. "Were you in the house yesterday when I came up the driveway?"

"Yes, sir." There was a doe and two fawns bedded down in the sage just off the shoulder of the road. "Do you think Mom's okay?"

"I don't know." The sheriff wiped his eyes. "They've no reason to hurt her." He sipped the coffee and placed it back in the cup holder. Checked his speed, looked at Billy, then back out the windshield. "Your mother's a powerfully spirited woman."

Rachel was sitting at the foot of the bed holding a cold pack to her jaw. A copy of her marriage license lay shredded on the floor.

When Jack proposed, one knee on the ash-covered plank floor of the yurt, he didn't present a diamond or engagement ring, but a package wrapped in white paper. She opened it and found a brick of crisp one-hundred-dollar bills. He called it a down payment, told her about a property at the foot of the Patriarch Run, and said they could build a house and raise bison to pay the mortgage.

Rachel had a vision of the baby in her womb, no larger than a kidney bean, growing up with horses.

The man ignored what Rachel had done to the marriage certificate.

"I don't know what it is he's done to you, and I don't defend it." That it had been about Jack meant Regan wasn't being threatened. She felt relieved. "But if you think Jack Erikson gives two shits about me or any human being on this planet other than Jack Erikson, you are sorely mistaken."

The man set a briefcase on the bed and opened it. "Did you know your husband was at the high school this morning?"

The firm lines of her face collapsed.

"You don't look well, Ms. Erikson."

She didn't respond.

"Ms. Erikson, when was the last time you saw your husband?"

"I told you, I don't have a husband. He's been gone near a decade. Billy was only a child then."

"Why are you protecting a terrorist?"

"I don't know what you're talking about."

He gave her a manila folder.

"What's this?"

Inside the folder was a printed image of a Lincoln Town Car. Its front doors were open. Two men, bullet wounds in their heads, lay on the highway.

The man closed the briefcase. "Your husband did that."

Rachel only glared.

"Billy was with him."

She cupped her hands over her nose and mouth.

"A lot of people want to talk to your son about what happened on the highway."

Rachel closed her fists and narrowed her eyes. One of the men wheeled in a television.

"Surely, an incident like the one in the photograph would have made the news." He pressed the power button.

Rachel saw the Town Car surrounded by a cluster of emergency vehicles on Highway 132. There was an image of the high school followed by Billy's senior picture.

The SHERIFF FLOODED ALL EIGHT CYLINDERS. THE AUTOMATIC TRANSMISSION shifted down, the engine roared, and Billy was thrown against the seat.

"He's gonna PIT us."

Billy didn't know what that meant, but the sheriff spoke so casually if it wasn't for the violent surge in speed, he would have thought it had a friendly connotation.

He turned around.

The front end of a black Mercedes tapped the patrol car just behind the rear wheel. Billy could hardly hear the impact.

The mountains and trees spun.

The sheriff steered through it and came out accelerating behind the black Mercedes. He switched on the lightbar and sirens.

"Ain't a law I can think of forbids you from loading that magazine."

The brake lights of the Mercedes flashed.

The patrol car closed all but forty yards before the sheriff could stand on his own brake pedal.

Tires screeched. Billy's body was thrust forward against the seatbelt.

White donuts began appearing on the windshield.

"Get down."

The sheriff was bleeding from the head. The Mercedes pulled away. The sheriff slammed the gas pedal to the floor, and Billy's skull was jerked backwards into the headrest.

A man in the backseat of the Mercedes used a boot to knock what was left of the glass from the rear window. Billy could see untied laces whipping in the wind. The man let go of the boot and presented a semiautomatic pistol.

"Down, Billy! Down!"

The patrol car kept accelerating.

Each new hole appearing in the windshield was surrounded by an opaque disk of laminated glass.

The sheriff took the Colt Python from its holster, aimed through the perforated windshield, and fired two rounds into the Mercedes.

Bullets ripped through the patrol car, ringing the sheet metal; safety glass sprayed through the cabin; stuffing oozed from the sheriff's seat; the rear window wasn't there anymore; beams of sunlight came through two holes in the roof liner.

Billy unbuckled his seat belt and curled up on the floor. He saw the fabric of the roof liner flapping and noticed the screaming wind.

The back of his head cracked the plastic door of the glove compartment. He bit his tongue. Heard crunching metal. Billy didn't realize they had rammed the other car until he noticed the airbags deflating.

The sheriff broke through what was left of the driver's side windshield with the steel barrel of the Colt. He thrust the revolver through the hole and emptied the cylinder.

The patrol car accelerated again.

The sheriff picked up the microphone—blood running from his wrist—and spoke as coolly as if he were talking about supper. "I got Billy Erikson in the car about a mile south of the airport on Highway 132. We're taking fire from three men in a black Mercedes echo-five-five-zero sedan. Over."

Billy swallowed the blood in his mouth. Then he opened the baggie and started cramming .30-30 cartridges through the loading gate of the '94.

The radio chatter was slow and hesitant for a moment.

"Say again? Over."

"Copy that, Sheriff. Charlie is inbound."

Billy couldn't see anything and tried to sit up.

"Billy, you just stay where you are."

Then the radio erupted, deputies talking over Nancy so that no one could be heard.

"So much for radio protocol." The sheriff switched it off. He looked up and slammed on the brakes.

He threw his torso on top of Billy. The patrol car was in a skid. Bullets ripped apart the dashboard, steering wheel, and driver's seat. The sheriff kept a hand on the bottom of the wheel and steered through the skid. Chunks of glass and plastic whizzed through the cabin.

The patrol car jumped off the shoulder of the road where the highway cut a trench through a low hill. The sheriff looked over the dash and corrected his steering. The corner of the front bumper burrowed into the embankment. The patrol car leapt up, bounced, and came to a stop on the white line. Its right front wheel was folded under. Steam poured from the hood. There was blood splattered on the instrument panel. The driver's side of the windshield was all but gone.

"You okay?" Blood ran down the right half of the sheriff's face. There were bullet holes in his uniform.

Billy's neck hurt. His head felt like it was exploding. He thought his arm was broken. "Yeah, I'm fine." He squeezed the bones, following them with the fingers of his other hand to check.

"I'm sorry I didn't issue you a vest." The sheriff opened his door, reloaded the Colt with a speedloader, then reloaded the empty speedloader. "One of 'em's dead. The passenger is now in the backseat with an MP5. They both looked Mexican to me."

Billy noticed that the sheriff's left shoulder was bleeding. That all the damage was on the driver's side of the vehicle.

"We'll make a stand right here. Stay behind the engine block."

Billy dropped the revolver in his coat pocket, opened the door, and got out. He rested the forearm of the rifle on his palm, the back of his hand on the hood of the patrol car.

"You stay behind that engine block."

The Mercedes was racing toward them. The man in the backseat was firing the MP5 out the window.

"When he's in range, take out the driver. If they get close enough for accurate fire, I want you to lie on the ground and cover your head with your hands. Do you understand?"

"Yes, sir."

The '94 was sighted in with a two hundred yard zero. Billy placed the post of the front sight well over the roof of the Mercedes, above the dark shape of the driver's head. He paused his breathing and squeezed the trigger.

He could see the fleshy color of the driver's face now and levered in a second cartridge. He lowered the sight to the roof line, took his time, and fired.

The Mercedes was at maybe two hundred yards.

He levered in another cartridge and fired again.

The Mercedes swerved.

"Keep hitting that driver."

Billy emptied the remainder of the magazine into the torso behind the wheel.

At seventy yards, the E550 was no longer on the highway. It was bouncing through the grass and rapidly losing speed. Then the front end disappeared into the Patriarch River.

Billy raised his head to get a better look and lead began ringing the sheet metal of the patrol car.

"Billy, get down!"

He dropped to his stomach and fumbled with the baggie. Billy couldn't control the trembling of his body, and the cartridges rolled off the shoulder of the road. He flung out a hand, accidentally knocking the hat off his head, but was only able to save a single round.

The roar of the sheriff's .357 magnum startled Billy. He looked under the car—the front end was collapsed over the broken axle—and saw the sheriff kneeling behind the door frame.

The MP5 was scattering bullets all over the asphalt. They were thudding into the engine block, piercing the sheriff's door.

Billy shoved the cartridge into the loading gate then levered it into the chamber. He heard the sheriff empty his spent brass onto the highway, reload, fire all six rounds, empty the spent brass, and reload again.

"You okay?"

Billy lay on his stomach behind the wheel, his rifle trained on the back of the sedan. "Yeah, I'm okay." He looked under the patrol car and saw the sheriff's knees. "How 'bout you?"

"Listen to me, Billy. The driver's dead. I hit the MP5, but he's still fightin'. They want you alive. Use that to your advantage. Keep your head cool, and you'll come out on top."

All but one of the windows were shot out on the Mercedes. The rear driver's-side door looked as if someone had sprayed it with silver dollars.

"Billy?"

"Yeah?"

"You did good, son."

Billy saw movement behind the Mercedes and started putting pressure on the trigger. He waited for what seemed like minutes. Until he heard the heavy steel of the sheriff's revolver fall against the asphalt.

He looked under the car. The sheriff was lying on his side. Billy couldn't see his face. Blood flowed through the spent brass.

"Sheriff?" Until now, he had felt scared. "Sheriff?"

BILLY EASED OFF THE SHOULDER OF THE ROAD—AN ANGER HEATING HIM unlike anything he had ever known.

He crawled on his belly thirty yards beyond the rear of the patrol car and slid into the river. Cold water tugged on his boots and pulled against his jeans. He stepped onto the ice then crawled inside the corrugated steel culvert, inching his way beneath the road.

When he came out the other side of the culvert, he saw that the front bumper of the Mercedes was under water. From the blue smoke in the exhaust, he knew the engine was still running.

Billy sat on the ice, the current burbling several inches beneath him. He spread his legs around a stone and leaned forward, using the stone as a rest. He could see by the man's legs that he was lying prone.

He could hear sirens.

The man got to his hands and knees, and Billy thought he could see an elbow through the grass. The fragmented target was no different from that of a deer in the woods. He visualized a line that passed through the rear passenger tire of the Mercedes and penetrated the man's torso. The bullet might ricochet when it hit the steel-belted tire. He couldn't control that. With a ricochet, it was possible that he could miss the man completely. But Billy didn't dwell on that thought. He focused on a single point, where the line he had visualized entered the tire. Then he checked his breath and squeezed the trigger.

Billy saw a puff of red mist, and the man collapsed. The Mercedes was now sitting on the wheel's rim.

The sirens grew louder.

Billy cycled the action. He was out of cartridges. He stood on the ice and searched his pockets. The only weapon he had left was the revolver.

He set the rifle next to the ejected piece of brass on the stony bank and climbed up to the highway.

A car approached. It was the wood-paneled Plymouth Voyager. As the van crept closer, he saw the kids pressed against the windows waving at him. They hadn't seen the sheriff's body under the open door of the patrol car. He could tell by Javier's eyes that he had.

The passenger door slid open as the minivan stopped. Javier called his name and beckoned to him with an arm out the window. It had been a long time since Billy heard it pronounced with a Mexican accent.

He walked around the back of the van. In the window glass, Billy could see the reflection of the sheriff's blood on his coat, his face.

RACHEL PULLED THE PIECE OF TRIM SHE PREPPED FROM BEHIND THE TOILET. She didn't have the information she needed to make the right decision. Who was outside the bedroom door? How many men? How much time would she have once they heard the breaking glass? Without that information, it was meaningless for her to plan.

She hobbled over to the bed, her hands bound in front of her body. She rolled onto the mattress, got to her knees then stood on the pillows. She felt dizzy and gripped the headrest for balance. She was thinking about Billy again. "Focus," she whispered to herself. What good will you do him?

Rachel raised the piece of trim to the window glass then remembered the plastic restraint on her wrists.

"Shit."

What frustrated her was that she could no longer trust herself, her own judgment. She had been through this already. How far could she get? She could make noise. She could hope to be seen or heard, but she could not hope to escape. Not unless she found a way to free her ankles and wrists.

Rachel stuffed the piece of trim between the mattress and box spring then studied her restraints. The ends of the plastic strap were secured in a pair of roller-locks. She bit the strap with her canines. Then she tried to crush the roller-lock housing with her molars.

Her jaw throbbed.

She took the finishing nails from the waistband of her skirt, under which she found a rash on her skin raised nearly a quarter inch.

Rachel tried to pierce the plastic strap with one of the nails. She tried to break the yellow teeth in the roller-lock housing. She stabbed at the roller itself. The roller gave a little, but did not break. She stabbed it again. Again. Out of frustration, over and over again. Until she saw it in her mind. The roller had a little play in it, allowing the teeth to feed through the housing. If she could slip something in there and lift the rollers, the lock would release.

The finishing nails were too big. Rachel studied the room. She considered the Van Gogh and tried to think of a way to get the nails out of the wooden frame.

They would be too big, too.

She looked at the shoe molding along the base of the wall. Then she got on the floor and peered under the molding into the gap between the carpet and the unpainted drywall. She wormed her way around the perimeter of the room, looking for a staple, something. She moved the nightstand, studied its footprint in the carpet then pushed the nightstand back into place.

She crawled into the walk-in closet, stood, and turned in a little circle examining the ceiling, the brass hanging rods, the empty shelving. There had to be something. She got back on her hands and knees and looked under the shoe molding, where she saw a red dot in the almond colored carpet.

It couldn't be . . . Her heart beat faster. She scratched at the glass head with her fingernail and was out of breath when she extracted the sewing pin.

RACHEL PUT HER EAR TO THE WALL AND LISTENED.

One chance, she told herself. Free the feet, free the hands, smash the window, climb out, and run.

She held the pin with her thumb and forefinger. "Don't you break," she was praying. "Please don't break." She inserted the pin into the roller-lock housing and lifted the roller. The strap loosened and she pulled her right ankle out of the plastic loop. Then she loosened the other side and pulled the restraint off her feet. She freed her wrists.

Rachel stuffed the restraints under the mattress, found the trim piece she took from the bathroom, and stepped onto the bed. She'd have to work quickly once she broke the glass. All she had to do was get to the ground. She felt certain that if she could get to the ground, she could get away.

She drove the wood through the glass and broke through the black plastic stapled to the exterior of the townhouse. Then she knocked out the little pieces of glass hanging from the top rail, folded the duvet, and used it to pad the glass shards she needed to climb over in the bottom rail. Rachel looked at the bedroom door. It was still shut. She stepped on the headboard and thrust her torso outside.

She was upside down. She hadn't thought about how to land. She didn't care either; she recognized the street.

There was a hand on her calf. She felt arms around her legs. They yanked her back and her chin struck the bottom rail. There were men pulling on her, shouting. The duvet no longer protected her from the broken glass. She was kicking, screaming. She was horizontal over the bed and bit the hand covering her mouth. She clung to the window sill, to chips of glass, to the wooden frame, anything she could grab.

Twenty-seven 3rd Street was a single story, red brick Catholic church with narrow, stained-glass windows the height of the building. A flagstone path in the back led through an iron gate into a walled court-yard, where there was a flower garden and statues of saints. He found an arched, paneled door on the side of the building.

When Jack pulled on the long, brass handle, he was pretty sure the door wouldn't open. But it did. He stepped into the carpeted hall and let the wooden door close against his back. There were offices on his right. He could see the foyer at the end of the hall. He stood still and listened.

He expected to find his contact in a public space, which meant the nave. He walked quietly past the offices, a closet, and stopped between the doors of the men's and women's restrooms.

The lights were off. Nobody seemed to be in the building.

Jack passed a glass display case in the foyer and stopped to study the empty nave through the window.

Then he opened one of the double doors and walked down the center aisle.

Rachel's phone rang.

Jack created a sling for his wounded right arm by leaving it out of the sleeve of his leather jacket; he kept the arm under the jacket and rested it on the partially-closed zipper. He answered the phone with his left hand.

"Walk toward the altar." It was a man's voice, deep.

Jack did as he was told.

"Turn left."

Jack turned into the north transept.

"Open the door and cross the courtyard."

The path led through a garden to a stone-crafted building.

"Open the door and step inside."

It was a dormitory. Jack let the wooden door shut behind him.

"I'm a friend, Jack, the only one you have left."

"I'm listening."

Bunk beds lined the granite walls of the dormitory. They were fitted with wool blankets.

"I brought you here because you need to remember."

"Tell me what you want me to remember."

"First things first. What did you see at the house?"

"I saw pictures of my family."

"They're in real trouble, Jack."

The voice on the phone was triggering a montage of memories. Jack walked the length of the room and turned around. "Who were the bombers in DC?"

"We're working on that. They're blue. That's been confirmed."

By blue, Jack understood that the men were Americans working for his own government.

After the detonation of the bomb in Washington DC, Jack remembered stepping out of an over-turned vehicle into a firefight. The driver of the vehicle was dead. The other man who had been in the vehicle was dying.

Jack asked, "And my two escorts?"

"They were mine."

Jack's mind was flooded with images from the bombing. "Who am I?"

"You were born in that dormitory. Nobody knows what happened to her after that, so there's no point in asking about your mother."

Jack opened the door and stepped into the garden.

WASHINGTON, D.C.
A FEW WEEKS AGO

THE SILENCE WAS RUPTURED BY A HORN BLAST.

Jack opened his eyes and saw the white, fluted columns of a courthouse. Pedestrians on the sidewalk.

His head was ponderous and difficult to turn.

A man in a black suit–a briefcase in his lap–was sitting beside him. The vehicle they were in was at a stoplight in heavy traffic. Jack's tongue was stuck to the roof of his mouth. It felt swollen and chalky, as if he had ingested a narcotic. He sucked his teeth but could not swallow.

When the mass of people huddled at the street corner began to cross the intersection, Jack noticed that a pale-skinned man with an earpiece stayed behind. They made eye contact.

The left side of Jack's head pulsed so violently from the drug the vision in that eye went white.

The SUV accelerated. Jack noticed the driver for the first time, the Ford Oval on the steering wheel. Then he bent forward and vomited between his knees. The man beside him in the backseat didn't respond.

Jack's attention was drawn through the crowd at the next intersection to another man talking into an earpiece.

He tried to press his palm against the side of his head, but couldn't.

A white van slowed to a stop beside him. The driver of the van wore the same earpiece. It seemed unlikely that the pattern was a coincidence. Beads of sweat dripped from the driver's nose. His jaw muscles were knotted.

Jack leaned forward to get a better look. But the van's door was now open, the driver gone.

Compelled by decades of training, he shouted, "Bomb!" The warning resonated with an unemotional authority he did not anticipate or comprehend.

The Ford he was in jumped forward, accelerating at full throttle into the heavy cross traffic. Tires screeched in the intersection. A white Civic swerved. Jack heard metal smashing metal. The Ford kept accelerating and punched the rear quarter panel of a blue Camry. It pushed through the lanes of cross traffic and T-boned a silver Tahoe.

JACK WAS COUGHING AND TRIED TO SIT UP, BUT HE COULDN'T. HE COULDN'T move his arms. He hit his head on the steering wheel and lay his cheek on the leather-trimmed door panel, in too much pain to curse. He kept his eyes shut to stop the skewer of light from plunging into his brain.

Bursts of automatic rifle fire punctuated the wailing and screams of terror.

He allowed his right eye to squint and saw jagged glass in a window frame. He closed the eye and slowly turned his head. He opened the one eye again and saw black asphalt and shattered glass beneath him.

He realized that he was in the front seat, that the Ford was on its side.

He put one knee on the asphalt, pressed his back against the roof, and stooped. He was standing in the broken-out window. His hands were bound behind his back.

Eight rapid, semi-automatic pistol shots fired from close by were followed by the clinking of a steel magazine against the pavement. Then he heard the familiar snap of supersonic projectiles passing close to his head and saw in the roof three pinholes of light.

Jack dropped and curled up on the broken glass. He assumed from the sound of the gunfire and from the small diameter of the holes appearing in the vehicle's roof liner that it was a 5.56×45mm NATO cartridge, probably being fired from an M4, a weapon commonly used by the armed forces of the United States.

Jack couldn't stop coughing. He couldn't recall how it was he came to be in the vehicle, and he didn't know where the two men in suits had gone.

When the gunfire ceased, he kicked out what remained of the windshield.

He remembered the briefcase and squeezed into the backseat. The combination briefcase was lying on the door. He used the sides of his feet to stand it upright between his ankles. Then he squatted with his hands behind his back and picked it up.

Civilians were calling for help. Others were crouching. There was a man prone on the asphalt, his hands shielding his head. From every direction came howls of pain. The air was black with smoke. Vehicles were on fire.

He found the driver of the Ford Expedition. There were bullet holes in his face and neck. Gray ashes speckled his cheek and black suit.

The Camry was upside down, on top of another sedan. Its windows were shattered. The paint was blackened, and three of its tires were ablaze like torches over the carnage.

A man thrashed his arms: his hair, back, and sleeves were on fire. A teenage girl ran out from behind the barricade of an overturned Prius, knocked the burning man down, and beat the flames with her cotton trench coat. Another burst of gunfire drove her to her belly. She lay on the man, smothering the flames.

He heard sirens. Everyone was coughing.

By the time he located the source of the gunfire through the black plumes of soot and smoke, the gunman was dead, splayed over the yellow hood of a Dodge Charger.

It was the man he saw at the first intersection.

He searched for the guy in the suit who was beside him in the Expedition. Gray ash fell from the smoke. A man crawled toward the sidewalk, coughing, dragging his right arm–a splintered, white bone protruding from his pant leg.

Jack stepped forward to help the man then remembered the handcuffs on his wrists and looked around.

The keys, he was certain, were in the locked briefcase he was holding behind his back.

A fire truck, sounding its air horn, pressed through the clogged street.

Then he found him, the guy from the backseat, lying prone in a pool of blood beside the burning Tahoe. There was a Colt Commander in his hand. By the position of the slide, Jack knew there was a round in the chamber. The pistol's thumb safety was off, the hammer was cocked, and the man's right hand was wrapped around the grip. His index finger was still on the trigger.

Jack set the briefcase in the street and sat in a pool of the man's blood. The blood was hot and soaked through his cotton pants. He eased the Colt out of the man's hand. Then he stood up, holding the gun behind his back. He brought the weapon to his left side, where he could see the muzzle, held his breath to suppress the coughing, and shot the brass lock on the briefcase.

Jack opened the latch and found the key inside.

THE MAN IN THE BLACK SUIT WAS MOANING. JACK ROLLED HIM OVER AND unbuttoned the suit jacket. Then he seized the bloody, silk shirt in both fists and pulled the shirt apart. Buttons sprung from their threads. The man was going to die. Jack pressed his bare hands against the wounds.

The man coughed, and blood misted Jack's face. Sirens and howls filled the street. He wiped the man's blood from his eyes, tore strips of silk from the shirt, wadded the fabric, and plugged the holes in the man's chest.

But the man's life, no matter how hard he pressed, welled up through Jack's fingers.

THE CRIES FOR HELP GREW MORE INSISTENT WITH THE ARRIVAL OF THE FIRST emergency crews.

The man in the suit was dead for minutes before Jack took his hands off his chest. He felt confused.

Barely visible through the sooty smoke, an uniformed officer, his weapon drawn, was making his way toward the Expedition.

It was time to leave.

Jack pressed the magazine release and counted the two remaining .45 ACP cartridges. There was a third cartridge in the chamber. He counted four spent stainless-steel magazines in the blood at his feet. Then he slammed the nearly empty magazine home and hid the Colt in his waistband. He searched the dead man for spare magazines, for identification, and found nothing.

Jack staggered away from the approaching officer, past the yellow

Charger with the dead gunman on the hood. There was a red hole above his ear. An M4 carbine lay in the street.

The dizziness nearly overwhelmed Jack.

Whoever the man in the black suit was, he had known what he was doing. Lying prone in a pool of his own blood, the man shot through the Charger's rear driver's-side window. The bullet passed through the cabin, exited through the roof, near the passenger-side windshield pillar, and struck the gunman in the head: a target not in the shooter's field of vision.

PRESENT

It was snowing when they unloaded—all eleven of them—behind the Holiday Inn. The children held hands; the eldest carried the youngest, and the two infants were under a blanket in Lola's arms.

The engine of the Plymouth Voyager idled as Billy followed the procession into the hotel and down the concrete stairs.

The basement hall smelled of laundry soap. The wallpaper was peeling, and the carpet was worn through. They passed a half-dozen canvas laundry carts parked against the wall. Then they passed an open door through which Billy saw a teenage girl folding white sheets. Behind her was a floor-to-ceiling bank of stainless-steel laundry machines.

The young laundress raised her head, as if to look at Billy as he passed. She had no eyes.

They stood at the last door in the hallway, and Javier spoke to Lola.

She was afraid and whispered, *"Tenga cuidado, Javier."*

Lola chewed her bottom lip and waited with the children in the hall. Less than a minute passed before she asked Billy to please accompany her brother-in-law inside.

The air in the windowless room was opaque with smoke. A young Mexican in a white tank top was shaving over a rusty bathroom sink, a cigarette in his lips. Another was smoking on the twin bed. Two middle-aged men were seated in metal folding chairs, cigarettes in their fingers. A man with pocked skin stood smoking against the wall—one arm resting on top of his protrusive belly.

Unemptied ashtrays cluttered every surface. The shag carpet was orange and littered with beer cans, tequila and whiskey bottles, Pepsi cans, cigarette butts, and a plate with desiccated scraps of chicken and green beans.

One of the men was shirtless, his chest black with tattoos. He nodded at Billy and grinned. In that grin, there was a threat.

Billy nodded back and, in that moment, realized he was missing his Cabela's hat. Nobody else seemed interested in his presence.

Javier was in the midst of a transaction. The man on the bed recorded the terms in a notebook, pulled out a roll of bills then peeled off two hundred dollars for Javier.

JAVIER PUT LOLA AND THE CHILDREN IN ONE OF THE LITTLE BASEMENT ROOMS. The toilet needed plunging. The sink was black with grime. He spoke to her then took Billy out to the idling van.

It was snowing harder.

The tires spun as the Voyager tried to climb the hill out of the parking lot. Billy stepped out of the van and pushed against the door frame. The air smelled of burning rubber.

The van inched forward then accelerated until Billy was jogging beside it. He jumped in and the Voyager shot across the street into the parking lot of the tire shop.

Javier told Billy that the children weren't his. Some of them were Lola's and the rest were her sister's. She and her husband were walking home together from the church when a police truck came around the corner, pursued by two bigger trucks from the cartel. The couple found themselves in the crossfire.

The pile of used tires behind the cinderblock building was covered in snow. They dug through it together, selected a mismatched set of four tires, and carried them, two apiece, around the building into the heated bay. There was a waiting room, but they stood with the vehicle.

"The houses on that street," Javier told him, "were behind high walls. There was nowhere for the couple to go. The same bullet killed them both. He died covering her body."

They stood shoulder-to-shoulder and watched the technician mount the first wheel on the balancer.

"Ciudad Juárez is at war. These things happen."

The technician took the wheel off the machine, rolled it over to the Voyager, and leaned it against the studs. The brake pad was worn nearly through.

"Lola has a good heart . . . to a fault. Although she could not feed them, she took the orphaned children into her own home. My brother did not complain, but he needed more income to feed so many children. He had only two real choices, the cartel or the police. Because he understood the situation in Ciudad Juárez, he chose the cartel. But Lola was more naive and would not allow it. So he appeased her and, in the end, applied for a job with the police."

The technician opened the hood on the balancer and hammered a lead weight to the wheel's rim.

"Lola came to me Tuesday night. She said he was killed in a bombing. What could I say to her? He was my brother."

Out of respect, Billy didn't speak during the long silences. The technician put the fourth wheel on the balancer.

"I knew I would be hauling refrigerated produce in a couple days, so I told her to purchase winter coats and to wait for me on the side of the highway."

THEY WATCHED THE WHEEL SPIN ON THE BALANCER. THE MACHINE STOPPED and the technician raised the hood.

The pneumatic drill whined as the lug nuts were attached to the rear studs.

"My father lives in Leadville. I will deliver Lola and the children in the morning. Then I have to drive back to Chihuahua."

The technician asked Javier if he wanted new pads on the front brakes. Javier shook his head, and the technician mounted the wheels.

Javier gestured to the minivan with his chin, "I rented it from some guys in New Mexico."

THEY GOT IN THE VAN AND DROVE BACK TO THE HOTEL.

"Was it drugs that caused the killings on the highway?"

Billy told him he didn't know. Only that it was about his father.

Javier nodded and said that the sheriff had been a good man.

Billy accepted the condolences without correcting the misunderstanding.

BILLY SAW HER AND SHOULDERED THE RIFLE. SHE WAS AT THIRTY YARDS, AND *her head was buried in the high grass. Billy could feel Regan's presence behind him, but he did not take his eye off the front sight, which was covering the shoulder of the deer. He was listening for Regan, for some sort of approval.*

Then it occurred to Billy that this was his doe, his decision. From the sheriff's silence Billy understood that, regardless of the company he kept, when it came to this type of commitment, he was alone. It occurred to him, in that lodgepole forest at eleven years old, that he would in this sense always be alone.

She lifted her head. Her ears rotated forward.

Billy knew that she had heard him. Knew that he had betrayed himself with a sound. Maybe he had released the breath he had been holding too quickly. Whatever it was, she was now searching for him in the trees.

Billy didn't hear the crack of the rifle. He saw her jump into the air and turn and run. She fell.

She was on her side. One of her legs still kicked, as if she were running in a dream. There was grass on her tongue. Blood frothed in her nostrils.

Billy turned to find Regan and realized that the sheriff had crossed the meadow with him. Then he saw the fawn for the first time. It stood at the edge of the clearing looking back at Billy.

Billy felt Regan's hand on his shoulder. It was the strength of the hand that set loose the grief.

BILLY WOKE. HE PICKED THE DENIM SHIRT HE WAS USING FOR A PILLOW OFF the floor and dried the sweat on his brow. He mopped the back of his neck and his face.

He put his arms through the dampened shirt sleeves, felt for his hat, remembered it was gone, picked up his coat, his boots, and stepped over the sleeping bodies in his stocking feet. He didn't want to let light into the hotel room and opened the door only a few inches, enough for him to squeeze into the hall. Then he pulled the door until he heard the bolt latch.

There was no place he could go. Billy fell against the wall in the lighted hallway with his jaw open. His eyes were squeezed shut. No sound came from his throat. But he was sobbing.

He forced himself to stop. Not because he thought it unfitting: but he had fallen to the floor. He didn't want to wake them. He stepped into his boots and laced them.

Billy carried his coat in his arms and looked into the laundry as he passed. The girl without eyes was asleep on a cot.

Alone…didn't describe the feeling. It was as if he had come to the end of the world.

He climbed the concrete stairs, opened the glass door, and stood in the falling snow—his shirt unbuttoned. He wished he would have walked back to the sheriff, seen his face. Touched it.

Halos of lightning encompassed the town, illuminating low clouds. Vertical strikes. Simultaneous cracks of thunder. The descending snow was radiant in the storm.

Billy buttoned his shirt, tucked it into his Wranglers, and saw a deer on the other side of the parking lot. It was crossing toward him. Crooked fingers of lightning, parallel to the ground, ripped through the falling snow. The accompanying thunder knocked Billy on his heels and set off alarms in the parking lot.

He held his coat in his hands and watched the deer approach by the light of the storm. Then he realized it walked on its hind legs.

Billy was unsure what this might mean. He had studied the book of Revelation in his English class, and by the way things stood, no manner of beast or sign would have astonished him.

Nickel-sized snowflakes already covered his boots, knees, and shirt-sleeves. The lightning had seemed unceasing so it confounded Billy when he could no longer see. He put his hand on the grip of the revolver.

After several heartbeats, he came to understand that the light storm had paused. Without his sight, he listened for footsteps.

In the next flash he saw that the creature had transmogrified into the shape of a man. It looked to be at about twenty yards. Billy heard its breath and advanced to meet it.

The old man closed the distance and grabbed his arm.

THUNDER RATTLED THE GLASS AS BILLY LED HIM—STOOPED AND NO MORE than five feet tall—through the doorway. Whatever his age, it didn't seem possible to be any older.

Billy brushed the snow from his hair and shoulders. Then the old Mexican took his arm again.

They descended into the basement.

The old man rested at the bottom of the stairs. The snow had sloughed from his poncho by the time he started shuffling down the hallway, past the laundry. He stopped at the first door.

Billy opened it, and they went inside.

The room had no windows. The bathroom light was on, its door ajar. Billy could see a man in the twin bed, another rolled in a sheet on the floor. The old man gestured to a glass coffee pot and told Billy in Spanish to get the water from the bathroom sink.

Billy did as he was asked and handed the pot to the Mexican.

More water spilt onto the table than was poured into the reservoir of the coffee maker. The old man pushed the power switch with two fingers of his gnarled hand.

Beside the coffee maker was an empty tequila bottle.

The Mexican did not take off his hat or poncho. He sat hunched on a metal chair beside the table and invited Billy to sit on the foot of the bed.

Water dripped from the heating element of the coffee maker as clear as it came out of the tap. The glass pot was less than half full when the old man poured himself a cup of hot water and offered the pot to Billy.

Water, still dripping from the reservoir, sizzled on the empty burner.

Billy thanked him for the offer but declined the water for the reason that there was no other cup, which he did not state. He sat down on the bed, inches from a pair of feet under the blanket.

The Mexican returned the pot to the burner. His ceramic mug was badly stained. He held it by the broken handle and sipped the hot water.

The old man asked where Billy was from.

"I was born in these mountains. I have always lived here, and god willing, I always will."

The old man nodded his head, looked into his lap, and repeated, "*Si Dios quiere.*" His mind was elsewhere.

Billy waited for the man to look at him again before he asked about the laundress.

He only said that she had no eyes.

The man on the floor rolled and farted so loudly it sounded as if he tore the sheet.

"And that one complains I talk in my sleep."

Billy looked at the man in the bed.

"Nothing wakes them when they are drunk."

Billy asked if that was the reason he went out in the snowstorm.

"No. I dreamt the world was ending. And if that were so, I'd rather go out and meet the end than have it find me in my bed."

Billy nodded. "What is it you met?"

"The snow. The cold. After that, bed seemed like a good place to be."

"*Dígame cómo terminó,*" Billy asked.

"What? The world?"

"*Sí, viejo, en su sueño.*"

The old man told him that there was nothing to eat.

"And how did it come to be in your dream that there was nothing to eat?"

"In my dream, the world was a corpse. People were laying their eggs in the corpse like insects. Crawling about and eating her flesh. Each generation produced more insects until her flesh undulated with larvae. They burrowed inside and ate her organs, her brain. Once she was consumed, there was nothing left to eat."

Billy thought about the image until the old man set the mug on the card table and switched off the coffee maker.

"What does it mean?"

"I don't know." The old man took off his hat and set it on the table. "Perhaps it is better for everyone not to fix any of the problems."

"Which problems do you mean?"

He shrugged. "The problems they talk about on television. The problems with the world: the famine, the global warming."

"I don't understand."

"In the beginning, there were only two insects, and it seemed there would always be abundance."

Billy waited a long time for him to say more. But he didn't.

The old Mexican folded the metal chair, leaned it against the wall, and lay on the floor beneath where he had sat. He tucked the hem of the poncho under his hip.

Billy asked if he required anything.

"Apague la luz del baño."

Billy did as he was asked.

He opened the door to leave. Then he froze, straining to hear the old man's voice.

"Every problem solved leads to the same thing."

Billy stood in the hall and stared into the blackness of the room trying to comprehend what was happening. His father had returned; Sheriff Regan Dowell had been gunned down; his mother was missing. He himself was being stalked by death.

When the old man did not explain the statement, Billy asked, "What does it lead to?"

"More mouths to feed."

SOMALIA
1991

JACK HAD NO PROFESSIONAL BUSINESS IN AFRICA. HE WAS IN SOMALIA FOR personal reasons—eating a breakfast of anjero and tea—when a college kid, maybe twenty-one or twenty-two, stopped at his table and asked, "You're an American?"

Jack wasn't looking for company, and he didn't smile, "Yes."

"Can I sit down?"

Before Jack could answer, the kid pulled out a chair and sat in it.

Jack continued eating.

"I'm a freelance journalist writing a piece about the famine and its historical antecedents. Do you mind if I ask you a couple of questions?"

"I do," Jack said.

The kid looked startled. He fidgeted, uncomfortable with the tension, but he didn't get up from the table. He didn't quit.

Jack admired that.

After a minute, the kid's body seemed to deflate. "I'm not really a journalist. I'm a journalism major. I bought a one-way ticket. And I need to build some contacts."

"Your parents know you're here?"

"Yeah."

Jack looked into his tea. "They approve?"

"No."

"A civil war is a dangerous place to go find yourself."

"I know."

"Not yet, you don't."

The kid looked away.

"Are your parents rich?"

"Yeah."

Jack's eyes were hard. "Does that piss you off?"

"Maybe."

"What's your name?"

"Malcolm."

Jack drank his tea and studied the kid for a long time. Then he guessed at his motivation for being in the country. "Malcolm, do you really believe a news story can put pressure on the United States to intervene in Somalia?"

"Maybe."

"What makes you think that will make things better?"

"You can't just watch people die and do nothing."

"That's an interesting statement." Jack's voice was stern. "Do you have plans for tomorrow?"

The kid didn't answer.

"Meet me here at eight."

THE BUS WAS A MODIFIED DUMP TRUCK. THE ONLY WOMAN ON THE BUS covered her head and shoulders with a green and black shawl. Most of the men wore slacks and Western-style shirts. Jack stood in the open-box bed beside an old man wearing a macawis around his waist and a cotton prayer cap on his head. It wasn't polite to converse in a language the other riders couldn't understand, so Jack ignored the kid's questions.

Jack climbed down from the bed when the bus stopped at a crossroad, and the journalist followed. All that could be seen from where they stood in the East African desert were the red, dusty roads intersecting at their feet and the surrounding acacia shrubs.

"Now what?" the kid asked.

Jack swung his backpack onto his shoulder, "We walk."

"Where?"

Jack started walking. "This way."

"Is it safe?"

"No." Jack didn't look back. "We're in Somalia."

AN HOUR LATER, THEY MET A MAN LYING ON THE ROAD UNDER A FILTHY blanket. His body was hardly more than a skeleton and skin. There were flies in his ear. The insects were crawling out of his mouth and nostrils.

The kid used his camera to document what he thought was a corpse.

Then the eyes came alive, focused, and looked into his.

The kid leapt backwards and let out an unconscious shout. The starving man twisted in the dirt–rib cage and collar bones bulging from his skin–and crawled toward the kid.

THE VILLAGE WAS SMALL. THE YOUNG JOURNALIST COULD SEE THE WHOLE OF it from where he stood on the road. The huts were round. They were made of sticks and grass and were surrounded by brush fences, most of which were falling apart.

Jack left the road and took a footpath that led through the village. The kid was almost tripping over his heels.

He could see men digging in the cemetery.

"It's been growing by ten graves per day."

The kid stopped walking, trying to comprehend that: how such a tiny village could supply so many graves? He saw mounds of freshly dug dirt, dozens of them. The new graves were covered with small sticks.

He followed Jack around a shrub fence, mostly collapsed, and saw an emaciated man flexing a long twig over his head. He was shaping it to repair the roof of his hut.

The Somali man recognized Jack and greeted him with a handshake. The two talked for several minutes before Jack introduced the journalist.

When the Somali man greeted him, the kid felt like a tourist. He was ashamed of himself. He could feel the man's nearly fleshless finger bones as they wrapped around his hand, the sliding and popping of tendons.

Jack continued to talk to the man, and the kid watched the children huddled against the wall of the hut. Impossibly thin arms and legs. Spherical shoulders. Pelvic bones protruding at grotesque angles. The youngest was eating her clothes.

Jack took a box out of his backpack and gave it to the man.

"WHAT'D YOU GIVE HIM?"

"Ammunition. I owed him a payment for a service he performed."

"Ammunition? What good is that to him?"

"Weapons and ammunition always hold their value. The greater the crisis the greater the value."

"He'll trade it?"

"It was very specialized ammunition. He'll know what to do with it."

"Where are we going now?"

"Back to the hotel."

"That's it? We walked a half a day to deliver a box of ammunition?"

"I guess it's up to you what you walked here for."

Jack led him through the rest of the village on the footpath.

The journalist saw a mother and her infant. The baby's face was wasted by hunger, her brown eyes sunken and stretched so wide she looked otherworldly. The infant's tiny fingers clutched her mother's withered breast.

The mother wore bracelets, a necklace. She was just a kid, around fifteen, but she looked like an old woman. Too feeble to stand, she lifted her baby to him. Her spindly arms shook spastically from the effort. The plea in the woman's brown eyes was the most desperate act he had ever witnessed.

The kid looked up and down the path then at Jack. He was frantic. "What? What does she want me to do?"

They stood at the crossroad waiting alone for the bus.

"Let it go," Jack said.

"I can't." Tears streaked his dirty face. "How do you explain to someone that a mother pleaded with you for the life of her baby?"

"You don't explain it. With some things, you're alone."

"We just passed by . . . "

"You haven't been here long enough. You'll understand once you have."

"I hope not." The kid wiped his nose with the back of his hand. "Not if being here makes me like you."

"If you'd have taken that child, what then?"

"I don't know. I'd find someone, a family."

"Is that right?"

"Yes."

"Before we get back to the hotel, there will be another child. Another mother just like the one you saw. You'd take her, too?"

The kid didn't respond.

"There are four-and-a-half million people starving here. You can't carry them all."

The kid looked away.

An hour passed as they waited for the bus.

"What you do with your time is a choice," Jack finally offered.

"That's supposed to make me feel better?"

"You misunderstand me. This is a famine. I'm not interested in how you feel."

The kid looked at the dirt at his feet. Then he met Jack's eyes and spat the question, "What do you choose to do with your time then?"

Jack knew the kid was starting to get it, the enormity of the problem. "You could spend all your money, your parents' money, your whole life here feeding people and not scratch the surface of this catastrophe. You're not powerful enough."

"So what do I do?"

"Bring the attention."

"So we just let them die. You know how that feels? That feels shitty."

"Yes, it does."

They heard an engine and turned to see a pickup approaching the crossroad. There were armed men seated in the bed.

"Don't say anything," Jack told the kid. "Don't do anything."

The truck came to a stop with one of the men in the back standing behind a DShK. The machine gun was mounted on a tripod and trained on Jack. The man in the passenger seat got out of the truck. He was wearing a macawis sarong.

He took their backpacks and tossed them into the cab. Then he asked Jack a question in a language the kid did not understand.

Jack answered the man and gestured with his head in the direction from which they came.

The man nodded then said in English to the kid, "Journalist." He offered a smile, absent of warmth, then got back into the passenger seat. The truck turned toward the city and in a minute was gone.

THEY BOARDED THE BUS. ON THE WAY BACK TO THE CITY, THEY PASSED ABANdoned villages. They passed a relief kitchen. Old men, women, naked children, all their bones visible, sitting in groups on the dirt. They saw bands of starving people as silent as the desert acacia all the way out to the horizon. Many of them were dead. The relief workers were equipped with enough supplies to feed maybe one in a hundred of those who had gathered there.

SEVERAL HOURS LATER, THE DUMP TRUCK IN WHICH THEY WERE RIDING CAME to a stop. The kid stood to look over the top of the cab and saw the pickup. It was blocking the road, and its machine gun was now trained on the bus. Beyond the roadblock was a village. The grass huts had been burned. Some were still smoldering in the red dirt.

Armed men forced the passengers off the bus.

There was a tree not twenty yards from where they were made to stand—young children, eviscerated babies, hanging from the branches.

Two young men were taken from the group of passengers. The others were made to re-board the bus, which drove around the pickup truck and passed through the village.

IT WAS DUSK. THEY WERE WALKING TO THE HOTEL WHEN THE KID SAID, "I don't know what to do with what I saw today. I really don't. Can I talk to you tomorrow?"

"I'm leaving tonight."

"Back home?"

"No."

"Will you be back?"

"I don't think so."

The kid's eyes were vacant, his shoulders caved in. "Okay then." He took a few more steps toward the hotel then stopped walking.

"You could've put that little girl in a hospital. She'd've still died." Jack was moving toward the hotel when he looked back and said, "It's not about hunger, Malcolm."

"What are you talking about?" Exasperated, the kid pointed into the desert. "What'd we just see?"

"There are, what, five-and-a-half billion people on the planet today?"

"Five-and-a-quarter."

Jack stopped walking and turned to face him. "That number has more than doubled in my lifetime."

The kid didn't comprehend Jack's statement. He couldn't make sense of the day. "You fed that man on the road. And that man you gave the ammunition to, you saved his family."

"That's not the point," Jack said.

"But you risked your life. You walked all the way out there just to save him."

Jack started walking again toward the hotel. "Don't miss the forest for the trees."

"What are you talking about?"

"Math."

"You're not making sense."

"No, it's you who's not making sense. If you want to help those people, write about the math."

The kid ran to catch up. "I don't understand you. I've tried. But I don't."

"If you want to help, treat the problem, not the symptom. What happened to the number of hungry people when the population doubled?"

The kid was out of breath and didn't answer.

"The hunger is a symptom. So is the violence. Run the numbers. If you want to understand what you saw today, you need to understand the math."

The kid shook his head, pain and confusion visible on his face.

"Listen to me, Malcolm. If the growth never stops, what you saw today is how it ends."

"For whom?"

"For all of us."

Present

Billy paid the Mexican who ran the basement for another night then lay on the floor in his room. He looked at the clock. 11:04. Javier was in Leadville by now. Billy had never felt so powerless. He had no idea what he would do. Only that he couldn't go home. He couldn't be seen.

There's still a law, he had told the sheriff. Now he was hiding among those outside of it.

He didn't notice the passing hours. He lay on the floor, looking at the ceiling.

He could turn himself in to Charlie, the only deputy he really knew. But if they could get at the sheriff, they could get at Charlie. He thought about the men at the Cedar Lodge, but he'd just be imprisoned in their custody again.

He needed a plan. But he didn't know where his mom was. He didn't know who had her or how to find out. Then he recognized his mistake. He shouldn't have killed the last gunman. What he needed was information.

He knew he couldn't be seen upstairs. But he had to eat. For his mom's sake, he had to keep his energy. Billy stepped into the hall. He would ask the old man to bring him some food.

The girl without eyes was with the canvas carts, separating the white sheets from the white towels. Billy recognized the shirtless man with her. The number thirteen was spelled out across his shoulders, and his torso was blackened with tattoos. The girl did nothing to rebuff the man's eager hands, and, at first, Billy thought her a whore.

Billy knocked on the door to the old man's room.

The shirtless man touched his cheek to the girl's. "Just let me taste the apples on your chest."

Billy watched her eyeless face, and it became clear: her refusals were subtle, shrewd, but they were refusals, nonetheless.

The shirtless man, aware of Billy's attention, offered the same knowing nod as the day before.

No one came to the door.

Billy wasn't intimidated by the man, but he couldn't afford to make a scene either. What made the matter complicated was that he simply didn't have it in him to walk away.

The shirtless man took a step toward Billy. "There's nobody there."

Billy's mind was clear for the first time that day. He kept looking at the door and said, "It's okay. I can wait."

He stood there for a minute, maybe more.

When Billy finally looked at the girl again, he saw the man pinching her breast. Fright opened the girl's mouth, her lips pulled tight with pain, but all that escaped audibly was a whimper.

The man approached Billy, looked him up and down, and offered a biting smile. "If you want her for yourself, why don't you say so?"

Billy didn't look him in the eye. He knew that as long as he stood as witness, no serious harm would come to her.

Billy used the pay phone in the parking lot.

He almost hung up when he heard the line switch to voicemail, but he didn't have any more change, and he doubted there'd be another opportunity to call.

Hello, this is Sally's voicemail. Please leave a message.

Billy heard her voice and felt sad all of a sudden. He didn't speak out of fear he'd choke up. Then Billy worried that the line might disconnect. "Sally . . . " He had cried in front of her before. " . . . it's Billy." He cried the first time they made love. But he couldn't allow himself to do that now, not on the phone. "It's good to hear your voice, even on a machine." His voice was strained. "I miss it." Billy really didn't have anything to say. He just wanted to be connected to her. He listened to the emptiness on the line. "I don't know how they're making it look on the news, but right now I'm okay." He couldn't think of anything else to tell her. "I probably won't be able to call again so I just wanted you to know that." He pictured the cellphone in her hand. She didn't answer calls from unknown numbers. "You should probably delete this message now that you've heard it."

THERE WAS A KNOCK AT THE DOOR. BILLY GLANCED AT THE CLOCK. 7:37. HE threw a sheet over the revolver, pointed it at the door, and called from the bed, "It's open."

Javier stepped into the room. He had returned to the hotel to pay his two-hundred-dollar debt, plus interest.

Billy asked, "Where will you go now?"

"To New Mexico. I'm scheduled to drive again in the morning."

"After that, will you return home?"

"No. I think there's been too much misfortune to return there."

Billy slipped the .44 into the breast pocket of his coat and stood to say goodbye.

"I can't leave yet," Javier said. "There's a problem with the car."

"What's wrong with it now?"

"It's cold outside. I just need you to hold the throttle while it starts."

THE PLYMOUTH VOYAGER WAS PARKED WITH THE EMPLOYEE VEHICLES AT THE back of the hotel. Billy found the throttle cable. Javier turned the ignition. The van started and a dark plume spilled from the exhaust.

Javier laughed.

Billy shut the hood, walked to the open window, and offered his hand, "Good luck to you."

Javier told him to walk with God and drove away.

The Voyager didn't make it thirty yards.

He could read the curses on Javier's lips in the side mirror. Billy took a step toward the van and heard gunfire. The driver's-side window glass sprinkled to the asphalt.

He heard the approaching engine and turned to see the white pickup. The truck was in a controlled skid. It swung around the parked cars and accelerated toward the van, snow spraying from all four fenders. The passenger hung out of the window, firing at Javier.

Billy already considered himself a dead man.

He drew the revolver and advanced. He tracked the approaching gunman with the sights. Then he remembered the sheriff's advice and switched to the driver. He squeezed off a 300 grain bullet that would penetrate the driver's torso, the seat, exit the sheet metal behind the cab, and the tailgate beyond that. The round made holes through elk an inch in diameter. The recoil lifted the revolver over Billy's head. He lowered the muzzle, sighted again on the arc of the steering wheel, and squeezed the trigger.

Billy leapt to his right.

The truck hurtled past, jumped the curb, smashed into the Holiday Inn, and disappeared in a veil of dust.

JAVIER WAS IN THE FETAL POSITION ON THE FLOORBOARD OF THE VAN WHEN Billy found him. "Are you hurt?"

Javier got onto his knees and looked out the window. "I don't know."

"I'll be right back. I need you to open the sliding door and pop the hood."

BILLY HELD HIS COAT OVER HIS FACE, STEPPED INTO THE CLOUD OF DUST, found the tailgate, and passed through the hotel wall in the bed of the truck. He jumped out on the passenger side and was standing in the room. The queen bed was underneath the front wheel. The carpet, the lamps, the television, the table and chairs were all buried in rubble and dust. The passenger window was down. Billy reached inside the cab and unlocked the door. The front end of the vehicle was so caved in he was surprised to hear the hinges groan, to see the door actually open.

The airbags were deflated. The footwell had been shoved back. Billy checked the passenger's pulse. He was crammed so tightly into the tiny space remaining under the dash that Billy wasn't sure he'd be able to pull him out. He took him by the armpits, and the man unfolded like an accordion. Billy stretched his body over the rubble. He felt the bones in his neck and spine, along his arms then his pelvis and legs. The right leg was broken. He felt his ribs. The only blood he could see was on his face. Lacerations from the glass. He looked in his mouth.

Billy found a black carbine on the floor of the cab. It had a red dot sight and some other high tech gear he didn't recognize. Billy had never had use for modern military weapons, but he only had four rounds left in his revolver. Any fool would have had sense enough to put more than a cylinder full of ammunition in his pocket. What made the carbine attractive to Billy was its thirty round magazine. But how would he conceal it? A gun like that would draw a lot of unwanted attention, and he couldn't risk attracting any more attention.

He decided against it, climbed into the cab, and checked the driver for an ID. He found a roll of hundred dollar bills and a cellphone. He claimed both and climbed out. According to the call history, the phone had only been used to contact one number.

He dialed it.

It rang once. *"Dígame."*

Billy didn't know what to say.

"¿Quién es éste?"

He tried to think of what he had to lose by being on the phone. Nothing came to mind. On the other hand, he couldn't afford to lose any more than he had. He shouldn't have called.

"Billy?" The voice spoke English now. "Billy, is it you? You are in a lot of danger, Billy. I'm trying to help you."

"Bullshit."

"Billy, I want you to listen to me."

"What have you done with my mom?"

"We're protecting her."

"Bullshit."

"Billy, you were smart to find this phone. Keep it with you so we can talk. Do you know where your father is? Once he's found, you and your mother will be safe."

Billy dropped the phone.

He propped the exterior door to the hotel room open with a piece of broken cinder block. Then he took the passenger by the elbows and dragged him through the snow into the parking lot.

People were gathering around the hole in the building.

Billy spoke without looking at anyone. "There's a baby in there. I heard it crying but couldn't find it."

Two men rushed through the door.

The left foot flopped from side-to-side as Billy dragged the man over the rutted snow.

Javier came around the van.

"Help me lift him."

They lifted him to the floor of the van and Billy slid the door shut.

"Try and start it."

Billy held the hood open with one hand and adjusted the throttle with the other. The crankshaft turned and the cylinders fired.

The van was already moving when Billy jumped in and shouted, "Go! Go!"

BILLY HAD NO ILLUSIONS ABOUT WHAT HAD JUST HAPPENED. IF THEY HAD meant to kill him, they would have.

Javier turned onto the highway. "This place is starting to remind me of home."

The sun was setting, which was a good thing because the shot-up van would draw a lot less attention at night. It started to snow. At fifty-five miles per hour, the holes in the sheet metal whistled and an icy wind ripped through the broken windows.

The man moaned.

Billy moved to the back and checked his pulse. He studied his face. The man worked for the people who killed the sheriff. He was sure of it. So in the end, it didn't matter whether he lived or died, as long as he lived long enough to talk. Billy thought about calling Rob. Then he realized that he didn't know what had happened to Rob after the raid on the clinic.

Javier caught Billy's eye in the mirror. It was obvious that the man needed a doctor.

Billy took the revolver out of his coat pocket, covered the man with his Carhartt, and shouted so Javier could hear, "Turn up the heat."

Once it was dark, they stopped at a Safeway. The snow flakes were large and falling heavily in the parking lot.

Billy gave Javier a hundred dollars and said, "I can't be seen inside."

By the time Javier came out of the grocery store, the windshield was blanketed in snow. He was carrying duct tape and plastic sheeting, a log of summer sausage, apples, a case of bottled water, and toilet paper.

They taped the man's wrists to the bolt on the rear seat then they taped the plastic over the windows.

The roads were almost empty because of the storm. Billy had no idea where he was going, only that he couldn't stay where he was.

THERE WERE THREE INCHES OF SNOW, AND THERE WAS NO OTHER TRAFFIC on the highway. Javier was leaning over the steering wheel, straining to see the shoulder of the road. The speedometer read ten miles per hour.

"Turn off the headlights," Billy suggested.

"What?"

"There's less glare."

Javier switched them off and the shoulders of the road seemed to suddenly appear.

"If you see any oncoming traffic, switch them back on."

THEY WERE TRAVELING A PLOWED SECTION OF HIGHWAY JUST SOUTH OF THE New Mexican border, and Javier had the Voyager up to thirty miles per hour.

"Do you know who they are?" Billy asked.

"Sicarios."

"Hit men?"

Javier pointed to his forearm. "The tattoo. He's from The Cartel."

Billy climbed to the back. He took his coat off the man and looked at his arm. The tattoo was an image of a richly plumed Aztec warrior. The face was portrayed as a skull.

Billy felt weak and sat on the floor.

It was hard to imagine how things could get worse. Surrounding the image of the Aztec warrior was the designation of the man's Army unit: Grupo Aeromóvil de Fuerzas Especiales. The tattoo was a modified insignia for the Mexican Army Special Forces.

"Some years ago," Javier told Billy, "a group of highly-trained soldiers hired themselves out as enforcers for the drug trade. At first, they served as bodyguards. They safeguarded smuggling routes and punished informers. Backed by drug money, their resources were unlimited. They purchased and stockpiled sophisticated weapons and communications equipment from military warehouses in Central and South America. They were better armed as enforcers than they were as an army unit. They could do anything, go anywhere. They even built training camps and recruited new members.

"They loved to fight and were eventually used as a paramilitary force in the war against the other cartels. There was nobody in Mexico who could withstand them. They were absolutely dominant.

"But their commander was smart. He realized that he no longer wanted to risk his life to enrich other men. So he slaughtered the leadership he was hired to protect and formed his own cartel, El Cártel.

"The reach of their brutality was unprecedented, even in the drug trade. They could strike anywhere. Kill anybody. El Cártel united the other cartels and grew more powerful than the Mexican government."

Billy decided to interrogate the sicario at the Blue Spruce, a motel just across the street from the San Juan County Medical Center. He needed every advantage available to him, including the nuances of his native tongue.

"Can you see the window?" He was sitting in a chair next to the bed and spoke English, hoping to be understood.

The man nodded.

Billy got up and pulled back the window curtain. "Can you see the clinic across the street?"

The man nodded again.

Billy shut the curtain. "You tell me what I need to know, and I'll make sure they find you."

"You are Billy?"

"I am."

"Mucho gusto."

Billy had removed the man's shoes. He also cut the black cargo pants to relieve the pressure from the swollen leg. A bottle of Tylenol sat on the round table.

"Where's your driver?"

"He had to go to work. Are you thirsty?"

The man nodded again.

Billy gave him a bottle of water.

The man was lying on his back with his wrists taped together. He sipped from the bottle. "You have earned a lot of respect."

"I'd just as soon none of it ever happened."

The man sighed. "But it did. Neither of us can change that."

Billy lifted the window curtain and watched the traffic on the street.

"You have to remember that, Billy. Neither of us caused this to happen. We were both doing our jobs."

Unaware of the fact that he had lost control of the conversation, Billy dropped the curtain.

"My job has required me to familiarize myself with your personality and habits." The man sipped from the bottle again. "May I make an observation?"

Billy leaned against the door and answered with bravado, "Go ahead."

"I think maybe you feel responsible for what is happening. I want to assure you that all this would be happening, even without you."

Billy sensed that he needed to retake the initiative. "I have an observation of my own. This is America. You . . . all this . . . belongs in Mexico."

"Billy . . ."

Billy stood over the bed. "Where's my mom?"

The man turned the conversation again. "You worked with the JROTC?"

"Yes."

"Are you familiar with the term operational security?"

Billy nodded.

"Then you'll understand why a separate team planned and executed that operation."

Billy felt confused. "What do they want with her?"

"To collect a ransom."

"From my father?" Billy walked to the other side of the room.

"Yes."

He was pacing. "How much is the ransom?"

"It's not money. It's a device. A very powerful weapon."

Billy couldn't wrap his mind around what he was hearing. "He stole it from you?"

"No, the Chinese."

WﬞHEN THE DOOR OPENED, JACK WAS APOLOGETIC. "DO YOU KNOW WHO owns that green Mazda?" He pointed to the snow-blanketed parking lot.

The homeowner leaned out the door to see what he was pointing at, and Jack cracked him with a sap behind the ear. Then he caught the man against his chest on the way down. The sap was made of a ten-inch length of rebar wrapped in leather, which he cut from the front seat of the green Mazda.

"Tom?" It was a woman's voice calling from another room. "Tom, who is it?"

Jack pulled the man inside and laid him on the tile floor. Then he shut and locked the door.

"Tom?"

Jack waited with his back against the wall.

"Tom?" The voice was urgent.

When she came around the corner, he gave her a crack behind the ear.

JACK SEARCHED THE TOWNHOUSE AND RETURNED TO THE COUPLE WITH A utility knife, an LED light, and a dispenser of packing tape. He put the knife and light in his coat pocket for later. He rolled the couple onto their sides and taped their wrists behind their backs. Then he taped their ankles together. He searched the kitchen drawers and found a rubber band, which he also put in his pocket. When he came back to the couple, he was carrying two dish towels. He gagged them with the towels and packing tape, then laid his finger over their upper lips to make sure they were breathing.

Jack found a prescription bottle of Nabumetone in a medicine cabinet and swallowed three of the pills. He poured the rest into his pocket. Then he found a first aid kit in a closet and changed his dressings.

Jack made a sandwich with the lunch meat and sliced cheese he found in the fridge, poured himself a glass of apple juice, and sat down at the table.

It even hurt to eat.

The phone rang. He rinsed the glass and put it in the dishwasher. Then he stood by the phone. The ringing reminded him of something. When he finally lifted the receiver, there was nothing to hear but dial tone.

Jack went into the bathroom again, put his ear to the wall, and listened to the Spanish speaking voices of the men in the neighboring townhouse.

Tehran
1979

Can you make it to the meeting?"

"Yes." Jack was in a safe house in Tehran, the capital of Iran.

The Colonel asked, "Do you need anything from me?"

"Yes, but it's not related." Jack was in the country to interrupt an exchange of nuclear secrets, but that problem seemed insignificant compared to the situation he had uncovered on the ground: the student protests, what he saw on the streets. "This whole thing is about to go. You've got to tell State to get their people out of here."

It wasn't just Tehran, it was the whole region. Jack had been to the Hindu Kush, and he didn't like what he saw in the mountains of Afghanistan and Pakistan either.

"It'll be okay."

"For who? The Ayatollah Khomeini?" The Ayatollah Khomeini was the leader of the Islamic Revolution in Iran. "These kids, I've seen the fervor in their eyes."

"Jihad," the Colonel offered.

"Yes. And Washington doesn't have a clue as to what the hell that is."

Jack was weary of the American foreign policy playbook: find a strong man to oppose the communists, stand him up, and close your eyes to the consequences. That strategy was unraveling in Iran.

"I got word from the CIA's Iran branch chief. He assured me that the situation would only get explosive if the Shah was let into the United States."

The Shah the Colonel was referring to had been deposed by the ayatollah's revolution and was now living in exile.

"And that comforts you? Which assumption are you making: that Kissinger is not that stupid or that he doesn't have that type of influence with the president?"

"Point taken."

As far as Jack was concerned, the CIA's only real success in the last thirty years had been the 1953 Iranian coup d'état which propped up the Shah as the dictator of Iran, an accomplishment that resulted in the present disaster.

"They got Howard Hart in there as station chief, don't they? He's a good man."

"Yes, he is." Jack conceded. "He told me headquarters buried his report."

The Colonel trusted Hart. "What else did he tell you?"

"That Tehran is going to explode. A group of the ayatollah's thugs almost executed him in January. He shot his way out of a second attack early this morning."

THE INCOMPETENCE IN WASHINGTON WAS STAGGERING. AMERICAN INTELLIgence could launch satellites. It could use them to count tanks on the ground, but for all its apparatus, for all its money, it could not collect any meaningful information about its enemies. Because Washington viewed Iran as little more than a battleground for a proxy war with the Soviet Union, it misunderstood the significance of the Iranian Revolution. What Washington needed to understand was the avarice of the Politburo. If it could just understand that, it would know how the Cold War would end. The Soviet system of government was beyond corrupt. All the Kremlin needed was time and it would defeat itself.

Jack knew that communism wouldn't be the battle of the future. The real threat was the religious extremism he saw in the streets of Tehran.

"I'll pass the word to Vance, but don't hold your breath."

"At least, we'll know we tried."

"Once you finish your business," the Colonel ordered, "get out."

PRESENT

JACK USED A KITCHEN KNIFE TO PRY OFF THE SHOE MOLDING IN THE BATH-room. Then he took the utility knife from his pocket and carefully scored the drywall. He quietly removed about a square foot of material so that he could look inside the wall. He marked the location of the studs then opened the entire cavity by removing a fifteen-inch-wide section of drywall along with a bat of sound dampening insulation. No matter how carefully he moved the pain in his rib cage was agonizing. He laid the drywall and insulation in the hall and took two more of the prescription pills.

There were disjointed memories parading through his mind: faces, streets, smells. Without context, the memories seemed meaningless. He couldn't focus on any of them. When he'd try, the images would just dissolve.

He waited in the living room for the sicarios in the neighboring townhouse to fall asleep. There was a dish of cinnamon candies on the coffee table. Jack tossed one into his mouth and used the rubber band in his pocket to secure the red, cellophane wrapper over the lens of the LED light.

It was when he stopped concentrating on the images that he recognized where the memories took place: the Nazi Abad district of Tehran.

Tehran
1979

THE WAY NORTH WAS BLOCKED BY A CROWD. ALTHOUGH THE ASSEMBLY WAS listening intently, Jack, at the back of the crowd, could neither see nor hear the orator. He stepped into the throng.

HE HAD TWO HOURS. THE MEETING HE AGREED ON THE PHONE TO ATTEND was located across town in the affluent Elahieh district. Peng Chuanzeng, a Chinese nuclear physicist, would be linking up with an agent working for the Libyan intelligence service in a restaurant on Fereshteh Street at noon.

What made the operation unique was that the Chinese were feeding Jack the intelligence. No government on Earth was willing to help Muammar Gaddafi build a nuclear weapon. He had tried them all.

Moreover, Peng Chuanzeng was a scourge to the Chinese Academy of Sciences. Not only did he peddle in unauthorized nuclear secrets, he sidelined in human traffic. Since the revolution, the market in Iran paid a premium for young boys. When Jack was briefed, he was presented with photographs of the rouge physicist in Dhaka, Bangladesh, where he spent the weekend. Accompanying Chuanzeng on the flight from Dhaka to Tehran was a nine-year-old Bangladeshi boy.

The restaurant on Fereshteh Street was about fourteen miles to the north. To make the meeting on time Jack needed transportation, something that could also get him to the boat waiting in the Persian Gulf, six hundred miles away.

WHAT HE SAW IN THE EYES OF THE MEN IN THE CROWD WAS THE SAME THING he saw in the eyes of the mujahideen fighting the communists in the mountains. Left to itself, the religious contagion wasn't dangerous. But if provoked . . .

That is what frightened him.

Not only was Washington oblivious to the threat, its national security bias was bent toward provocation. Compared to the conviction of these college students, other security concerns were myopic. No, it was worse than that. Washington's security concerns were misguided.

Jack checked his watch. He had a half hour. Although he wanted to hear what the orator was saying, he didn't have time.

Jack saw a man on a motorcycle looking for a way through the crowd. The man gave up and began to turn the bike around. Then he became interested in what was happening in the street and cut the engine.

"How much will you take for the motorcycle?"

"Excuse me?"

"How much will you take?"

"I don't know what it's worth. Besides it's not for sale."

Jack pulled a roll of US currency from his jacket.

"What's this?"

"Hold out your hand."

The man wrinkled his nose.

"Like this." Jack took the man's wrist and started stacking hundred dollar bills in his palm.

The Iranian's mouth opened. He muttered something unintelligible.

Jack kept counting bills into his hand.

The man looked around to see if anybody was watching.

Jack counted out eleven hundred dollars.

"Okay, that's enough."

Jack studied him for several seconds, assessing his astuteness. "Tell them it was stolen."

Present

Apart from a pair of black electrical wires strung between the exposed studs, the wall cavity in the bathroom was empty. Jack put his ear to the paper backing of the adjoining wall and listened. The men were still awake.

He paced off the distance from the bathroom to each of the bedrooms and rehearsed his assault. Then he went back to the kitchen and searched the fridge.

He tried to eat again, but it hurt. So he sat on the couch and read through an issue of *Allure*.

Tehran
1979

Jack started the bike before the target got out of the taxi. He esti-mated that from where the taxi was parked, the target would have about thirty meters of sidewalk to cover before he could reach the door to the restaurant. There were pedestrians in the area, but Jack knew from experience that they'd take care of themselves. When the target got out of the taxi, Jack rode the bike onto the sidewalk and approached him from behind. To avoid being hit by the motorcycle, a bystander pressed himself against the facade of a building. Another man leapt into the street.

When he heard the shouts from the frightened pedestrians behind him, the target turned around to look at the scene.

Jack swung the bike sideways and skidded to a stop a few steps from Peng Chuanzeng.

Chuanzeng clutched the handle of his brief case with both hands and brought it up to his chest. When he recovered from his shock, he asked in Persian, "Who are you?"

Jack could see that Chuanzeng understood the purpose of their encounter and chose not to answer the man's question.

"Who are you?" This time Chuanzeng asked in English.

Jack thumbed off the safety as he drew the M1911 A1 pistol from a shoulder holster. It was the same pistol he had modified and fought with nine years earlier in Vietnam.

Chuanzeng saw the .45 caliber muzzle and turned his head. It's what they all did. There had only been two targets who did not flinch at their own execution. One of them was a woman.

His voice cracked, "Please."

"You don't strike me," Jack was unhurried in his delivery, "as a man who has shown mercy."

Chuanzeng's eyes were squeezed tight. He dropped the briefcase. The action didn't seem voluntary. Despite all his mathematical training, his profound understanding of momentum, the physicist lifted both hands and pressed them together in order to shield his head—as if a few inches of flesh and bone could deter the speeding mass of the bullet.

Jack wasn't thinking about nuclear secrets. He wasn't thinking about safeguarding democracy. He was thinking about a nine-year-old boy.

His voice was high pitched and barely audible, "Please don't." The urine spread down the physicist's slacks, over his shoes, and onto the pavement.

Jack had time to see the hole bored through the palms before the target crumpled to the pavement.

Jack heard screeching tires and turned to locate the source of the sound. He found the vehicle and saw a series of muzzle flashes coming from the driver's open window.

Jack's visual world narrowed until it was composed of only two items—both of which he saw in high definition. The first was the front sight of his own weapon. He could make out the horizontal serrations milled into the blued steel. The other item was the muzzle of the revolver pointed at him. It couldn't have been more than a .38, but the black muzzle seemed huge.

A gun fight had a way of distorting reality. Time flowed differently, and the physical world often became other than what it was only moments ago.

Jack could not hear the reports, neither from his weapon nor his enemy's. But he could hear the screaming of the civilians around him. He could hear his ejected brass tinkling against the windshield of a parked car on the street. The front sight of his weapon kept returning to his enemy's muzzle, and he kept resetting then pulling the trigger.

Jack ejected the empty magazine, slammed a new magazine home, and released the slide without consciously thinking about it.

Then he finally saw the sedan and the Libyan driving it, just as it crashed head-on into an oncoming truck.

PRESENT

BILLY LOOKED THROUGH THE PEEPHOLE AND UNLATCHED THEN LATCHED the security lock on the motel door.

"This is bigger than you realize."

Billy rested his palms against the door then his forehead between his hands. He had read that the Mexican Army Special Forces cross-trained with the Navy SEALs. The man was tough, and Billy no longer knew what questions to ask.

"You and your mother are very small in this. Right now she is safe. But nobody counted on you . . . " the man took another sip from the water bottle, "your resourcefulness."

"Resourcefulness." Billy moved to the chair. "I'd give a lot for a little of that right now."

"Think about what you're saying. Do you really believe you have so much responsibility?"

Billy felt confused and didn't answer.

"What if I told you that you were making the situation more unstable, more dangerous."

"That's not what you said earlier." Billy sat in the chair then stood up and paced the room.

The man squeezed his eyes and clenched his teeth. Then he inhaled and relaxed, as if a wave of pain had passed. "Like me, you involved yourself as a player in these events. We can already see how that decision has turned out for me." He gestured to his leg. "It is too early to know the total impact, but your will has altered the overall outcome."

"That's not the way I see it." Billy came back to the chair. "My dad has nothing to do with us. There was no cause to bring my mom into this."

The man turned his palms upward in acquiescence. "I understand your frustration, but I'm afraid you've confused cause with culpability."

"I don't understand."

"Your concern for justice is an obstacle to you. You need to put yourself in the mindset of your enemies. Let me assure you, none of them are interested in justice."

Billy paced the room. "I think you miscalculated." He kept touching his face. He stopped at the foot of the bed. "He doesn't give two shits for my mom." He was talking quickly. "Besides, he doesn't remember us. He doesn't even know who we are."

"If you're telling the truth," the man's inflection was matter of fact, "you are running out of time."

Billy's jaw muscles tightened. "How much time does she have?"

"A day."

Billy massaged his chin. He ran his hand through his hair. "He doesn't have what you're looking for."

"I believe you."

The desperation raised the pitch of his voice, "Help me convince them."

"It can't be done."

Billy wiped his face with both hands and sat down on the empty bed.

"I'm sorry, Billy." The condolence sounded genuine.

The man's empathy had a calming effect on Billy. The weight he had been carrying felt lessened. Billy asked, "Are you in a lot of pain?"

The man nodded his head. Although he was sweating and his leg looked like a black balloon, he seemed philosophical about his fate.

Billy opened the bottle of Tylenol on the table and gave it to him. "I'm sorry."

The man shrugged. He poured the pills into his mouth and washed them down.

Billy paced the room. Then he thought of a new line of questioning and spun to face him. "If you were planning the operation against my mom, where would you take her?"

The man smiled. "That is a clever question. I'd use a straw buyer to pay cash for a house in an upper-class neighborhood."

Such a purchase would require something in the area of a million dollars. Billy was just beginning to comprehend the scope of the situation.

He asked, "How many teams do you have in Colorado?"

"Three. A team for your mom, a team for you, and a larger team for your dad."

"What are the orders for that team?"

"Your father's enemies are within his own government. They are at risk as long as he is alive. That team is instructed to find him before his enemies do, to capture him alive."

"And the device?"

"My employer wants it back."

"The Chinese?"

"Yes."

Billy sat in silence. His thoughts chaotic.

"Were you leading the team assigned to me?"

"Yes."

His eyes narrowed, "Did you give the order to kill Sheriff Dowell?"

"No."

"Bullshit!"

"In an operation like this, every effort is made to keep a low profile. This is not Mexico. In America, it is suicide to kill a member of law enforcement. It brings too much heat."

Billy's fists were clenched. He walked to the other side of the room. "I ought to shoot you dead."

The man grimaced and shut his eyes. When he finally exhaled, he spoke through his teeth. "The sheriff was a good man."

Billy glared. "What do you know about it?"

"I was supposed to be there. There was supposed to be another vehicle. Once the patrol car was forced to stop, it would be surrounded." The man's neck muscles flared, and his face was contorted in pain. He lifted his head, and Billy could see the sweat stain on the pillow. After several seconds, the man finished his statement. "With five armed men, we doubted the sheriff would risk your safety in a fight. Nobody was supposed to get hurt."

"Give me one reason why I shouldn't kill you right now."

The man nodded in acquiescence. "You would be within your rights."

Tears welled in Billy's eyes. "You have no idea what you've done."

"The situation is escalating. It is out of control."

Billy sat at the foot of the empty bed, his back to the man, and dried his face with his hands. "If you were me, what would you do now?"

"None of this is your fault. There is nothing you could have done to change the outcome on that highway."

Billy couldn't stop the flow of the tears.

"I know you think it is your responsibility to save your mother. Perhaps you could save her." He paused. "Or perhaps you will only get yourself killed."

Billy looked the man in the eyes, making no attempt now to disguise his grief. "My life is irrelevant."

The man held Billy's gaze. "To you."

"And that's all that matters."

He put his bound hands over his heart. "It seems to me that you're only focusing on one detail of the problem."

"I want her alive. What other detail is there?"

"From your point of view that makes sense, but you need to see the bigger picture, the picture from your mother's point of view."

"What would you know about that?"

"Perhaps your mother would choose your life over her own."

Billy bit his lower lip and looked up at the ceiling. Then it burst from his chest, the sound of his grief—his fear. The pain pulsed through his vocal chords like a pressurized fluid.

THE MAN SPOKE GENTLY, "IT'S NOT YOUR FAULT. NONE OF THIS IS. YOUR courage is remarkable."

"I don't feel courageous."

"That is because you are a man of action. We do not indulge our feelings of fear. We act in spite of them."

Billy wiped his face clean with his coat sleeve and paced the room. His mind was made up. Nothing would stop him from going after his mom. Then he felt suddenly foolish, manipulated even, when it occurred to him that he believed everything the man had said.

"There is one more thing. I wouldn't make any more phone calls."

Billy looked at the carpet and offered a self-conscious nod.

"When you got the room, did you go to the office? Were you seen by anybody?"

"No," Billy looked more confident now.

"Good. Your picture is all over the television."

BILLY PULLED THE PHONE CORD FROM THE WALL AND PUT IT IN HIS POCKET.
"I'll notify the clinic in an hour, let them know you're here."

The man clutched the sweat-soaked bedsheet and inhaled sharply against the pain. "Do me a favor, Billy."

"Okay."

"Don't notify the clinic."

WASHINGTON, D.C.
1984

Jack checked into a hotel room near Dulles International Airport. He didn't know where he'd be flying to in the morning, just the time he was instructed to be at the gate. He unlocked the door to the room, and before he could set down his kit, the phone rang.

He had been in the profession long enough to know that the timing was no coincidence.

He let it ring twice then picked up the receiver.

"We know some of the same people." The male voice did not identify itself. Rather, it established its credentials by naming a half-dozen Special Forces personnel with whom Jack had served in Vietnam.

Jack didn't respond.

The speaker requested a meeting at an Arlington restaurant.

Jack agreed, "Roger." The only word he spoke in the conversation. Then he hung up the receiver.

Although Jack was pretty sure he wasn't interested in what the voice on the phone was offering, he had been trained to value information, and he was going to collect as much of that as the speaker was willing to offer.

He took a taxi to the restaurant. It was a little sandwich shop with a single table on the floor. The only customer stood up when Jack opened the door. He introduced himself as Ed Wilson from Consultants International and showed Jack a corporate ID.

Jack nodded his head and sat down. By now he knew three things. That Consultants International was a front company for the CIA, that the operation was going to be black, and that its utility was likely to be of negative value to the United States.

"I know about your trip to Nicaragua."

That was the first Jack heard of his destination in the morning. That

Mr. Wilson knew Jack's destination while he himself did not signifi-
cantly elevated, in Jack's mind, Mr. Wilson's stature and the value of
any information he might share.

"Jack, you can do your country a favor . . . " It was the line Jack
always heard when men like Mr. Wilson offered him a job. He wanted
Jack to support the Nicaraguan Contra militia in its struggle against
the Sandinista government.

From Jack's point of view, the job was a career ender: the shortest
possible path he could take into the spotlight of courtroom and scandal.
The political reality was that Congress had it in for the Contras. And
the operation sounded as ill conceived as anything he had ever heard of
since Operation Eagle Claw, the culmination of the international debacle
he had warned the Colonel about five years ago in Iran.

The answer was no. Jack was certain of that. But the longer he let Mr.
Wilson talk the more he would learn. It was the law of conversation.
If you let a person talk long enough, he would begin telling you things
he didn't want you to know.

Mr. Wilson tried one last pitch, "It's up to people like you and me to
take a stand against evil in the world."

Jack knew better than to react, but the comment made him furious.
He was furious at the small-mindedness it represented. "What is evil?"
he asked in a subdued voice.

"We both know the answer to that."

"I'm not sure we do."

Mr. Wilson sat back in his chair. He was uncomfortable now and it
showed. "I'm not here to debate ethics with you. I'm offering you a job."

"To take a stand against evil?"

"They told me you were eccentric." By they, Jack knew Mr. Wilson
was referring to the DCI (Director of Central Intelligence). "They also
told me that you were, hands down, the best person for the job."

"In that case, I think it'd be best if you sometimes questioned the
DCI's judgment." Jack shook Mr. Wilson's hand and left the restaurant.

PRESENT

J ACK LISTENED AGAIN TO THE WALL IN THE BATHROOM. HE DIDN'T HEAR anything. So he switched on the LED and taped it to one of the exposed studs. Then he turned off all the other lights in the townhouse. The bathroom glowed red.

Jack retracted the blade of the utility knife to a depth that would not fully penetrate the drywall of the adjoining room. In the event that he did puncture the wall, the red filter of the candy wrapper would minimize the light signature. Using the studs as a guide, he slowly scored the brown paper backing.

Jack began a breathing exercise. He listened again to the adjoining unit, finished the breathing exercise, and pulled the flashlight off the stud. He took off the rubber band and red cellophane then he increased the power to the LED bulbs. He hoped the sicarios would be asleep, and he wanted the flashlight now to be as bright as possible, not only to find them but to blind them.

Jack drew the Colt from the shoulder holster. Then he put his ear to the wall again. He spread his feet and crouched. It was going to hurt, but there was nothing to be done for it. He exploded with his legs, drove his shoulder into the scored drywall, and stepped through the adjacent bathroom into the hallway.

The flashlight illuminated a man wearing a winter coat. He was seated in a chair in the hall. Jack shot him twice in the bridge of the nose. Then Jack turned around and kicked open the door to the back bedroom.

A man wearing a wool trench coat and dress shoes was rolling on top of the bed, away from the doorway. He was almost to the edge of the bed when he thrust out his arm, firing a burst from an MP5.

Jack held the beam of light on the man's head. He moved along the bedroom wall squeezing off rounds.

The man in the trench coat disappeared off the far side of the bed.

Then his weapon reemerged, spewing lead into the empty doorway.

Jack had already advanced three-quarters the length of the room. He changed magazines and fired seven rounds through the mattress. By the time he reached the corner, the man was dead.

Jack spun to cover the hall from which he came. There were bullet holes in the ceiling and around the bedroom doorjamb from the MP5.

He changed magazines and wiped the sweat from his forehead. With the cramping in his side, it was difficult to breathe.

He gripped the Colt in his strong hand and held the flashlight parallel to the slide in his weak hand. He walked back to the bathroom. It was still empty.

That left the living room, the kitchen, and the master bedroom.

Clearing a residence was no different from hunting game. It was tempting to project a specific location, to imagine where you would find the target. That temptation was a trap, as the specificity of the image was a distraction.

Jack stepped into the living room, which was empty. He cleared the kitchen.

The target would appear whenever and wherever it appeared. Its appearance would startle you. And you would react as your training conditioned you to react.

He moved back to the hall and stepped over the corpse.

He kicked open the door to the master bedroom. The mattress was bare, the room cold. The curtains lifted with the change of air pressure. There was shattered glass on the carpet. Behind the curtains, two-by-fours had been screwed to the wall like bars over the broken window. He advanced to the far corner of the room and checked behind the bed. Then he checked under it.

Nothing.

Then he pushed open the door to the master bathroom. The door stopped against flesh.

Jack recognized her from the photographs. She was in the fetal position, gagged, shivering on the bathroom tile. She wore a torn-up sweater, a badly stained skirt. Her feet were bare, her ankles bound. There was dried blood on her thighs, her buttocks. Her bloody hands were bound behind her back.

He held the flashlight in his teeth and cut the plastic cuffs on her wrists with the utility knife.

She used her hands to sit up. Her eyes were black and swollen. There were crusts of blood on her nostrils, on her chin. Her whole body convulsed.

At most, they had minutes before law enforcement would arrive.

Jack wanted to remember something. To feel something. He didn't.

"You don't have to come with me, but I can't stay." He freed her legs and loosened the gag. "Decide now. We can talk later." Jack stepped out of the master bathroom, rechecked the bedroom then the hallway.

He stepped over the corpse again, advanced to the living room, swept it and the kitchen, then moved to the front door.

He looked over his shoulder before he unlocked the door.

Rachel was wearing a pair of men's dress shoes. She had the bloody duvet from the back bedroom over her shoulders.

THE DRIVEWAY WAS COVERED IN UNTRACKED SNOW. NEITHER THE DECK NOR the front porch had been shoveled. There were lights on in the house, but Jack thought that was just to keep it from looking empty, which he was sure it was.

He heard rotors approaching in the sky.

Jack helped Rachel across the creek and pulled her under the wooden deck. To conceal their heat signature, they huddled against the basement window. Rachel's teeth were clattering. Her breath was shallow and quick.

The rotors faded to the west.

"Wait here."

It wasn't a good idea to leave her out there. But, as always, there was nothing to do for it.

Jack used the railing on the deck to climb onto the roof. He cut the screen and tried the bedroom window. It was locked. He broke the glass with his knee and stepped inside.

The spasm in his rib cage was making it hard to breathe. He stooped over, resting his hands on his thighs. Creek water pooled on the carpet at his feet. He took another pill from his pocket.

Then he checked the other two bedrooms with the flashlight. Both beds were made, the rooms empty.

He crept downstairs and found a Jeep Liberty in the garage. He searched the family room and den, where he found the thermostat and turned up the heat. Then he walked through the kitchen and opened the sliding-glass door.

Rachel was curled up in the bloody duvet and shivering. He dragged her out from under the deck.

She could no longer stand on her own.

He was familiar with the condition. To conserve heat Rachel's body had shut down at the extremities. It was trying to preserve her core. This, in itself, did not alarm Jack: hypothermia was one of the most powerful lifesaving techniques he knew. In cases of cardiac arrest, the rapid cooling of the brain and organs gave the patient a fighting chance to survive prolonged resuscitation. Although the condition was temporally crippling, he had the resources to warm her.

He picked Rachel up, grunted, and carried her into the house. Jack set her on the bathroom floor then doubled over, holding his side.

The bullet holes in his arm were bleeding.

Jack tested the temperature of the hot water with his hand. It was too hot. He added cold water to the flow and tested the temperature again. Then he scooped Rachel off the floor and set her, still wrapped in the duvet, inside the tub.

The water turned crimson.

Rachel's knuckles thumped against the porcelain. Her whole body shook. Jack kept his arm under her neck, supporting her head. Waves of water splashed over the side of the tub into his lap.

He shut off the faucet. The duvet was tangled around her feet. He freed her feet one at a time and set the duvet sopping on the bathroom tile. Then he added hot water, heating the bath.

Eyes closed, Rachel put her hand up and felt for his cheek, "Jack, you're home."

JACK FOUND A BOX OF GLAD THIRTY-GALLON TRASH BAGS ON A PANTRY SHELF and put his ear to the bathroom door.

The shower was running.

He stuffed the wet duvet in the trash bag then found a bag of roasted coffee beans in the cabinet above the coffee maker. He started the coffee then went upstairs.

As Jack looked through the armoire, he caught his reflection in the mirror and froze. It wasn't his reflection he was trying to keep hold of, but a remembrance. He felt that if he moved, if he altered anything at all, the image in his mind would disappear.

She wore a tiara of pine needles and juniper berries and a knee-length dress. There was snow on the ground. And there was a yurt. He was carrying Rachel up board steps.

AND THAT WAS IT. THERE WAS NO MORE TO IT. EXCEPT . . . THE HAPPINESS. It shocked him, the happiness.

He tried to get it back, but it was gone.

Jack took two photographs out of his pocket—the one of Billy, still a boy at Christmas, and the one of Rachel in the driver's seat of the pickup. He held the photographs and tried to remember more.

JACK WALKED DOWNSTAIRS AND LISTENED AGAIN AT THE BATHROOM DOOR. The water was off.

He told her, "There's women's clothing in the master bedroom."

The phone vibrated in his pocket. Jack moved away from the door and put it to his ear.

"You did good, Jack."

As he moved into the kitchen, he looked back at the bathroom.

"The blue team we spoke of already found the two Mexicans at the townhouse. They know you have Rachel. They're airborne and hunting as we speak."

"What do they want?"

"You."

"What did I do?"

"One step at a time, Jack. Be ready to move."

The line was empty.

RACHEL CAME DOWN THE STAIRS DRESSED IN BLUE JEANS, BOOTS, AND A GREEN, wool toggle coat. She wore white bandages on her wrists.

Jack poured her a mug of coffee and set it on the breakfast table.

Rachel stopped at the front door, contemplating the choice she had: to either turn the handle, open the door, and step out into the darkness or to walk into that kitchen and take her chances again with Jack. There was no question in her mind which was the wiser course to follow.

He rattled a bottle of prescription pills. "Percocet. I found it upstairs."

Rachel smelled the coffee and, against her better judgment, limped into the kitchen. She twisted the lid off the Percocet and swallowed the pills dry. Her hair was pulled tight in a pony tail. Her nose was black over the break—purple swelling on her cheeks. Her lower lip was split, and she wore a butterfly bandage over the deep gash in her chin.

She pulled the chair out from the table, hesitated, looked back at the front door, then sat down.

"Rachel," he was timid, "you need to know that I have no memory of our relationship." When she didn't respond, he pressed his knees together and fidgeted. Then he pulled two prints from his pocket, "I'm aware of it only through the photographs I found at the house."

His shoulders were rounded forward. He took up very little space. The contrast with the man she knew, with the man who killed those men hardly more than an hour ago, was stunning.

Rachel didn't want to look at the photographs. She didn't want to feel anything for him. But she did. She felt like that little girl who fell in love almost twenty years ago. It pissed her off.

"Where's Billy, Jack?"

His response contained no emotion. "He's safe."

Until Jack came along she was content to do for herself. It was a lesson she had learned from an early age: she knew better than to rely on anyone else. But his presence was intoxicating and carried with it a promise of security. Twenty years ago she could not control her hunger for that.

"Where, Jack? Tell me where he is."

"I met him behind the school." He tried to read her face, but it was swollen, discolored, and impenetrable. "Billy recognized me, but I didn't

144

know him at the time. When things got dangerous, I left him with the authorities."

"Where?"

"At Rob's clinic."

She assumed Billy was with Regan and felt relieved. "What were you doing at the clinic?"

He lifted his wounded arm a few inches then let it rest again on the zipper of his leather jacket.

"Tell me what's happening, Jack."

"I don't know."

Rachel had spent the last decade recovering from her youthful decision to give herself completely to the man who sat at the table before her, to the man who had stormed into her life and transported her to an exotic world of tenderness and safety. This was the same man who had abandoned her, who had abandoned her son, without a word of explanation.

"How did you find me?" Rachel braced herself. "Start with that."

"Someone contacted me two days ago on your cellphone."

Rachel wanted to know how he had gotten her cellphone, but she didn't ask. She needed to be disciplined. She needed to keep her guard up, and the more she talked the harder that was.

After a long silence, he looked up from his teacup. "It was someone I used to work for."

"I thought you said you had no memory."

"When I hear his voice, I can see his face."

"Who were those men?"

He shook his head.

"Why is all this so familiar, Jack?"

"I don't understand."

"Earl Grey tea, your love for secrets. Nothing's changed."

He didn't look up from his cup. "I wouldn't know."

"Well, I've had enough." Rachel stood. "I'm going to get Billy."

Jack didn't respond.

"Do you have my phone?"

He gave it to her.

She turned it on and tried to call Regan. "It doesn't work."

"Look at the SIM card."

She opened the phone and saw the device. It didn't look like a SIM card. "What is that?"

"That's the way I found it."

"Where?"

"At the house."

Rachel put the phone back together and set it on the table. She bit her thumb nail. Then she crossed the room and picked up the receiver on the kitchen wall. "The line's dead. Jack, what's happening?"

"I'm trying to figure that out."

"Why am I involved?"

"To get at me."

She was leaning against the kitchen counter. "Why?"

"What did they tell you?"

"That you have something they want."

"Did they say anything about it, anything about who I am, anything about what I've done?"

"They called you a terrorist."

Jack looked concerned.

Rachel asked, "Is it true?"

"I don't know."

The rotors came overhead again, this time rattling the house.

"Jesus," Rachel moved toward the sliding-glass door, "what is that?"

"No, Rachel!"

She couldn't hear him through the noise.

He went after her, "Stay away from the windows."

COLORADO
1990

He ate at the Mountainside the night Rachel quit. Average size. Average looks, for an older guy. He was polite when she took his order, no flirtation. Not that she minded that with other men. It was part of the job. But it stood out, the respect with which he spoke to her.

When she brought out the soup, he was holding a conversation in Spanish on the pay phone. That drew her attention. She noticed the athletic shoes, the jeans, the loose fitting shirt.

Unless he looked you in the eye, he wouldn't be a man you'd remember.

Rachel was helping the line cook garnish plates when her manager called her to his office. She had work to do on the floor and ignored him.

He found her at the soda fountain. "You best not put me off."

She set a pair of cokes on the serving tray she was holding and stepped around him.

Marvin expected extra from his female employees. Because she tolerated it, Jeani was able to pick her shifts. Nobody said anything either when her drawer came out short.

Marvin caught Rachel at the register. "I don't like your attitude . . ."

"That's fine." She took off her apron. "I never cared for yours."

Rachel started the Scottsdale and pulled onto the highway. She couldn't see the road through her tears and noticed the doe about the same time she felt the impact.

She stopped the truck and walked back to where it lay on the shoulder of the highway. The animal's neck was twisted like a towel that had been wrung.

Rachel sat next to the deer with her back to the road. A thunderstorm was rolling over the valley. She didn't hear the approaching vehicle.

Didn't hear it stop or back up.

When she heard the door shut, she turned around.

"You okay?" It was the man from the diner.

She stood and brushed herself off. She was embarrassed. "I'm fine."

He squatted and felt the animal's shoulder, ribs, and hindquarter. "I already looked at your truck. A busted headlight and a little tuft of hair in the chrome. It'd take me all of a minute to fix." He turned the doe over and felt the other side. "It looks like you only got her on the head."

He stood and shook her hand. "I'm Jack."

"Rachel."

He took the knife from his belt. "You can wait in the truck if you like. Without a job, I thought it might be nice for you to have a supply of steak."

"You don't have to do that."

"She gave herself to you, Rachel. It'd be disrespectful not to."

The man was strange. That much was certain. He went to his Jeep and came back with a pair of shirts. Then he got on his knees and boned out the meat. Jack wrapped the hindquarters in one shirt and the loins and forequarters in the other.

THEY BUTCHERED THE MEAT IN RACHEL'S KITCHEN.

"Maybe what the doe is trying to tell you is that this is an opportunity."

She laughed at that. "An opportunity?"

"It's easy to misinterpret the little gifts life offers."

He cut the loin into steaks, which she wrapped in butcher paper. The meat was dark red, red unlike anything Rachel had ever seen at the store.

"Maybe this is an opportunity to pursue your dream."

She ignored the statement.

"No?"

"Who has time to dream?"

JACK WAS GRILLING THE TENDERLOINS WHEN SHE CAME OUT TO THE PATIO with a selection of tea. "Water's ready."

He pointed to the box of Earl Grey.

Jack came inside with the steaks a few minutes later. All the furniture in the living room was pushed against the walls, making space for the roll of bleached canvas on the floor and the pile of wooden stretcher bars. There were a half-dozen nudes leaning against the couch.

"Are you the artist?" he asked.

"Yeah." She had never shown the self-portraits. Rachel felt herself blush and turned away to set the table.

The best she could do with what she had on hand was to slice apples to serve with a salad.

"If you're not ready to dream," he said after they sat down at the table, "maybe we should plot."

"Okay, what do we plot?"

The steaks were cooked rare, and Rachel presented the apples to look like fall leaves on the white plates.

"Your revenge, of course."

She laughed. Then she saw that he was serious. "I don't know."

"Are you afraid even to dream about that?"

"It's just . . . I don't know that I'm the vengeful type."

"Call it justice then." He sipped from his tea. "If you could make something happen, dream it into being, what would it be?"

"Dream it?" she didn't know what to make of him.

A buzzer sounded.

"Hold on." She got up to put his shirts in the dryer.

"Anything," he called after her.

"Anything?" She could still see him from down the hall.

He nodded his head.

"I don't know," Rachel said as she walked back to the table. "Maybe I'd just like his wife to find out what happens in that office."

"Why not a jury?"

"No. I wouldn't want to humiliate the other girls."

"You're twenty-three?"

She looked into her cup and blushed.

"I wasn't that considerate when I was twenty-three."

SHE SAW HIM AGAIN A MONTH LATER STACKING REDWOOD ON A CART AT THE lumber yard. Rachel was carrying a pair of hardwood one-by-twos and noticed him first.

"Jack?"

The affection communicated in his smile had a physiological impact on her body, and it took Rachel a moment to realize that he had asked her a question.

"I'm building a frame for a painting," she answered. Then after a few seconds she returned, "What about you?"

"I'm building a yurt."

"I wanted to thank you for helping me see the opportunity I had." He was still smiling, and Rachel found it distracting to look him in the eye. "I got a job in an art gallery."

"Sounds like a step up."

She kicked at the dirt floor. "I've been meaning to ask you something. My landlord said somebody paid the month's rent. Do you know anything about that?"

"I didn't know there were still people like that in the world."

"You know, I'd just like an opportunity to say thank you."

"Maybe if that was important to them, they would have left a note."

Her heart was pounding. "I guess so."

"I think you can feel good about the future, Rachel." He pushed his cart toward the registers. "Good luck with your frame."

Even though his back was to her, she raised her hand to wave. The ends of the one-by-twos she was holding crashed into a display of adhesives, knocking a tube to the ground.

Rachel called out, "Good luck with your yurt."

The owner of the gallery offered Rachel a show and pitched it as an event for local artists. It was the first time in two years Rachel wore makeup or heels or, now that she thought about it, a dress. She had worked for weeks selecting and framing the pieces, creating the catalogue, and changing her mind about it all. Her name, along with one of her landscapes, was on the poster hung at the Safeway and in the ad in the *Sentinel*.

Rachel hoped he'd see her printed name and show up.

She sold her first piece, ink on paper mounted on canvas, for four hundred dollars to a woman from Connecticut who told Rachel that her work reminded her of a non-ghoulish Lita Cabellut.

The opening was bigger than anyone had anticipated. They moved one of the walls just to create space for the guests.

Rachel suspended her conversation to watch his entrance. His presence seemed to charge the air. Her stomach was doing little flips.

Jack had spent forty minutes in the gallery and still hadn't approached her. She had paid attention to nothing else. She made note of the gold cufflinks. The narrow cut of the black tie. The shape of his sideburns.

She sold the second piece then was dragged into a back room by Jeani, the waitress from the Mountainside.

"Did you hear?"

"No. Hear what?"

"About Marvin. His wife received a videotape."

Rachel didn't understand.

"Somebody mailed her a videotape. A videotape with footage from the office at the diner."

"A videotape?"

"Supposedly, our faces are blurred out. Who do you think could have done it?"

When Rachel returned to the floor, Jack was standing at one of her paintings. In the crowded room, she had to stretch her neck to read his reaction and was off balance when he caught her eye.

Jack had seemed thin, so when he hugged her, she was surprised by the muscles in his back and shoulders, surprised by how firm his body was. Rachel was certain he could feel her runaway heart kicking against his chest.

He told her that he had seen her name on a flier.

Rachel thanked him for coming, but no matter how hard she tried, she couldn't come up with anything more to say. They looked at the painting.

It was an acrylic of a lone tree standing on a hill. Jack looked closely and saw the infinitesimally-small, parallel lines that formed the tree.

"They're birds." He stepped closer. "And bands of rain." Jack moved back to take in the whole. "You even milled the wood." He ran his finger over the finished frame.

She had indeed milled the one-by-twos by hand.

Although she was blushing and struggling to make conversation, Rachel felt satiated, more alive than she had ever been. All that mattered to her in that moment was to remain in Jack's presence.

He bought the painting for five hundred dollars then took her out to celebrate after the show.

"You know what I like about that piece?"

"Tell me." It took effort not to confess that the electric sensation in her chest was making her feel as if there were no gravity, as if she were floating away.

"It captures something remarkable about you. It's melancholy and hopeful at the same time."

Jack took her out twice the following week. Then he went out of town for nine days.

Rachel tortured herself with the fear that he would never return. What she hated most was the naiveté, the recklessness of her hope. It was stupid, so stupid. Her repetition of that word was compulsive. She was not aware of it, but each rebuke contained a line memorized by the child still living inside her heart. A line her mother had taught her. You're so stupid.

Jack took her to dinner the night he got back, and they spent the weekend together.

She tried to be cautious. What had she gotten herself into? But Rachel could not control her heart. She felt invincible in his presence. She created safeguards, attempted to slow things down, but she could not stop herself from wanting more.

They were hiking a trail that traversed the Patriarch Run.

"You know what I want?" Rachel asked.

Jack took her hand. "What?"

Rachel's worry, her fear, it all dissipated for that moment. "I want to create my life here," she told him, "in these mountains."

"Do you believe it?"

"What do you mean?"

"Do you believe that it can happen?"

It was how Jack spoke to her, as if her faith in herself was all that mattered.

She looked down the wide avalanche runout. "I don't know."

An enormous pile of boulders, many of which were larger than a passenger car, were in a deposit thirty or forty feet high on top of the original Patriarch townsite.

In September Jack asked her to move in with him. The only access to the yurt was by foot, a six-hour hike up the Milestone Valley. There was already snow on the ground. In another month the only access would be by snowshoes or skis. She'd have to quit her job. Put her furniture in storage.

Jack went out of town again, and his absence stoked her fears. She chastised herself for needing him, for being such a child. She decided to call it off.

Twelve days later he phoned from Africa.

"I'm in Dakar."

She didn't know where that was.

"I've got a little bungalow on the coast. There's a ticket waiting for you at the airport if you'd like to fly out and meet me."

Jack met her at Dakar Yoff International Airport.

"Are you hungry?"

When they arrived at the restaurant, a man wearing a loose flowing robe called Jack by his name and kissed him three times on the cheeks. Jack introduced Rachel. Then the two men engaged themselves for several minutes in what sounded like a ritual greeting.

The only language, other than English, Rachel had been exposed to was Spanish. "What language is that?"

"Wolof. But here in the city, the dialect contains French and Arabic."

It did not surprise her that Jack could speak it. As a matter of fact, she was beginning to believe that there was nothing about the man that could surprise her.

"How do you know him?"

"I helped his son get into an American university eight or nine years ago."

There was no glass in the restaurant windows, and the dining room was outfitted with plastic patio furniture.

Jack ordered fish with rice and vegetables for them both. The dish reminded Rachel of jambalaya.

"Do you like boats?"

"I've never been on a boat."

"I thought maybe we could go out in the morning and explore the coast."

Not only had Rachel never been on a boat, until today she had never seen the ocean, let alone a foreign shore. She had been out of the state once. That was to Wyoming. But she never got out of the truck, never left the Rocky Mountains.

When she applied for her passport two years ago, she did it for the same reason some people purchase a lottery ticket: it was a hope she never expected to actualize.

"Everywhere you look in this country, you see the residue of the French, from the language to the cuisine." Jack held a forkful of fish and tomatoes. "It's a window into the colonial past."

Rachel didn't know anybody else who talked like Jack. The word exotic wasn't novel enough to describe her experience of the last hour. The tropical climate, the ramshackle airport, the people, the Wolof language, a restaurant with plastic furniture and no window glass.

"What is it you do?"

"I'm a contractor for the Federal Government."

Rachel thought through the possible meanings of that statement. They were endless.

She angled for more. "Is it interesting?"

"Yes, always."

She felt like Jack was teasing her. "And you travel a lot?"

"Wherever my services are needed."

She debated whether or not to ask the question, but she could tell by the way he was leaning into the conversation that he expected it. "What type of services?"

Jack slowly laid his fork on the dish. Then he wiped his lips with his napkin. When he looked her in the eye, she felt naked. Pierced. She resisted the urge to look away.

"Rachel, although these are normal things for people to discuss, you need to know that I am not in a normal line of work. Which means we need to put a boundary around this conversation."

She dropped her eyes.

Jack moved his dish, clearing the space between them. "Ask me any question you want. If I can, I'll answer it. But when we get up from this table, we can never speak about this topic again."

She scrutinized his face. Beneath the reassuring tone was a take-it-or-leave-it deal. She had no illusions about that.

PRESENT

RACHEL WAS STANDING WITH HER BACK TO HIM ON THE FAR SIDE OF THE living room, her arms crossed. "Why is my son involved in this, Jack?"

"I know how this sounds to you, but the truth is that I don't know. I'm afraid you know more about who I am than I do." He was still seated at the breakfast table, an empty cup in his hands. "Right now, I need your help."

Jack's plea for help infuriated her. After he had abandoned her, abandoned her son, Rachel had picked herself up, built a new life. She had created a life for herself and Billy. A good life. And now that was gone. She had been kidnapped. Men Jack had wronged were after her son.

"You had no right . . . " She turned to face him. Her left eye was nearly swollen shut. "You had no right bringing my son into this."

"Rachel, please listen to me. I need your help. Who did I work for?"

"That was the deal, Jack." She wiped the tears from her cheeks. "We didn't talk about it. I agreed to that because I thought . . . I thought I was in love."

Jack gazed into his cup.

"But that chapter is shut." She massaged the bandages on her wrist as she limped across the living room. She could not stop the tears, and it angered her that he was able to see them. Rachel looked away and shielded her face with her hand. "That chapter is shut."

She squeezed her bottom lip in her teeth until it bled. A minute passed.

"You had no right to reopen it."

"Rachel, whoever that man was, you're not talking to him now. I don't know him. I don't know what he's done."

Rachel dropped her hand and glared.

"You're not safe." He met her stare. "Billy's not safe. Not unless I fix this."

She limped forward. "I don't think this is something you can just fix,

Jack." She stopped short of the kitchen. "Somehow, I gather repair was never one of your professional specialties."

"How many men did you see at the townhouse?"

She gasped at his calloused persistence then answered the question. "The two who picked me up, a third, then the asshole with the briefcase."

"What did the man with the briefcase say to you?"

"He showed me the aftermath of the gunfight you brought my son to. Then he asked about you." She limped over to the table. "When I didn't have the right answers, he did this."

"What did he want to know?"

"We'll get to that later, Jack." Rachel sat down. "There are a few things I need to know first."

Jack had no memory of his wrongdoing, and he accepted Rachel's grievance at face value. It was the inevitable consequence of the situation in which he found himself.

"Who were they?" she asked.

"I don't know."

"Who were they working for?"

"I don't know."

"What do you know?"

"The men in the helicopter outside tried to kill me in Washington about a week ago."

"How?"

"A car bomb. I have no memory before that."

"You don't make many friends in your line of work, do you?"

"What is my line of work, Rachel?"

"You're a contractor for the United States government."

"Which agency?"

She shook her head.

"What else have you heard?"

"That you're a wanted man. A traitor."

Jack nodded and waited for her to continue.

"They said something about a weapon of mass destruction."

Jack's jaw went slack.

She was tempted to reach for his hand across the table. Then she caught herself and recoiled. "Why did you come back?"

"I don't know. Maybe because you and I . . . "

"That was a lifetime ago. I put myself back together, my family. Billy leaves for college in the fall. Until Tuesday, I had forgotten about you."

SENEGAL
1990

AFTER DINNER, JACK WALKED HER TO THE BEACH WHERE THEY WATCHED the sunset. She took off her shoes and felt the hot sand between her toes. Then she rolled up her pants and stood in the warm surf.

She kissed him and said, "Jack, it's like a dream."

"You know the best part?"

"What?"

He pointed to the house not thirty yards behind her. "That's our bungalow."

She woke to breakfast: a tray on which there was a bowl of porridge, a baguette, and a cup of coffee. Rachel ate in bed then got dressed an hour later and went out onto the covered porch, where she found a small taboret with an easel, brushes, and paints.

"I wasn't sure what you'd need." Jack told her. "I tried to remember the tools and materials I've seen you use."

There was a stack of wood, a bucket of gesso, canvas pliers, shears, a staple gun.

Rachel didn't know what to say to him.

She looked out at the beach. There was a man standing inside what looked like a brightly painted canoe. He was watching them.

"That's Ousmane. He's waiting for us. If you're ready, we can go."

The water was more powerful than Rachel had imagined. Her image of the ocean had been of something soft, something romantic. But the waves slapped the wooden boat with force. She had to learn to move with it to avoid being hurt.

They motored out past the surf then turned east.

Jack pointed. "Look. You see it?"

Rachel had been watching the dorsal fin since the boat changed course to pass nearer by. "Is it a shark?"

"A swordfish. It's sunning itself."

The fish disappeared then breached not eight yards from the boat. She saw its silver back and white belly.

"It's beautiful."

Ousmane spoke in Wolof, but she understood him by his hands. He told her that the fish jumped to stun the little fish, to make them easier to catch.

"What's that over there?"

"That is Gorée Island," Jack told her, "the location of one of the first European settlements in Africa."

Even though Gorée Island was hardly more than a rock in the water, its possession had been contested since 1444 by four European powers: Portugal, the Netherlands, England, and France. In 1960 the French gave the island back to Senegal.

Jack continued, "Gorée Island is known best today for the House of Slaves."

They watched as the island appeared to come along side then drift behind them.

"I knew a biologist," Jack said, "who argued that colonization is a survival strategy hardwired into our genes."

OUSMANE REFILLED THE BOAT'S FUEL TANKS IN BARGNY-GOUDDAU, WHERE they ate fruit, fresh vegetables, and rice for lunch.

They spent the afternoon swimming in the ocean. Then they walked the beach.

As she watched the tide recede, Rachel found herself caught between two desires. There was a voice inside her head telling her to stop. She knew she was heading down a dangerous path, but she could not quell her longing for the kindness, for the strength that radiated from this man.

WHEN THE SUN SET, THEY WERE FIVE MILES OFFSHORE. OUSMANE CUT THE engine, and water lapped against the wooden hull. Rachel could not discern the difference between the fire in the clouds and the fire on the water. Her heart was so open she could discern no difference between her hopes and what lay out there on the horizon, between her own soul and Jack's.

She decided in that boat that she would move into the yurt.

THEY CAME ASHORE FOR DINNER IN MBAO. THE LITTLE PATIO OVERLOOKED the starlit ocean and was just big enough for two tables. The woman who took their order was over eighty years old and spoke English with a French accent. She was also the cook.

Rachel was looking out over the water. "Do you think we can just build our lives, make things the way we want?"

"I think so."

"If we can do that, I want to use my hands." She held them up for Jack to see. "I want a piece of land. I want to tend it."

The old woman brought out thieboudienne and a bowl of mangos. Rachel could see Ousmane sitting alone at his cook fire on the beach.

As they ate, both of them considered Rachel's vision of the future. They could build a life together.

When the old woman came back for their dishes, Jack looked at her mischievously.

She demanded, "What?"

"Do you like motorcycles?"

Rachel remembered a similar question about boats from the night before. She cocked her head and waited for the explanation.

"I thought in the morning we could explore the Savannah."

PRESENT

JACK OPENED A DOOR IN THE HALLWAY, LOOKING FOR THE LINEN CLOSET. What he found was a two-drawer steel filing cabinet, on top of which was an open instruction manual. The page showing was written in Chinese.

Jack was surprised to discover that he understood the text. He picked it up. It was a set of instructions for the installation of a dishwasher. He glanced over his shoulder then back at the manual in his hand.

The fact that he understood it was disorienting. He turned the page and continued reading. The translation seemed effortless. Then he realized that there was no translation. Jack was thinking in Mandarin Chinese.

The manual fell to the floor.

Jack remembered the convention center. The university. He could remember Beijing.

He was in a massive hall. The signs were written in both Chinese characters and English. As the signs passed overhead, Jack realized that he was riding down an escalator. A Chinese man was talking to another man on the crowded landing. His name badge read: Jihong Zhang.

That was it.

Jack tried to recall more, but the effort only pushed the memory away. He saw it retreating down a tunnel in his mind. The harder he worked to recall it the further away it went. The tunnel got narrower and narrower, until whatever light remained from Jack's past was squeezed out.

RACHEL LAY ON THE LEATHER COUCH WITH A BAG OF FROZEN PEAS OVER HER eyes and nose.

Jack spread the cotton blanket he found in the linen closet over her legs. Then he twisted the lid off the Percocet and handed the bottle to Rachel.

"The clothes fit?" he asked as he refilled her coffee.

"The jeans are alright with a belt." Rachel was in too many pieces to know what to feel anymore. "The boots are too small."

Jack sat on the love seat. "Did I ever say anything about China?"

"China?" She swallowed two pills. "No, Jack, you never told me anything."

"Did I ever go to China?"

"I don't know."

"Did I ever mention a man named Zhang?"

"No." She sat up and looked around the room. "I don't feel right being here. I need to see Billy. I need to talk to Regan."

"There's a car in the garage. Before we go, is there anything else you can tell me?"

"They also said something about a computer. They wanted to know if I'd seen it, if you'd talked about it."

"What did you tell them?"

She didn't respond.

"Rachel, is there anything else?"

They heard the overhead door opening. Rachel shot up. The frozen peas landed at her feet.

There were headlights in the driveway.

Jack drew the phone from his pocket, and Rachel could hear the voice in the speaker.

"Keep her with you. Get out of the house."

She watched Jack cross to the sliding-glass door.

"Rachel, come on."

"Who was the man on the phone?"

Jack didn't answer.

They heard a pair of car doors shut. Heard the overhead door in the garage begin to close.

"Who was he?"

"The Colonel, my old boss."

"No, he wasn't."

Jack looked confused.

"I know his voice. That wasn't him."

Colorado
2001

Because the Colonel walked with a limp, the duffle bag he carried lurched against his leg. He wore a black polo shirt tucked into his jeans. Even with his age and injuries, there was no fat on his body.

Rachel brought him into the house through her studio.

"It looks finished." The last time he had seen the house they were building the doors.

"There's still some fencing to do."

She sat him at the kitchen table, on which there was a partially played game of chess. Then she brought him a can of Coors beer. "Jack's been teaching him to play."

"The kid's cornered." The Colonel's voice resonated with an authority that made every statement seem factual.

Rachel brought him a plate of lunch meats, a loaf of homemade bread, lettuce, and a dish of sliced tomatoes.

"Why didn't they finish their game?"

"Billy was losing and giving his pieces away."

The Colonel nodded.

"Jack took him outdoors to change his mindset. They're scouting for deer."

"I bet you're happy here." The Colonel built himself a sandwich. "Billy's, what, nine years old?"

"That's right."

The Colonel was looking at a framed photograph of the family on the wall. "It's a beautiful thing. That boy. This place."

Rachel sat down at the table, and the Colonel took one of Jack's knights with Billy's king.

"Billy's never won a game against his dad. He still asks to play every night."

The Colonel gestured for Rachel to take Jack's turn.

She put him in check.

The Colonel moved his king toward the edge of the board. "I apologize for taking your husband."

"It pays the bills."

"I've known Jack a long time. You've been good for him."

"How long will he be gone?"

"Let's start with a month."

The two of them studied the board.

"He talks about retiring." Rachel moved her queen and put the Colonel in check again.

The Colonel moved the king to the edge of the board.

Rachel brought in her bishop and asked, "Will you let him?"

"I'm afraid that's stalemate."

JACK TOOK THE COLONEL OUT AT DAWN TO HUNT. THEY RODE BACK TO THE house with a buck apiece just as Billy was getting out of bed. He saw them coming from his bedroom window and ran out to meet them wearing nothing but his underwear.

The men unloaded the game in the garage. Billy led the horses to the barn, removed the saddles and bridles, and washed off the blood. He brushed the horses. Then he got dressed and helped the men with the butchering.

Rachel packed the Colonel's share of the meat in a cooler with dry ice. They grilled deer steaks for lunch.

"You ever read any Chinese mythology, Billy?"

Billy's napkin was tucked into the neck of his shirt. He wiped his mouth and said, "I like westerns and comic books."

"I never studied the literature coming out of China either," the Colonel drank from a can of beer. "Never considered it. Not until recently." The Colonel watched Billy eat. The boy's appetite was that of a grown man's. Then he put down his can and said, "About three thousand years ago there was a Chinese artificer named Yan Shi who made a robot that looked like a person. It could walk, sing, and dance. And it had an eye for women."

Billy expressed his skepticism with a raised eyebrow.

"One day Yan Shi brought his robot to the king. Nobody had ever seen anything like it. The exhibition went perfectly until the robot started being lewd with the women. That incensed the king.

"Yan Shi knew he would lose his life if he couldn't get the king to excuse the robot's behavior, so he dismantled it.

"When the king saw all the parts, he was amazed. The robot had muscles over the bones. Tendons and ligaments. It had hair and teeth."

Billy had stopped eating. His eyes were slits, and he was looking at the Colonel sideways. "How did he make it?"

"I don't know."

"How come the Chinese can't make one like that today?"

"Maybe they can."

Present

IT WAS TOO LATE. TOO LATE TO GET OUT OF THE HOUSE WITHOUT BEING SEEN. An emergency call from the homeowners would bring the helicopter. Jack drew the Colt from its shoulder holster.

Rachel saw the gun and turned to see a middle-aged couple entering the house from the garage.

"On the ground! Now!"

The woman dropped her purse and held her hands at her shoulders, showing her palms. The man stood speechless behind her. Neither of them had yet stepped into the hallway.

"My god!" Rachel said. But, to her, the voice sounded like it came from somewhere else.

Jack advanced through the kitchen keeping the front sight of the weapon trained on the man's torso. "Down! Now! On the ground!"

The woman grasped the man's hand. She was trembling. She knelt down slowly, but the man was still paralyzed. She pulled him to his knees.

"Lie down! Now!"

Jack kicked the man over.

"Oh no." The woman's voice was so melodic Rachel didn't connect the words to what was happening, not until the woman repeated the words.

The couple was prostrate on the garage floor.

"Turn your heads and face the wall."

The woman obeyed.

Jack stepped into the garage and kicked the man in the mouth. "Face the wall." He crossed the garage and took a roll of black electrical tape from a shelf.

"Oh no."

They wouldn't survive the cold. Rachel helped the woman to her hands and knees and led her inside the house, where Jack taped her wrists and ankles.

The man was muttering. A string of blood swung from his bottom lip. Rachel led him inside. The stench of excrement hung in the hall. She saw the stain on the back of his slacks.

Jack searched the man's pockets, took his phone. Then he found the keys in the woman's purse.

"I'm not going to help you take their car."

Rachel was done with Jack. She had been done with him for nearly a decade. Her mind was confused. Tired. But she knew this. She knew it in the core of her being. She wanted nothing more to do with the man who had bedazzled her when she was twenty-three.

She could only think about one thing: her family. And Jack was not part of that. She needed Regan. She wanted to see her son.

"You won't make it on foot. They'll reach you before you reach the sheriff."

The truth of the statement exasperated her. She still needed him. It was a source of shame to Rachel: that she ever needed him.

She had to step over the couple to enter the garage.

"I don't like this. It isn't right."

Jack chose the BMW X5 over the Jeep. He studied the GPS in the dashboard as he pulled out of the garage.

Rachel's phone vibrated. Jack held it rattling in his hand.

"How do you know it isn't him?" It was spoken more like a demand than a question.

"I knew the Colonel, Jack. You hunted together at the ranch. It's not him."

The phone kept vibrating.

"You're sure?"

"It's not him."

Jack answered. "Who are you?"

"We've been through this."

"I remember the Colonel. You're not him."

The line was silent.

"Fuck with me," Jack said, "and I drop the phone."

"The Colonel is AWOL." The voice now had a pleading tone. "You and I worked together on Talon in Beijing."

Jack couldn't remember his name, but he could see the face that went with the voice. The situation was finally starting to make some sense. "I'm listening."

"I have reason to believe the Colonel intends to undermine your mission."

"What was your role in Beijing?"

"I led the team that took care of you. I put together your cover and handled your papers."

"What do you want from me?"

"Yan Shi, Jack. You need to tell me where you hid it."

The plows were still clearing the side streets. Jack turned onto Main Street and heard the rotors of a helicopter. It was approaching the vehicle from behind.

"It's just a search pattern. We're intercepting their communications traffic. They don't know where you are."

The sound was deafening. Rachel turned around in her seat, afraid the helicopter was landing on the car. It passed slowly overhead. The noise drowned out the conversation for nearly a minute.

"What is the blue team after?"

"Like the Colonel, they're in theater to terminate you."

"Why?" Jack thrust his head out the window to locate the silhouette of the blacked-out helicopter against the stars.

"Turn right here."

Jack slowed for the turn.

"The oncoming vehicle is equipped with facial recognition scanners."

He completed the turn before observing, "It's dark."

"Doesn't matter."

"Then a lot has changed."

"Yes, it has."

Jack looked at Rachel. "Tell me what she has to do with this?"

"Nothing."

"She's not safe with me. I'm taking her in."

"Pull into the parking lot on your right."

A John Deere frontloader was clearing snow from the far side of the parking lot.

"Why terminate me?"

"Your government doesn't want Yan Shi to be found."

Jack left the transmission in gear and parked with his foot on the brake pedal. "Who's Zhang?"

COLORADO
2001

W HAT WAS THAT STORY YOU TOLD BILLY?" JACK WAS DRIVING.

"About the robot?" The Colonel saw history as a perpetual retelling of the same theme, which made him fond of allusions. "The important thing about that story is that the robot was absolutely true to the Chinese understanding of human anatomy. Without a heart, it couldn't speak. Without a liver, it couldn't see. Without kidneys, it couldn't walk. And so on."

"What does that have to do with us?"

The Colonel looked in the passenger side mirror. "There's a professor Zhang heading an artificial intelligence project in the Department of Computer Science and Technology at Tsinghua University in Beijing."

"You want me to go to Beijing."

"Zhang's team is developing an AI platform that makes the high tech gadgets of Silicon Valley look like Stone Age artifacts."

Jack waited for the explanation.

"Zhang's software writes its own code."

Jack shifted down, trying to comprehend the Colonel's statement.

"Guess what he calls it."

"Surprise me."

"Yan Shi."

"After the artificer?"

"It would be a hell of a coincidence."

Jack shifted up as he came over the hill. Computers weren't his typical line of work.

"The Chinese have been content until now to steal American technology. They've got an army of kids over there hacking into secure servers from Microsoft to the Pentagon. That they've designed something of their own is actually a surprising development."

Jack slowed and turned into the airport, which was little more than a paved strip boxed in by mountains.

"There will be a conference on artificial intelligence next week in Beijing, which means there will be a lot of Westerners at the university. The computer itself is too large to be moved. Your assignment is to steal Yan Shi's memory."

Jack parked the Jeep. There were no other travelers at the rural airport. The two got out and headed for the gate. A Cessna Citation was waiting for them on the other side of a chain-link fence.

THE COLONEL ASKED, "WHAT DO YOU KNOW ABOUT AI?"

"Just what I've learned in the last five minutes."

"I'm not here just because the Chinese have a better computer than us. Software that can optimize its own code can evolve at an exponential rate. Whatever it can do now, it can do better tomorrow. It can design its own hardware, design the machines to build that hardware." The Colonel led Jack through the gate and across the tarmac to the Cessna's gangway. "With access to nanotech manufacturing, a computer like Yan Shi can build anything, do anything. Evolve at a pace never seen before on this planet. In the intelligence community, we call this the Technological Singularity."

"As in a black hole?"

"We are living at the event horizon." The Colonel was standing at the top of the gangway. "Nobody knows what happens once you cross the horizon. Only that everything changes. It's all theory. Theory that is taken very seriously by a heretofore neglected niche of the intelligence community."

"To be clear," Jack offered, "we're talking about *Terminator*, *The Matrix*?"

The jet was outfitted with black leathers seats, a forward cabin galley, and an aft lavatory. They sat facing each other on opposite sides of a wooden table.

"How long do you think it would take for a computer brain evolving at an exponential rate to become intelligent enough to make the entire digital security apparatus of the United States obsolete?"

"I don't know."

"Neither does anybody else."

Jack opened the window shade.

"We've known that the country has been vulnerable to a cyber attack on its power grid for years. Such an attack wouldn't require a super-intelligent computer. It could be done from a college dorm. Now imagine what a cyber attack planned by Yan Shi might look like."

"I'm guessing somebody already has."

The Citation accelerated down the runway, lifted its nose, and was airborne.

Jack looked out the window and could see the 3,000-vertical-foot scar of the Patriarch Run. The bottom of the avalanche runout marked the southern fence line of his property.

He was having a hard time imagining how a power outage could pose an existential threat to the nation.

The Colonel anticipated his question. There was a file sitting on the table titled Vulnerable Infrastructure. He pushed it forward.

Jack opened the folder to find a briefing dated two days ago. The first section of the report outlined the three main constituents of the power system: generation, transmission, and distribution.

"The part that kept me up the last two nights," the Colonel said, "was transmission. How long do you think it takes to replace a fried substation?"

Jack was skimming the document. "I haven't read that far."

"Two years. That's without a crisis, when you're only replacing one."

Jack found the relevant paragraph of the document and learned that there were thousands of vulnerable substations in the system. Those substations were constructed with large transformers, which were no longer manufactured in America.

There were other vulnerabilities outlined in the report. Scattered throughout the power grid were SCADA (supervisory control and data acquisition) systems. At minimum, these systems would need to be rebooted. Many of them would have to be replaced.

Jack looked up from the folder. "Sounds like a real goat-fuck."

"You haven't gotten to the good part yet." The Colonel directed him to the paragraphs on power generation.

A cyber attack could manipulate the control systems of a power plant to irreparably damage the vulnerable hardware, such as the power generators.

"You wouldn't be able to flip a switch and have power again," the Colonel explained. "Even if you could mobilize, transport, and feed all the trained workers in the country, it would take years to fully recover."

"But you wouldn't be able to mobilize, transport, and feed them."

"That's right," the Colonel smiled grimly. "Keep reading."

The next section was about fossil fuels. In short, it stated that the refineries and pipelines were as vulnerable as the power grid. A sophisticated cyber attack could deny the country fuel, which meant there'd be no transportation.

Jack drew the conclusion, "Without the ability to generate power or to produce fuel, the whole country would simply stop."

"We're talking about raw sewage overwhelming the nation's waterways," the Colonel cracked his neck. "No drinking water. No food in the grocery store."

The next section of the report detailed the dependency of the country's food infrastructure on electricity and petroleum. That infrastructure included irrigation systems, food processing plants, refrigerated warehouses, supermarkets, trucks, trains.

The report stated that the population of the United States at the turn of the century was 76 million. It was 285 million in 2001. America was feeding 209 million more people than it was at the turn of the century, but it had only increased the amount of land it farmed by six percent. To accomplish this feat, the American farmer increased food yield by more than fifty-fold. Technology made that increase possible: machines, fertilizers, and pesticides. All of which were either made from or powered by petroleum. All of which were manufactured with electricity.

The section concluded that without a functioning power grid and plentiful fuel, the nation would revert back to untreated water and pre-electricity food yields, which would feed only a fraction of the population.

Jack laid the open folder on the table.

"The food supply is the weak link in the security of a nation." The Colonel stood up in the tube-like cabin of the airplane and stretched his back. "We might be the first civilization in history that has grown enough food for the population to have forgotten that." He walked forward to the galley, took a Coke from the fridge, and offered it to Jack.

"No thanks."

"It gets worse," the Colonel pointed at the file on the table. "Keep reading."

Jack skimmed the next three sections and learned that any device connected to the internet, a telephone network, or a satellite could be hacked. The banking system could collapse. With it, all commerce. Software worms could be hidden within the computer controls of the nation's chemical processing plants. These worms could cause explosions that could release poisonous clouds into the air and chemical waste into the nation's waterways.

The final section of the report was titled "Nuclear Disasters." Jack read that a super-intelligent attack could take over the electronic control systems of the country's 104 commercial nuclear reactors simultaneously. Even if all the plant operators managed to shut down all the reactors safely, they couldn't avert catastrophe because there is no shutting down the half-life of a radioactive isotope. It takes electrically-powered cooling pumps to keep the spent fuel in these facilities from overheating. In the wake of such an attack, there would be no diesel fuel available. Once the emergency generators ran out of diesel, the cooling pumps would shut down. Then the radioactive fuel would melt through the reactor cores.

The report was a modern vision of Armageddon. Its final paragraph detailed an apocalypse in which the American people could wake up to radiation, toxic clouds, fires at oil refineries. Using the finite resources available, POTUS (President of the United States) could communicate by messenger and make strategic choices. Select installations could be saved or, at least, catastrophic failure postponed. But there wouldn't be enough calculative power in the Federal Government to cope with the magnitude of the disaster.

"Here's the kicker," the Colonel sat down again across from Jack.

"The spectacular explosions, the threat of nuclear meltdown, it would all amount to a dazzling distraction. The real threat is, and always has been, starvation."

Jack closed the folder and put it back on the table.

"If you can't distribute food, you don't have a civilization. Wealth will be counted in canned goods and the guns and ammunition stockpiled to defend them."

The briefing offered the conservative estimate of 153 million casualties by the end of the first year. The middle of the road estimate was 200 million.

Jack looked out the window at the city beneath them. Then he pointed to the folder on the table. "Doesn't all this assume the Chinese have a will to destroy us?"

"No. No rational state would jeopardize its own existence to strike at the United States of America. If China were to attack us, it would be obliterated."

"If China's not the threat, who is?"

"Yan Shi is essentially software. Software that can be sold and distributed to the highest bidder. If you were POTUS, would you take that risk?"

Jack shook his head. "It doesn't make sense for the Chinese to sell it. They would want to control it."

"Yes, but could the Chinese prevent it from being stolen?" The Citation was banking and descending. "Without a power grid, you'd have a medieval paradise for an Islamist extremist."

"Why me? Why not abduct professor Zhang and take out the computer?"

"Those details are being handled by whiter agencies."

PRESENT

RACHEL SAW THE LIGHTS AS SOON AS JACK TURNED ONTO K STREET. FROM afar, the front steps of the Sheriff's Office looked like a city viewed from a mountain at night. As they drove closer, she realized that each of the lights was a burning wick. There were candles arranged in the shape of a cross on the cleared-off sidewalk, a peace sign made of candles in the handicap space.

Jack pulled into the parking lot. The headlights illuminated a snow-enveloped lawn colored by countless bouquets.

She stepped out of the car.

Rachel couldn't approach the building for the barricade of candles and flowers. There were teddy bears. Paper signs.

She stood at the steps. There was a Hot Wheel's patrol car. Balloons. American flags, hundreds of them. But her eyes were drawn to the flames flickering in colored jars, ordinary table glasses, paper gift bags, and plastic cups.

There was a newspaper arranged with three framed photographs of the deceased. She picked up the paper.

When she turned around, the car was still running, its front doors were open, but Jack was gone.

Jack didn't know Regan was dead until he saw the makeshift memorial at the Sheriff's Office. It felt cruel to leave Rachel in the parking lot, but it was too dangerous to keep her with him.

He called his contact.

"I got someone on the phone now," the voice told him. "Rachel will be taken into protective custody."

Jack saw a pair of headlights swing onto K Street ahead of him.

"You've got company. Turn left," the voice said.

Jack headed for the town park. "I want her far away from this."

"She'll be taken care of."

There was no sidewalk, so he hurried through the tire tracks on the unplowed street. "Why didn't you didn't tell me the sheriff was dead?"

"Things are moving fast. I lost track of the detail."

"We're not talking about a detail." The word angered Jack. "Regan was acting as my son's father."

"He was killed by sicarios."

"Mexicans?" Jack looked behind him and saw the headlights slowly enter the intersection on K Street. "What am I missing?"

"While you were away, GAFE entered the illicit drug trade." GAFE (*Grupo Aeromóvil de Fuerzas Especiales*) was the acronym for the Mexican Special Forces. "To make a long story short, there was a war and GAFE won."

Jack glanced again and saw that the vehicle had stopped. "They're working with the Chinese?" The vehicle was backing up through the intersection. He had no time to process what he was hearing. The headlights swung onto the street behind him.

"The point is the Chinese want their computer back."

He could make out the gazebo in the town park and beyond it, the

178

silhouette of a grove of pine trees. "Why didn't they just build another one?" Jack hurried through the snow-covered field.

"They've been working on that for ten years now. You've been gone a long time."

He thought about using the gazebo for cover, but decided against it. The trees would attract less attention in the dark. "What's next?"

"Yan Shi, Jack. Where is it?"

He answered before he had time to think about the question. "The ranch."

"Where?"

Now that he was thinking about it, he couldn't remember. "I don't know. But it's there."

"Then you need to go back."

By being bold, clever, and very lucky, Jack had gotten away with that once, but the blue team would have learned from his incursion. Jack knew it wouldn't be possible to get inside their perimeter again.

The voice on the phone addressed Jack's concern. "We'll leak the location to the Mexicans and use them to keep the blue team occupied."

Jack was in the pine trees. The vehicle that was pursuing him was stopped on the street. The dome light in the cab came on, and he could see the silhouette of someone examining his footprints in the snow.

By taking advantage of the distraction, Jack could probably get himself in. But the firefight would be decided quickly, and he was now sure of this: the man on the phone, who had already lied to him once, had no intention of getting him out. Jack looked up, saw a satellite coursing among the stars, and ended the call.

He watched as the vehicle climbed onto the field and swept the park with its headlights.

Rachel staggered through the snow. Unaware of herself. Of anything. Her vision tapered, and she began to list sideways. Her shoulder caught a tree. She stood slanted against the pine trunk. The shock had drained her body. Her legs no longer held her. She slid down the bark of the tree and sat in the snow.

Although she remembered the headline, "Sheriff Regan Dowell Gunned Down by Mexican Cartel," Rachel was no longer aware of the newspaper in her hand. Beneath the headline she had seen a photograph of the sheriff's body on the highway. It was partially zipped in a black bag. His uniform was visible. Next to the sheriff was a second body in a bag. Beside which was Billy's .30-30 Winchester rifle and his Cabela's hat, stained with blood.

She might have sat in the snow under that tree for an hour. She didn't hear Charlie's voice, or any of the other deputies calling her name. When she stood, she thought nothing. She didn't feel cold. She wasn't aware of her body's shuddering attempt to warm itself or that she was walking. Only that her men were dead.

Rachel walked uphill through the forest, stumbling. Sometimes crawling through the snow. Unaware of the night. Her baby was dead.

BILLY PULLED HIS COLLAR UP AND WALKED HEAD-DOWN THROUGH THE snow on the shoulder of the highway with his thumb out. He knew the risk, but by the way he figured it, unless he wanted to become more of an outlaw than he already was, he didn't have much of a choice. He had given all but twenty dollars to Javier.

They must have taken the picture they were using of him on the TV from the yearbook. Sally had him dress up all unnatural for that. The whole episode had been an embarrassment. Now he was grateful: it didn't look a thing like him.

He walked north, toward Colorado, for about a mile and a half before a red Chevy S-10 slowed and stopped. It sat about a hundred yards up the road. When he got there, the driver's window was down.

"Go ahead, get in." She had long, gray hair and bright blue eyes.

Billy walked around the bed, opened the passenger door, kicked the snow off his boots, and sat down.

"Seat belt."

Billy buckled, and she pulled onto the highway.

"Sophie." She held out her hand.

Billy shook it. "Tom."

Rachel woke in an unfinished basement. She didn't know how she'd gotten there. It wasn't even a question she asked. Upon waking, she was skewered by the memory of the newspaper headline, the memorial at the Sheriff's Office. Billy was dead. The pain was physical. She curled herself in a ball—her whole body clenched as a brace against it.

It wasn't a nightmare. She had hoped it was just a nightmare. Regan was gone. How could they be gone?

When she heard voices upstairs, Rachel climbed out the broken window. She didn't notice the dawn. The driveway. She couldn't feel her own body. She didn't have any thoughts—other than the repetition of the realization that they were dead. Every time she realized they were dead, it was another shock.

She didn't know how long she had been climbing. She didn't think about the mountain, the snow. Only that it seemed fitting—that it was arduous to move. She didn't feel cold. Not even tired. She was numb.

Then she was aware that she was sliding. That she had slipped and was on her side. She did nothing to change what was happening to her body. She felt relieved by the thought that she might die.

She had survived all those years in her mother's house. She had come of age fatherless, and she had survived that. She had survived being abandoned by her husband. She had survived being taken at gunpoint from the home she built. She had survived being stuffed into a trunk. She had endured torture, heatstroke. She had withstood the terror she suffered over the whereabouts and the safety of her son. She had survived being helpless to protect him. But this: Regan's death, Billy's death, broke her.

She heard the cracking of the branches, but did not feel them striking her limbs. It was as if she were sledding down the mountainside, but she was hollow and sledless. She let her arms flop over her head. She was unaware of the snow packed in her open mouth and nostrils. She felt herself suffocating, but it was what she wanted.

She left the earth and tumbled. In her flight, she sheared branches from their trunks. Then she hit the mountain slope and bounced, cartwheeling through the air.

Rachel lay twisted, facedown, one leg above her, unaware that the falling had stopped. She coughed involuntarily, expelling snow. Then she remained as she was.

WHEN SHE HEARD SNORTING, SHE SAT UP.

Something large approached. Rachel stood knee deep in snow. She saw movement to her left and turned to face it. She felt no fear. But she was curious. She made out a silhouette in the dense forest. It was huge. Assuming it was Death, she watched it advance.

The creature came on through the trees until she recognized it was a horse.

Maiden nuzzled Rachel's chest and brought her back to her body.

THEY WERE AN HOUR NORTH OF THE COLORADO BORDER WHEN SHE ASKED, "You headin' home?"

"More or less." Billy didn't intend to come this far south. He didn't intend anything. It was all just happening.

"Your folks keep horses?"

Billy couldn't think of a simple answer.

"I can smell it on you."

He eyed her, trying to decide whether or not she was serious.

"At my age, I can't think of a better companion. What's her name, your mare?"

"How'd you know she's a mare?"

"You wear it in on you."

Billy thought she was messing with him and said, "Maiden. She's a buckskin mustang."

"That's a rugged breed."

"She's a good horse."

"You miss her?"

"Haven't had much time to think about it."

They were being passed on the left by a tractor-trailer rig hauling some type of heavy equipment under a green drop tarp.

"You hungry, Tom?"

"Yeah, I'm hungry."

"There's a burrito place I like to visit about ninety minutes up the road. What do you say we make a stop?"

"Okay." Billy looked at the speedometer again. She never broke fifty-five.

"I buried my daughter Friday. I'm comin' home from that."

"I'm sorry to hear that."

"She was forty-two and had no family of her own. Wasn't in her to settle down. I guess some people are like that."

"I guess so."

"I was in her room the morning she passed. I suppose that's a blessing. We hadn't seen each other for over a decade. You couldn't really call it a feud as the grudge was one-sided. Held against me."

"I'm sorry to hear that, too."

"I'm sure she was justified."

The woman had to be in her sixties, but her skin didn't show it. If she colored her hair, there'd be little about her appearance to suggest her true age.

"What I should've done was drove down there ten years ago. I didn't because I knew she wouldn't've had me. I should've done it anyway. Why it took something like her dying for me to understand that I'll never know."

"Tell me about her."

Sophie's eyes were soft, and there was a depth to them that Billy had never seen before. She looked at him for so long he began to worry about the road.

"You know, Tom, since she passed I might have talked to two dozen people. All of them kind. But no one has asked me that." She smiled. "I didn't realize I wanted to answer it."

They were being passed again. Sophie pulled over as far as she could onto the snow-covered shoulder and a trio of cars soared by.

"She was the apple of her daddy's eye. He loved her spunk. But she and I tended to clash. Once, when she was two years old, she refused to brush her teeth. Her daddy advised me to let it be. But I couldn't. One way or another, I was going to get those teeth brushed. I guess she knew it too 'cause she took off. I went into the bathroom to get her toothbrush and toothpaste, and when I came out she was gone. Simply gone.

"We found her diaper in the front lawn. When we found her, she was naked strutting down the sidewalk a block away from the house. She had her Pooh Bear."

"What's her name?"

"Samantha." Sophie didn't even try to dry the tears. "Everybody called her Sam. She was a bit of a Tomboy and never grew out of it. The first girl to play the boys' sports at her high school."

There was a box of tissues on the dash. Billy passed it. "What'd she play?"

"Football, baseball. You name it. She got a scholarship to play soccer in college and turned it down to enlist in the army. They wouldn't let her fight so she became a pilot. Sam served in the First Iraq War and Somalia."

Sophie looked at him again. "You know, Tom, you're an easy person to talk to. I appreciate you listening to all this."

She drove another five miles. "You look tired."

"I make it a point not to sleep on account of the bad dreams."

"What sort of dreams?"

"I prefer not to discuss it." Billy looked out the windshield. "What about her dad?"

"He's been dead a decade now. Cancer. I'm afraid the manner of his passing was why Sam was mad at me. It took a full year for the cancer to finally kill him. It's a horrible business."

There were a dozen antelope bedded in the snow just off the highway. They both turned to look at them.

"Jim couldn't eat. Couldn't control his bowels. He could barely communicate. IV's. Horrible machines. He knew. He knew, and I didn't. He'd been asking me for months, but I just couldn't do it. So he asked her. He asked his daughter to take him into the mountains. By this time, he didn't weigh but ninety-two pounds. To this place we'd been to as a family. To leave him there. To carry him in and just leave him there.

"The thought of it. Vultures picking at him. I couldn't. I just couldn't. I didn't let her. She tried to take him anyway. I came back from the store and caught them in the driveway. I called the police."

They were entering a town. Plows and tractors were clearing the streets. She decelerated then stopped at the traffic light.

"To make him go on like that. Just wasting away. And the pain he was in. Because I couldn't, because . . . "

She took two tissues from the box and cleaned her face. The light turned. Neither of them spoke for a full minute. The light turned red again.

"After that, I didn't see Sam for ten years. Not until Sunday."

A car stopped behind them.

"I blame myself." She looked at Billy and saw that he was crying. "Oh bless your heart, Tom, I'm sorry." She pulled a clean tissue.

Billy waved it away. He was thinking about the sheriff and looked out his window.

The car behind them sounded its horn, and she started driving again. Billy could see the sign for the burrito place.

Sophie signaled and got into the lane to turn. "Last summer they had a little drive-through window installed. We can go through that."

"Okay."

"It'll be more anonymous that way."

Billy turned so far in his seat that his back was against the door.

"Oh, relax. There's not but one in a hundred people who wouldn't recognize you, Billy. For five days now, you've been the only thing on the news."

Five days? That didn't seem real. "How many days has it been since . . . ?"

She studied him for a long time before she answered. "Sheriff Dowell was gunned down on Wednesday."

He had no idea which day it was now, and because of the look of concern on her face, he didn't ask.

"Billy, were you with the sheriff on that highway?"

"Yes."

"Because the news didn't say anything about that."

WHEN SOPHIE TRIED TO PAY FOR THE BURRITOS, BILLY REACHED ACROSS THE cab, held her arm, and handed the cashier a twenty.

"I won't feel comfortable if you don't let me contribute something."

When they got back on the highway, she talked about roses. "You ever eat a freshly picked rose hip?"

Green salsa ran down Billy's fingers. He licked it off then wiped his fingers on his Carhartt. "I don't think so."

"You ever cooked with rose water?"

"I never paid much attention to roses." Billy's hand went up to his hat, which wasn't there. He ran it through his hair. "I'm sorry I lied to you."

"What about?"

"My name. I feel embarrassed about it."

"That's nonsense. You did the right thing."

"What is the news saying about me?"

"Read it for yourself." She pointed to the floor beneath Billy's feet.

He picked up the newspaper and read the front page: "Elite American Unit Deployed to Colorado to Crush Mexican Drug Cartel."

SOPHIE STOPPED FOR GAS. SHE SAW THE SHREDDED CHEESE STILL ON HIS LAP, a salsa stain on the sleeve of his coat, which he had used to clean his mouth. His fingernails were all bit down. Some were bleeding.

"You best stay in the truck, Billy."

He gathered up the trash from the burritos and handed it to her through the window. Then he fell asleep against the door.

IN HIS DREAMS, BILLY HEARD THE SHERIFF'S REVOLVER HITTING THE PAVEMENT. He could hear the submachine gun. He would ignore the gunfire, walk around the patrol car to the sheriff's body, and search for his face. He never did find it.

WHEN BILLY WOKE, HE FELT AS IF SOMEBODY HAD LOADED HIS CHEST WITH lead.

"Did you have a good nap?"

"I dreamt about my dad."

"I'll tell you something, Billy. Learn it if it's possible. There ain't a soul on this planet without just cause to hold a grudge. Holding is the easy part."

Billy was looking out the window. "What's the hard part?"

"Letting go. He's family. Remember that. Before you know it, the day'll come when it'll be too late."

They passed about fifteen miles without talking.

She turned on the radio. "What are you gonna do now?"

"I don't know. I ain't never been an outlaw before."

She laughed so hard the truck swerved. "You're no outlaw, Billy."

She saw the anxiety on his face and grew serious. "Is that why you're running? The news is referring to you and your mom as missing persons."

She looked in the rearview mirror and eased over to let the faster traffic pass. Then she looked at him again and saw the fuzz under his sideburns, above his lip. "Why, you're just a kid."

THROUGH A BREAK IN THE CLOUDS, RACHEL SAW A RED PICKUP TRUCK PARKED on the otherwise empty highway. From her view of the three Matriarchs on the other side of the valley, she recognized the trail she was on. Maiden was taking her home. She was wet and shivering so fiercely it was all she could do to stay on the horse.

YOU SURE YOU WANT OUT HERE? IT'S SUPPOSED TO SNOW AGAIN."

"I'm sure." Billy opened the door.

"I'm going right through town."

He got out. "I appreciate everything you've done." He shut the door and started walking.

Billy studied the highway and found the skid marks, which disappeared into the snow-covered grass. He looked for the spot in the river where the Mercedes had crashed. Then he studied the site from the side of the road. The river looked different with all the new snow.

He heard Sophie's truck begin to accelerate.

"Okay, Billy. Take care."

His back was to the highway. He put up a hand.

ONCE HE WAS ALONE, HE CROSSED THE HIGHWAY AND WALKED THE OPPOSITE shoulder.

He felt nauseous.

Even under all the snow, he could see where the patrol car had left the road, where it had carved out a piece of the embankment. He walked closer and smelled the antifreeze. Although the shoulder had been plowed, there were still pieces of glass.

Billy heard someone advancing behind him and froze. The footfalls grew louder. He reached inside his coat for the revolver and spun around to face the threat.

He saw an empty highway, vast forests, snow covered peaks, storm clouds.

Then Billy realized that what he was hearing was his own heartbeat. His heart grew so loud he thought it might burst his chest.

HE TURNED BACK TO WHERE THE PATROL CAR HAD CRASHED.

Although washed out, the blood was still visible. Billy felt dizzy and stood in the lane and wept.

Jack's broken rib throbbed, and although the temperature was well below freezing, he was sweating, wading through thigh-deep snow. His jeans were crusted with ice. To conceal his track from any watchful eyes he made his descent along a game trail.

He had passed the night beside a fire in the cave Billy pointed out to him. In that cave he began to remember details about his life, whole narratives. He went to school at the Catholic church on 27 3rd Street. His first car was a 1966 Camaro. He was sixteen and bought the Camaro new with money he had earned framing houses. He could remember Somalia, Iran. But he still couldn't remember anything pertinent to the mission. He couldn't remember why it mattered.

From his position on the mountain, Jack could see Main Street, the highway at the bottom of the valley, and the road that led up to the house. He was pretty sure that Yan Shi wasn't hidden inside the house. If it was, the blue team would have found it. Which meant it was somewhere else on the property. But where? He hoped the right landmark would trigger the memory. To find that landmark, he wanted a view of the entire ranch.

The phone vibrated in his pocket. Jack didn't trust his handler and ignored it. A black helicopter rose from the town and flew toward the mountain. No doubt the subject of the text he just received.

Jack squatted under the canopy of an Engelmann spruce tree. He put his hands in his coat pockets and ducked his chin into his leather collar for warmth. Now that his legs were no longer generating heat, the snowmelt iced his thighs.

What would the cartel do? Come up the long driveway? That would be suicide. No vehicle would get very far up that road. But what choice did they have? A competent assault would take more manpower than Jack imagined they had on hand.

He had minutes before the blue team would destroy the cartel's sicarios—by which time, he'd have to be gone.

He watched the Little Bird circle the property below then raise a whirlwind of snow as it landed near the ranch house.

He was shaking from the cold and eager to get moving, but the Little Bird was airborne again. It flew up the mountainside and passed directly overhead, stirring snow from the trees which fell in clumps all around him. The helicopter carried four armed passengers in black fatigues on its side benches and was armed with a Minigun and rockets. It kept climbing then disappeared into the clouds as it flew west.

When he stood up, the ice pulled out the hair on his thighs.

Billy saw a black sedan parked in the northbound lane. A truck passed going south. Then the driver's door opened, and the Colonel stepped out of the sedan.

"Billy? Jesus Christ, this is a hell of a place for you to be. Get in the car."

The dizziness was getting worse. Billy stepped forward, but the world was spinning.

"Christ, son," the Colonel took his arm. "Come on, before someone sees you."

Billy heard the passenger door open. The Colonel stuffed him into the seat and shut the door. He walked around the front of the car and got in.

"Jesus, Billy. This is where it happened, isn't it? Jesus."

THE FIRST SNOWFLAKES FELL AS JACK DESCENDED THROUGH THE LODGEPOLES. Snowfall would normally be welcome cover, but he needed good visibility to find his landmark.

There was a treed ridge about a half mile below him and to the left. Jack's exertion was generating heat, and although the skin of his thighs was wet with snowmelt, his jeans were iced over. He didn't want to get to the ridge early because if he stopped moving, he'd freeze.

But he didn't want to arrive late, either. He needed to be on that ridge before the firefight began and before the snowfall veiled the terrain he needed to study.

THE LAST TIME I SAW YOU, YOU WERE JUST A KID."

Billy watched the spring snow falling outside the passenger window. "The last time I saw you, my dad didn't come back."

The Colonel wiped the back of his hand across his mouth. He hadn't shaved in over a week. Billy had never known him to let his hair grow more than a quarter inch. Now it was lying on his ears. His slacks were wrinkled.

He reached for the radio then brought his hand back to the steering wheel without turning it on. "Billy, I had nothing to do with that."

"But you know what happened."

"Yes, I do." The Colonel had a voice like an unmuffled hotrod.

"I need to know."

"Billy . . . "

"They've got my mom."

The wiper blades crossed the windshield a dozen times in the silence.

The Colonel slowed and turned the car around. "When I met your dad, he was a good man. A true believer."

"What'd he do for you, kill communists, that type of thing?"

"No. Not that type of thing." The Colonel turned up the fan for the windshield defroster. "He wasn't an asset politicians had access to. He took care of third-world psychopaths. Criminals who trafficked in nuclear secrets. What you need to know about your dad is that he served his country, that he made it his life's work to make the world a better place."

"Then what happened to him?"

"Maybe he believed in his country a little too much. He was a lot like you, Billy."

Billy looked away.

"You might not want to hear it. But Jack was a patriot. He gave up more for this country than most people ever dream of."

"Patriots don't turn."

The Colonel put out his lower lip and nodded.

"Then how can you call him that?"

"When you get older, Billy, youthful patriotism can come off as a little naive."

"What's that supposed to mean?"

"It means that good and bad gets a little gray."

"Is that what happened to him? He got like you?"

The Colonel massaged the silver stubble on his chin, put both hands back on the steering wheel, and looked hard at Billy.

Billy reached for his hat. It wasn't there. He sunk lower in his seat and looked out the passenger window.

"The world is a corrupt and corrupting place. What happened to your dad is that he grew up. Saw more."

The Colonel's nose had been broken an untold number of times. It was crooked and scarred. And he was missing the lobe of his right ear. Billy found it hard not to stare at the deformities.

"Saw more of what?"

"Reality. When your dad was young, he assumed everyone else was like him, a true believer. He didn't understand how rare that was. It was incomprehensible to him what other men did. What motivated them. When he first started to see it, it sickened him. The money. The dark side of government. You look behind the curtain of power in America and you'll find something wholly un-American."

"So he turned?"

"No. It doesn't happen like that. Each betrayal takes another piece of you. Chips you down. Decades go by. The change is slow. Then one day you wake up and see America entirely differently. You realize the woman you fell in love with as a young man has always been a whore."

"I don't see it that way."

"There's no point in debating it. I'm telling you your dad was a good man. You can believe it or not believe it."

"But he changed."

"Or the world changed him."

"I don't see the difference."

"Because you're young."

"Shit." Billy shook his head and looked out the passenger window.

"Well, I guess since you know everything already . . ."

The snow was beginning to stick to the road and visibility was less than a hundred yards.

"Why didn't he come home?"

"Your dad's outlook on people got dark. He was doing mercenary work in order to see what he called the consequence. What you and I would call suffering. He was alienated by his outlook. Crippled, you could say. Other people go to Paris. They see cathedrals. That wasn't his interest. Your dad was interested in atrocity, wars that nobody in the West cared about. Eradicated villages. Nameless people. The dead. He thought of himself as their witness."

Billy could make little sense of what he was hearing, but the story had a pull on him more powerful than anything else he had ever listened to.

"He was interested in different forms of revolution. He's the only one I know who predicted the collapse of the Soviet Empire. That was right before he met your mom." The Colonel leaned over the steering wheel and looked into the snowfall, toward the ranch. "I left him alone with her for awhile hoping he'd get better."

The Colonel let off the accelerator to negotiate a curve in the road. He wasn't driving more than thirty miles per hour, but the sedan went into a slide. It crossed into the oncoming lane before he steered his way out of it.

"I came to see him after you were born. He looked happy. All of you looked happy."

Billy pursed his lips and looked away. "You still haven't told me why he left."

The Colonel concentrated on the road, and it was a long time before he answered. "He stole something."

"From the government?"

"No, the government sent him to steal it."

Ice was beginning to build up on the windshield. Visibility worsened.

"And?"

"He didn't come home."

"Because he got caught?"

"No." The Colonel leaned forward over the steering wheel. "He took the wrong path."

COLORADO
1990

WHEN JACK CAME HOME FROM EAST BERLIN, HE MET RACHEL IN A DINER. He read the name tag on her apron as she took his order. Although her demeanor was friendly, he could sense her desperation. Her hand was darting in and out of her apron pocket, and she kept looking behind her. Jack empathized with the behavior. She was scanning for threats. As she served his soup, he noted the hungry eyes of her manager and fantasized about doing something on Rachel's behalf, about taking her with him. But he didn't give the fantasy serious consideration. It was just another variation of an old theme: the hope of a new life, a family, love. Jack fantasized mostly about love. About taking care of someone.

But he knew better. A woman could not change what the world was. There would be no end to the loneliness, not even in her arms.

When the manager cornered her at the register, Rachel blew up and stormed out the front door of the restaurant. At that moment, Jack thought it might actually be possible: to disappear, to tell no one where he was or what he was doing, to build a yurt in these mountains.

To take her with him.

But by the time he finished his meal, his mind was back to Central America. He paid his bill. And moved on.

Jack had returned to Colorado in search of something, but he had no idea what it was. He was only vaguely aware that he was looking.

Then there she was again—grieving over a deer on the side of the road. He stopped his truck and stood unnoticed behind her. Jack had come of age on the battlefield. He was accustomed to blood, to the smell of death. Although he admired her fire—what he had witnessed in the diner—he fell in love with Rachel's innocence.

The America that existed in Jack's mind never squared with what he encountered on the ground in Washington, and although he had long since lost his American religion, he never could relinquish the romantic aspects of its spirit. Jack felt a profound and irrational desire to protect Rachel. To take care of her. To make sure no one could ever hurt her again.

He told himself to walk away. It was a fantasy. He knew that she could not save him. That he could not save her. He told himself again to turn around and leave. But he could not bring himself to walk away.

When he offered his name, Rachel blushed, and he wanted to hide deep in the mountains with her. Just the two of them. In love.

He went to her apartment and processed the meat. He saw her self-portraits. And she laundered the blood from his clothes. They ate together. He paid her rent. And moved on.

Or so he thought. His encounter with Rachel had shifted something profound within him. He had never felt so much before. Jack was forty years old, and for the first time in his life, he would cry at night. He had no idea why. He would lie there and open his chest and wail. The sobbing shook the bed. He didn't understand it, wasn't sure of its purpose. Whether it was good or bad. But he didn't try to stop it either. It went on for months. Sometimes when he screamed he could feel the pain tearing his sternum. He could feel his throat ripping open, as if to make room for the grief to flow out of his mouth. When the screaming stopped, it would surprise him to still be alive.

Once he was no longer in her presence, two long-standing habits, reason and discipline, convinced Jack to do it. To build the yurt. To build it far from any road or trail or habitation. To leave the world to the world and to disappear. But he wouldn't bring Rachel. He wouldn't indulge that particular fantasy.

He brought the lumber for the decking in on his back, carved a bow out of a juniper limb, and made the bowstring from the sinew of the deer Rachel took with her truck. He didn't have to hunt. The deer came to him in either the first or the last of the light. He used scavenged metal for broadheads and shot the animals as they grazed around his camp. He dried the meat on racks, tanned the skins, and sewed them together.

Every day he thought about Rachel. And every day he reminded himself that it was a fantasy.

He pulled the stove up the mountain on a wood-framed sled over the course of a week. Jack didn't like being in town. He went down for the last time to purchase a stovepipe.

He passed the Safeway and, in a moment of weakness, turned back and went inside. All summer long he had been craving strawberries. He bought as many as he could carry in his backpack. He had finished the first tray and was pushing the plastic into the trash when he saw Rachel's name. It was on a bulletin board covered in handwritten advertisements: index cards and other sheets of paper pinned to the cork. Apartments for rent, cars for sale. He pulled her poster for the art show and folded it into his pocket.

PRESENT

THE RIDGE WAS, INDEED, A PERFECT OVERWATCH POSITION, BUT BY THE TIME Jack arrived, the ranch below was concealed behind a wall of falling snow. He needed to remember where he hid it, but more than that, he needed to remember why. What was driving him to do this?

Jack felt cold, and he was getting colder. He took one of the photographs from his pocket.

Billy's pajamas were patterned in camouflage. The crumpled wrapping paper was red. Jack remembered harvesting the tree.

Billy pointed to a full-grown blue spruce. "That one."

"I'm not sure it'd fit inside the house."

Billy stepped back in his snowshoes to survey the tree more carefully.

Jack pulled on a branch of the tiny tree beside it. "How about this one?"

"It's puny."

"Let's give it a try. If you don't like the way it fits, we'll come back for the other."

They took off their snowshoes, and Jack lifted the bottom branches while Billy hacked at the trunk with the axe.

They dragged the tree down the mountain, pulled it into the living room, and stood it by the window. The top three feet of the crown was bent against the ceiling.

Jack studied the image until the snow crystals nearly covered the paper.

HE WAS SHIVERING AND NEEDED TO MOVE TO GENERATE HEAT. HE COULDN'T be sure where the perimeter would be. And watching motionless, a sentry, if they were using one, would have every advantage. Moreover, the wind was wrong. And there was no time to circle the target to make it right. Even if he had time, he didn't know where the target was located, which meant he didn't know how to go around it.

Jack repeated that fact to himself. He was walking into a situation in which he had no idea where the target was located.

It was one thing to understand what was wrong. It was another to be distracted by that understanding. Jack had to learn the hard way that once all the missteps and misfortunes have been acknowledged, you have to accept them. Then you have to let them go.

Shaking from the cold, he descended the ridge one step with every three breaths. Listening. Eyes scanning the ponderosa forest. It was no worse than Belarus.

Just do your job.

Colorado
1993

Jack was splitting firewood when he saw the Colonel walk out of the aspen trees and into the meadow. He had been expecting it since the day he stepped out of his life as an operator and disappeared. Jack kept swinging the axe. He let the Colonel cross through the high grass, thistles, and wild flowers and come to him.

Rachel was seated on a wooden step nursing Billy. When she saw the man approaching, the first visitor they had seen, she put away her breast.

So Billy was crying when the Colonel introduced himself. Then he looked down at the grass and apologized. "I'm sorry. I really am."

As Jack led the Colonel out of earshot, he turned and said to Rachel, "Just give me a minute to talk to the man. Then I'll send him on his way."

"There's a problem in Mogadishu."

Jack didn't ask the Colonel how he found him. He didn't ask him anything. The answers were already known. Jack's eyes were watering. The desperation pinched his voice, "Don't come to me with this."

"There's nowhere else to go."

Jack shut his eyes. When he opened them, he was looking at his son in Rachel's arms. "I'm not going back. Aidid can be resolved a thousand different ways." He turned his back on the Colonel and walked toward his son. "Tell them you couldn't find me."

"It's not Aidid."

PRESENT

THERE WERE BRAKE LIGHTS AHEAD. NOTHING ELSE WAS VISIBLE IN THE storm. The Colonel let off the accelerator and looked at Billy. "I have very few regrets in my life. At my age, I think that's rare."

He stopped the car.

"Looks like an accident." Billy opened the window and put his head out.

"I'm a civilian now."

Billy closed the window. "I still don't understand why you're here."

"Your dad's alive because my men died defending him."

Billy was struggling to understand the conversation. What in the past several days had he understood? For the first time in his life he appreciated what they meant by the word surreal.

He looked out the passenger window. He just felt sad.

"Listen, Billy, this thing has to be put right." The Colonel opened his window and stuck his head out.

"See anything?"

"Snow."

They sat in the traffic on the highway looking through the windshield.

"To tell you the truth, I don't know if it can be put right."

The snowflakes were fat and falling slowly.

The Colonel got out of the car. "I realize now that I was wrong. Somebody has to stop your dad."

Billy watched as the Colonel walked past the brake lights ahead of them and disappeared in the snowfall.

As Jack descended through a grove of aspen trees, he realized that his toes were no longer burning. The absence of sensation meant the frostbite was progressing. The only sound in the forest came from his own movement through the snow, yet he kept turning his head, listening for something. The demands of the silence strained his attention.

Then he was certain he heard it, Rachel's voice.

Jack held his breath and listened.

There were deer bedded in the snow sixty meters up the mountainside. The sleeping animals were curled up in the snow with their noses tucked under their hindlegs for warmth. They weren't aware of his presence. Nor would they be. The wind was bringing them to him, which also meant it was bringing him to wherever he was heading.

He was moving too slowly now to generate any significant body heat. He took a step, broke the snow then listened again. When Jack finally oriented himself to the sound, he saw her in an art gallery. There were other voices, but he could only hear Rachel's. He saw how shy she was. It was irresistible—her melancholy, the hopefulness it expressed. He felt the emotions as if they were new to him, as if Rachel, all those years ago, were right now present beside him.

Jack broke the snow with the heel of his shoe and felt for branches, anything that would make noise. He was overcome with happiness. Then the love he felt for Rachel began to split his chest. It throbbed like his shattered rib.

Jack was disoriented. He shifted his weight and stood listening. He could smell her. The mountain and the trees now seemed more ephemeral than his memories. He could feel Rachel in his arms.

It was as if it were ten years ago.

Then his confusion gave way to anxiety, a panic that constricted his chest and doubled his breath. Jack kept his feet planted in the snow and, seeing the trees again, looked franticly through the forest. He didn't know why he was out in the cold. He didn't even have boots. It was so cold. Why had he come? As he looked through the trees, he realized that he was searching for Rachel. Was she really here?

If he loved her, he asked himself, why was he still trying to find Yan Shi?

When the Colonel opened the driver's door, the falling snow swirled through the cabin. He got back in the car, pulled into the oncoming lane, and passed the parked traffic. A passenger van had lost control and hit a Ford Escort.

"There's nothing we can do for those people, Billy."

Emergency crews had not yet arrived, and motorists were extracting the driver of the Escort through the passenger door.

The Colonel drove around them. "The driver of the van survived."

"Is this it?" The Colonel was hunched over the wheel, his face nearly touching the windshield.

"If we're going to my place."

"There's something I need to show you."

Several inches of snow had already accumulated on the dirt road that led to Billy's long driveway. As the car climbed the hill, snow shot out from under the front tires and flew past Billy's window.

The Colonel slowed for the bend in the road.

"You need your momentum." Billy pointed up the hill.

When the Colonel tried to accelerate, they heard the whining of the spinning tires. The vehicle slowed nearly to a stop. The tires kept spinning and the front end began to slide off the shoulder.

"You'll put us in the ditch."

The Colonel took his foot off the accelerator and rested it on the brake pedal. Then he shifted the transmission into reverse and backed down the length of the hill.

"I thought it was May."

"Welcome to Colorado."

He came up the hill again. And again, he decelerated ahead of the turn.

Billy shook his head.

The tires spun and pulled the front end to the side of the road. The Colonel lifted his foot from the accelerator and pressed the brake pedal just before they slid into the ditch.

He put the vehicle in park.

"Alright, let's see you try." He left the driver's door open, walked around the back of the car, and stood at the passenger door waiting for Billy to open it.

Billy was embarrassed and got out without making eye contact with the Colonel.

The Colonel sat in the passenger seat with his arms crossed.

Billy backed down the length of the hill. He opened the front windows, listened for traffic on the highway then backed across both lanes to get a running start. He left the windows open, put the vehicle in drive, and accelerated as much as he could without spinning the tires.

He carefully let his foot off the accelerator to keep the tires from spinning as they climbed the hill. He couldn't see well so he stuck his head out the window. That wasn't any better so Billy opened the door. Holding the open door with one hand and the steering wheel with the other, he watched the tire carve its track through the snow.

When they got to the curve, Billy did not let off the accelerator, save to keep the tires from spinning. The Colonel uncrossed his arms and braced himself on the dash.

Billy left the door open, came back inside, pulled the emergency brake, and the vehicle slid into the curve. He released the emergency brake, straightened the front end, and came within an inch of putting them in the ditch. Then he thrust his head outside so he could see the tire and continued climbing the road.

The Colonel pulled his hands off the dashboard. "I guess you've done that before."

JACK LEFT THE GAME TRAIL HE HAD BEEN FOLLOWING AND FELT SOMETHING inside his mind burst. The pressure had been building since he left the cave. He shut his eyes. But the memories kept coming. It was as if a barrier had ruptured. Jack was being assaulted by a flood of images. The smell of burning flesh in Somalia. Atrocities he did not want to recall. Decapitated villagers. He saw babies, still breathing, suspended by their own intestines from the branches of an acacia tree.

There was so much killing.

Jack felt as if he were being swept down the river of his own life to drown. He saw a woman running from an explosion in Burma. The longyi she wore and the child in her arms were on fire. He could feel the heat of her burning skin.

The disorientation was absolute. Jack was surrounded by the dead and no longer knew where he stood in time. He saw dozens of people moaning at the bottom of a village well in Panama.

He was at Billy's birth, making eye contact with his son. Those eyes were so blue, so penetrating. Jack felt shame, as if the newborn child had already discerned his failure as a father. He was in the corral teaching Billy to ride a horse. He was holding a book in Billy's bed. His son's head lay on his chest. Billy was pointing at the pictures. Now he was carrying Billy through the alfalfa the afternoon he broke his arm. He could smell blood and human feces on the battlefield. Then it broke him: the quiet manner in which the littlest of the boy soldiers wept after the firefight.

Nauseous, Jack put his good arm around the trunk of a tree. Who was he to have done so much killing?

Just do your job. He kept repeating that. But it didn't help. He had no temporal bearing.

EVERYTHING WAS QUIET. SQUIRRELS. BIRDS. ALL BEDDED DOWN FOR THE storm. So when the four-by-five elk came trotting up the mountainside, fresh powder sliding off its back, Jack squatted on his haunches.

Being startled by the elk sharpened his awareness. He told himself to focus. But the pulsing memories raised a question more powerful than his discipline. He needed to know who he was.

The bull stopped, not eight meters from Jack, and swung its head to look over its back-trail. As it took in the air, Jack could see its nostrils flare. Its ears twitched as they tracked a sound Jack could not hear. The elk lifted its tail and released a staccato stream of scat which disappeared into the snow. Then it swung its huge head and trotted up the mountain.

Someone was down there.

BILLY, STOP THE CAR."

It was the only downhill section of road on the climb to the driveway. "Why?"

The Colonel pulled an envelope from his chest pocket and unfolded it. "Just stop the car."

Billy kept his hands on the steering wheel and studied the wrinkled envelope for a minute or more.

"It's from your dad."

Billy slowly shook his head.

"It might answer some of your questions."

"Have you read it?"

"Yes, I have."

Billy didn't respond.

The Colonel was looking out the windshield. "I made a mistake when I interfered with the decision to terminate your dad." He looked at Billy, who was not looking at him. "You know the event as the Washington bombing."

Billy narrowed his eyes and glanced at the Colonel.

"Your dad spent much of the last decade in a prison very few people have heard of."

Billy let go of the steering wheel. "What'd he do?"

The Colonel held the letter between them. "I'll let him answer that."

Billy,

You're nine years old. It may be that it doesn't matter how old you are, it may be that you will never sympathize with the contents of this letter. Which means, in part, I must be writing it for myself. I acknowledge that and I'm grateful to you for the audience.

I met your mother a little more than ten years ago. She changed my life. Before I met her I was lost. My career, you can say, has not been conducive to stability, and stability, I have learned the hard way, is a human need.

I'm not lost anymore.

Your birth was the most important event in my life. Being your father is a sacred task so it is heartbreaking to me to only have the nine years we've had. I wish the timing were different, I wish the circumstances were different, but they are not and each man has to carry his burden. Mine is abandoning you.

What I've said so far is more important than what I am about to say, for what I've said is that I love you and what I'm about to offer is a rationale, a rationale for what it is I've left you to do.

There isn't much more I want to say about my life or my career. What I regret about the career are all the parts of myself that I've had to kill in order to be good at it. In this regard, being your father and being in love with your mother were a great redemption. The truth is I am good at what I do. One of the skills I acquired from my service in Vietnam is the ability to look beyond the emotion of the moment, to look into the future, and to weigh the long-term benefit of an action against the present hardship.

I want you to know that I love humanity. And even more than that, I love life. I hope to preserve both.

When you were six years old, Billy, you asked me if I hated the elk.

"No," I told you, "I love them."

You looked me straight in the eye and said, "Then why do you always want to kill them?"

"I don't always want to kill them," I explained. I took you into my arms and I carried you to the window where we could see the forest and I told you, "I hunt them in the fall because it's good for them and it's good for our family."

You didn't let me off the hook. You asked me to put you down. You wanted to know how it was good for the elk to be killed.

It was a good question. You've always had a penetrating mind.

I told you that there were no more wolves in Colorado, only the ones that have snuck back into these mountains, and there weren't enough of those, not yet, to keep the elk herds in balance.

I asked you who was left to prey on the elk. You didn't have an answer. There are no more brown bears in our mountains and the lions here prefer to eat the deer.

That was all you needed. At that point, you understood.

But let me write this anyway, let me write it just to see the words on the page, the idea. I'll write it for me.

Elk reproduce at a robust rate. Without predators to keep the herds in check the population would swell and the herds would destroy their habitat. Once their habitat was destroyed the elk, in turn, would starve. There simply wouldn't be enough food to feed them all.

Given our choice to remove their natural predator it would be cruel not to hunt the elk because harvesting a limited number preserves the whole. In the end, culling the herd saves lives.

We accept this as a biological truth, I think, that everything has to be kept in balance. The chasm between our understanding of ourselves as human beings and biological reality can be bridged by asking the following question, where is the wolf?

In the effort to make ourselves more secure we have exterminated our competition. Thousands of years ago, on the scale of a few million human beings trying to make it in the world, the strategy made sense for our species because the human population was fragile.

It makes sense to eliminate the competition, to kill the wolf, today only if the lens is focused on the individual. If the harvest of an elk is detrimental to the individual elk but beneficial to the species, how can it be any different with a human being? Do we not reproduce, eat, and starve? The truth is that we need predators. Because of our birth rate, like the elk, we need strong competition to survive.

In our zeal to exterminate that competition our species has created a wolf more dangerous than any previous predator. This wolf will come in the form of our own hunger. There will be a collapse. I think we all know this. Somehow we sense it. This is true for every part of the world to which I've traveled. People see it coming.

The growth rate of the human population is governed by the same mathematical equations, the same biological laws that govern the elk. The only remaining question is one of scale. How catastrophic will the collapse be? That is up to us. That is up to me.

Without action, the hunger will extend far beyond our own suffering. To do nothing is to preside over the next mass extinction.

The sooner the population is restored to balance the gentler, the more humane will be the collapse.

That, in a nutshell, is my job. To save lives. Just as I kept the elk, I have been given an opportunity to be humanity's keeper.

I love you more than anything in the world,
Dad

Billy wiped his fingers down his face. "I'm not sure what it is I just read."

"Your dad had a gift. Those who knew him called him a prophet." The Colonel's lips tightened against his teeth. "But his gift made him arrogant." He clenched his jaw. "I'm afraid your dad has lost touch with reality."

From the expression on Billy's face, it was obvious that he wasn't listening. The Colonel waited for the kid to look at him. "It's not an easy letter to read."

"What's it supposed to mean?" Billy waved the pages. "What's he trying to say?"

"Your dad stole a device powerful enough to act as the wolf he was searching for. He's the only one who knows where it is. With the notable exception of the organization I used to work for, the United States government wants the threat to expire with your dad."

The Colonel gestured to the road with his eyes, and Billy put the car in gear. He felt as if he wasn't really there.

The snow got deeper as he climbed. Five miles per hour was all he could coax out of the sedan. The driver's window was still open. Both Billy's hair and the leather door panel were layered with snow.

"What is that?" Billy asked.

Two black SUVs were parked at the gate. One facing the road, the other facing the driveway.

"Billy, turn the car around."

All four doors of the SUV facing the road opened simultaneously. Four armed men in black fatigues and load-bearing vests encircled the sedan.

He FOUND THE BED THE BULL HAD BEEN STARTLED FROM. IT WAS ICED, AS if it had been occupied for some time. Then he found the track in the snow made by the patrol who had startled it.

Jack had made a track coming down from the ridge not much different from this one. There was no way to hide it. The next patrol to come through here would give the whole thing away.

The Mexicans had better arrive before then.

His body was beginning to shut down from the cold. He accepted that and stepped over the track of the patrol and continued his slow pace down the mountain.

Jack's memory was relentless in its proffering of the dead. He was re-living a catalogue of atrocities he could not justify, an archive of horror he could not comprehend. It wasn't the blood. It wasn't the screaming. It wasn't the children. It was their eyes. No matter how young or old, the dying watched him with Billy's blue eyes. He needed a switch to turn it off, but there was none. It was as if his mind was besieged by its own history. A convoluted set of images without context, without a narrative he could employ to make meaning.

The memories of the killings unleashed conflicts, passions Jack's training had taught him to ignore. What had he done? He felt outrage, abhorrence. Could he even trust himself?

He stopped and told himself to concentrate.

He was inside the perimeter, attempting to penetrate the security of some of the most sophisticated operators the world had ever known. There would be time for introspection later.

But he could not concentrate. The question was insistent. He needed to know why he was doing this. He needed to know who he was.

I'M SORRY, BILLY."

Billy couldn't see the two men behind the sedan, but the two in front had their weapons shouldered. Both were sighting on the Colonel.

"Are these the same guys?"

The Colonel kept his hands above the dash, palms open and facing the soldiers in front of him. "I wish you didn't have to see this."

There was a hand signal. Billy watched through the passenger side mirror as a soldier came into view, approaching from behind. The passenger door opened, and the Colonel was pulled from the sedan.

Billy heard the Colonel say, "Think it through. Without me, you won't be able to stop him."

JACK DIDN'T SEE THE HORSE UNTIL IT STOPPED. IT STOOD TWENTY METERS away and carried a rider who looked like a ghost, diaphanous in the snowfall. Jack was motionless as he watched. He couldn't see the rider's legs, arms, or weapon. The calculation was simple. Either Jack had been seen or he hadn't. If he moved, he was certain he would be seen. Shortly after which, he'd be dead.

The horse didn't move. There was no sound in the forest. He could still feel the air moving down the mountainside.

Jack stared until he could make out the hunched torso. It was no soldier. Jack took a step toward the horse.

The animal did not move.

Jack advanced again. The rider's hair was covered with snow. So was her coat and thighs.

He touched her hand. It was blue. Rachel's fingers were cold. He felt her pulse.

"How long have you been out here?"

She didn't respond. How long had it been since she had stopped shivering? It wasn't a good situation. He looked at her eyes. She was someplace else. Rachel had no idea that he was even there.

"Rachel."

Her head moved, but she looked past him.

"Oh god, Rachel."

It made him sad. He had brought her back once. He didn't think it would be possible to do it again.

Jack took Rachel off the horse and set her in the snow. It wasn't the way he would have had it. Her bruised face looked euphoric.

Two soldiers led the Colonel to the SUV. Billy opened the car door and got out. He was immediately pushed to his knees.

"Put your hands on your head."

Before he could comply, he heard the diesel engines. They sounded like four-by-fours screaming up the road.

The Colonel stood with his legs spread, his hands on top of an SUV. But the man who was about to search him was now sighting his M4, like the others, through the snowfall—down the road they could not see.

"Stay down, kid."

Billy saw the spewing fire, fell face-first against the road, and put his hands over his head before he understood that a tailgate had dropped open and that the terror he was experiencing was being unleashed by a .50 caliber machine gun. He felt his urine melting the snow beneath him and was glad for it—his body had sunk a few millimeters deeper.

Although he heard their weapons firing, he could no longer see the four soldiers who had surrounded the sedan. He wasn't about to lift his head to search for them either. The best use he could think of for the revolver he was lying on was to get rid of it so he could get closer to the earth.

The paralysis he was experiencing wouldn't even allow that.

The .50 caliber fired burst after burst.

He squeezed his eyes shut. It felt like the machine gun was shooting directly over his head. When he opened his eyes, he saw the Colonel bolting into the trees.

The prospect of being separated from the Colonel was more terrifying than the machine gun. In Billy's compressed state of mind, closing the gap between himself and the only man who seemed to understand what was happening to his family was the priority in that moment. He felt certain of it. That this is what he had to do. He was not aware of choice. He only felt the impulse to lessen the space between them.

Billy shifted his weight onto his knees and elbows and raised his body into the lead-rent air. He saw the muzzle flashes. He drove his legs harder than he had ever done before, but the ground was snow covered, and it felt like no matter how many strides he took, he was getting no closer to the trees. He kept repeating the word, "Shit."

Although he could not hear the explosion, he felt the concussion. Saw the blanket of snow on the road erupt and burst skyward. He, himself, was flying.

JACK MOUNTED THE HORSE AND HEARD A BURST FROM A .50 CALIBER MACHINE gun. He heard a second burst before there was any response. As he turned the horse toward the sound, the mountain below him erupted with small-arms fire.

He told Maiden, "The clock is ticking."

There was a second .50 caliber machine gun and explosions that sounded like 40mm grenades.

Jack listened to the firefight long enough to locate the blue team's positions then he squeezed the horse with his legs and started down the mountain.

THE COLONEL PULLED BILLY BY HIS BELT OUT OF THE DITCH THEN LIFTED him to his feet. He mouthed the word, "Move!" and pushed him into the trees.

Jack felt a presence and turned the horse.

Rachel was seated where he left her. Just above that, the mountain moved. It seemed to flow along the contour of the ridge. Jack couldn't see more than thirty meters through the snowfall, and he could barely make out the huge bull leading the herd.

That's when he remembered. He remembered where he had hidden Yan Shi.

He rode back up the hill.

They were like spirits: dozens of bison, snow piled on their backs, streaming soundlessly through the trees. He heard the explosions of the firefight beneath him and felt as if he were riding up the mountain into another world. With all the snow on their backs, the animals looked like flora or some undiscovered constituent of the forest.

Jack stopped the horse beside Rachel. She was too far gone to know she was in trouble. If left alone, she would die. There had to be another way.

Jack squeezed the horse forward and followed the herd. He pushed Maiden harder, and as the horse crashed though the lower limbs of the trees, clumps of snow fell from the branches. Jack pushed the horse until he found himself alongside the enormous bull at the head of the herd.

He called him by name and brought the mare against the bull's flank.

Moses swung his colossal head and turned up the mountain. The herd followed.

Jack turned Moses between the trees. Moses dropped his head, and the exhalations from his nostrils blew divots in the snow. Jack turned him again. The animal's eyes bulged. He leapt forward, as if to break into a gallop, but before the bull had any momentum, Jack turned him again. Jack turned him until the bull grunted and stopped.

The intensity of the firefight below them had waned. Jack could still hear the .50 caliber machine guns and occasional bursts from the M4s.

It was the pungency of the scent, the bull's musky odor that brought it all back. There it finally was: his purpose. Jack leaned down to breathe it in. He could smell the fermentation of the grass on Moses's breath. He remembered the letter he wrote to Billy. All of it was coming back. He remembered the Colonel's briefing about Yan Shi aboard the Cessna. And most importantly, he remembered why he was on the mountain.

He had come to cull the herd.

Jack drew the Colt from his leather jacket. The temporal shifts that had been disorienting him during his descent, the torment, the doubt: they were all gone. There remained unanswered questions, but they would have to wait. Jack was certain of his target.

Snow was piled on Moses's wooly head and on the base of his great horns. Jack held the muzzle of the gun just off the animal's ear and squeezed the trigger.

Moses collapsed.

When Jack dismounted, he saw that his leg and Maiden's side were sprayed with blood. He walked around the carcass.

Blood dribbled from Moses's black nose. His gray tongue hung from his open jaw. The sweet smell of blood was invigorating.

The foreleg was twitching. Jack squatted and tried to pull it out from under the immense body.

He couldn't move it.

The herd was encircling Moses. The bison came in and stood shoulder-to-shoulder, horns facing outward.

Jack looked over their backs for Maiden. Then he watched her move down the mountain until she disappeared in the falling snow.

He needed that horse.

He looked at the huge animal at his feet. Then again at the herd that had encircled him. It wasn't the first goat-fuck he'd gotten himself into.

Jack stepped around to the other side of the carcass and took Moses by the horns. He pulled the head until the carcass shifted in the snow. Then he came back to the foreleg, pulled the knee out from under the animal, and unfolded the twitching leg. His hands stung from the cold. He walked the leg up so it rested on his own shoulder then knelt in the snow and felt for the utility knife in his pocket.

The fine motor skills of his fingers were gone, and his whole body was shaking. He dropped the knife and had to dig for it in the snow.

The retractable blade was frozen inside the handle. As he thawed the knife in his mouth, the phone in his pocket vibrated, indicating that he had received another text. Now that he remembered why he had stolen Yan Shi, Jack had no intention of giving it up.

Because his frozen fingers had little feeling, he wiped the back of his hand through Moses's armpit and found the squared edge of the device. Jack's shuddering body made it difficult to control the utility knife. He held it in a fist and that fist in his other hand. The incision was jagged and hardly penetrated Moses's thick hide. The phone vibrated again in his pocket. The cold was painful. Jack trembled so fiercely the foreleg fell off his shoulder. Still kneeling, he exposed the animal's armpit by lifting the heavy leg in one hand. Then he hacked along the length of the device hidden beneath the skin. He deepened the gash until the frozen blade of the utility knife snapped.

Jack examined the broken blade and determined that the knife was useless. He dropped it in the snow. Then he ripped the stringy facial tissue with his fingers and forced his hand underneath the aluminum housing of the device. His fingers stung from the animal's heat. When Jack pulled the miniaturized harddrive out of the leg, the tissue made a sucking sound.

The phone vibrated. Without reading the display, Jack pulled the phone out of his pocket and let it fall in the snow.

Billy waited for the Colonel at the newly flattened fence. His ears were ringing. He looked at the back of his leg. His jeans were torn and the leg was bleeding.

"That might have been the stupidest thing I have ever witnessed." The Colonel was out of breath and leaned on one of the upright fence posts. "Take off your coat. Let me look at you."

Billy took off his Carhartt and held it by the revolver still inside the pocket. The canvas was shredded.

"Lift your shirt and turn around."

The grave expression on the Colonel's face communicated to Billy the implications of the shredded coat he was holding in his hand. Billy didn't feel any pain. Then he realized that was irrelevant: a person could die without ever knowing it.

"They're all scratches." The Colonel's statement was a matter of hope, not fact. He could see the shrapnel imbedded in Billy's back. "Put your coat back on."

Billy did as he was told.

"You were safe where I left you."

"You ran."

"Those boys would give their lives to protect you, Billy." The Colonel gestured to the trampled fence and the trail the bison had made up the mountain. "Moses?"

"Yep."

"I oughta leave you right here."

"I know the property. If we get in with them, it'll make us harder to find."

THEY HAD SURROUNDED MOSES TO PROTECT HIM. INSTINCT WOULD HAVE compelled them to do the same for any member of the herd. Jack admired that. He admired the bull he had just slain.

Jack chose Moses to conceal Yan Shi for several reasons, the first of which was the tactical advantage of the hiding place. He knew it would work. He also appreciated the irony. The software housed on the harddrive, kept secure inside the body of a genetically pure bison, had the ability to return the great plains of North America to grassland. A grassland inhabited not by people living in towns and cities, but by nomadic tribes. In Jack's vision of the future, Moses's offspring would repopulate the North American plains.

There was no gap in the ring of bison that had surrounded him. They were nervous, and the smallest among them could maim him by simply taking a step. He had little time to finesse the predicament.

He wasn't sure there was anything he could do for Rachel. The hypothermia wasn't the immediate concern, not as long as he could warm her. The immediate concern was the tissue damage. Once frozen, human tissue cannot be repaired. It might already be too late to save her limbs.

Jack picked a cow whose tail was relaxed. She weighed over three-quarters of a ton and was nearly as tall as he was. He talked to her before he put his hand on her hindquarter. The muscles twitched. When he squeezed between her and the other cow, she stepped sideways letting him through. He talked his way up to the hump then paused before he got in front of the horns. Her eyes were blinking. He spoke soothingly and promised the animal that one day she'd be fenceless.

THE HERD HAD TRAMPLED THE SNOW DOWN TO THE GRASS. THE TRAIL WAS thigh deep. Stooped over, the Colonel led Billy up the ridge.

"He said something about being humanity's keeper. Is that what he wants it for?"

"Your dad has the ambition of a madman."

"Can it do that?"

"Do what? Return human civilization back to the Stone Age? Everybody here thinks so."

"And the soldiers, they're here to kill him?"

"Yes." The Colonel was winded, but he didn't stop climbing. "They also have orders to eliminate me."

"But the sheriff said they're the good guys."

"Most days they are."

"I don't understand."

The Colonel turned to face him, "Billy, you need to listen to me. I don't think it's possible for your dad to get out of this alive. He already knows that. That knowledge did not deter him from coming. Hidden somewhere on this property is a device that would fit in your pocket. If your dad is permitted to turn it on, there will be precious few tomorrows."

H<small>E FOLLOWED</small> M<small>AIDEN'S TRACK IN THE SNOW, UNABLE TO SEE PAST THE</small> trees immediately around him. His own feet were all but frozen, and it was difficult to walk.

The firefight was over. If the storm held and he had the horse, Rachel just might survive. The device he had used to store Yan Shi was equipped with a broadcaster. He switched it on.

T<small>HE MARE WAS NUZZLING</small> R<small>ACHEL, WHO WAS SEATED WHERE HE HAD LEFT</small> her in the snow. She was talking incoherently. She was talking about Billy.

Jack pulled the icy strands of hair away from her eyes. She was beautiful.

He told himself that he could stop what he was doing. That he could turn. That he could take a different path from the one he was on.

Jack brushed the snow off the horse's back.

He had a family. He could be a father. Isn't that what he wanted? Before him was a choice. He could pick Rachel up, take her with him. Or he could finish what he had started.

By THE TIME BILLY SAW THE MARE, IT WAS LESS THAN THIRTY YARDS AWAY. He thought she was an elk. Then he saw his dad standing on the other side of it.

When his dad saw him, he ducked behind Maiden, which bewildered Billy until he saw the snubnosed revolver outstretched in the Colonel's arms.

When his dad reappeared on the other side of the horse, he was holding someone.

"Mom!" Billy started toward her.

He was stopped by the Colonel's palm colliding into his sternum.

"He'll kill you, Billy. Don't misunderstand this."

"Mom!"

She didn't respond, and he couldn't see through the snowfall to read the expression on her face.

The Colonel's voice cracked with authority, "I can't let you do this, Jack."

His dad was leading Maiden away. As they walked up the ridge, it looked as if his mom was being erased by snowfall. Billy pushed against the Colonel's arm.

"Talk to me, Jack. I don't understand why you're doing this."

"I'm the keeper." The answer sounded disembodied in the falling snow.

"For Christ's sake, they're your family."

Billy's mom was all but dissolved.

"It'd be hypocritical," Jack said, "not to share the sacrifice."

At that moment, the Colonel knew whatever hope he had harbored for the man was not only naive, but exhausted. Jack was gone. Lost.

He didn't want it to end this way, but he was out of options. It hurt more than he thought it would.

The Colonel could barely see his sights. Jack was using the horse for cover, and it was hard to distinguish between Jack's and Rachel's heads. He needed a carbine. With such a tiny gun and the snowfall, it was an impossible shot. The blue team had already cleaned up the Mexican sicarios, which meant Jack would be reluctant to shoot first. A gunfight would bring the whole unit down on them.

He decided to hit the animal, which was quartering away. To try to open up the target.

Billy flinched at the shot. He saw Maiden bolt into the trees. The second shot sounded like a rifle cartridge. He assumed it was because his ears were ruined from the firefight.

His dad was kneeling in the snow, still holding his mom.

Billy tried to run toward her, but his legs were stuck.

Although he couldn't make out the gun in his dad's outstretched hand, he saw the muzzle flashes and was puzzled by how little it hurt. His face felt hot. When he wiped it, his hand came away wet. He looked down at the snow. It was red. Hair and a piece of scalp. Then he saw the Colonel over his feet. He didn't understand what had happened until he saw the brains.

As Billy waited for himself to fall, he saw his mom being pulled to her feet and called out, "Mom!"

When he still didn't fall, he turned around in search of an explanation and saw a carbine lying in the snow behind him. Next to it, he saw a wool cap then the black battledress of a dead soldier.

Which confused Billy. He looked again at the Colonel's blood in the snow and realized that he, himself, wasn't hit.

Then he remembered his mom. His dad was leading her away. He had yet to comprehend what had just taken place.

Billy drew the revolver. "Mom!" He could hardly see through the falling snow, but he could tell that she had fallen down. "Let her go."

His dad picked her up with one arm. The other was extended toward Billy.

The confusion he felt, all the questions he had, narrowed. Leaving a single thought in his mind. Billy knew he had to be first. That if he wasn't, he'd never know it. But Billy couldn't squeeze the trigger.

DYING WASN'T ANYTHING LIKE SHE THOUGHT IT WOULD BE. HER SKIN WAS on fire. It was like a nightmare in which she knew Billy was there—she could hear him calling for help. She tried to go to him, but her body would not cooperate.

Billy kept calling her name.

Rachel needed to find her son. She writhed against the paralysis. But she could not move.

When she stopped struggling, she found herself simply getting up. It took no effort. She was taller than she used to be. She was as tall as the pine trees, looking down at Jack. It took her awhile to understand that what she saw at his side was her own body. After some time, she noticed that Jack's arm was extended. At what she didn't know. So she looked.

Billy was there. He was covered in blood.

Rachel was moving away. She didn't want to leave Billy. But now that she had gotten up, she couldn't stop. She felt as if she were being pulled along a cord. No. It was a tunnel. She was being pulled through a tunnel of color and light.

She conceded to this, too. And left Billy. That's when she saw Regan. He was waiting for her. She felt eager now to get through the tunnel, to reach him.

Regan's body had changed. It was pellucid—to see him was to know him. She worried that he might be able to see as much about her. Then that concern left her, along with every other concern. For what she was experiencing in Regan's presence was compassion. She had never felt so loved. So known.

All she wanted was to remain in his presence.

There was something Regan wanted to show her. When she looked, she realized that it was everything she had ever done. Transparent. Her life laid out panoramic before them.

Rachel could barely recognize herself. It was as if Regan was showing her someone else's story. She admired the woman. Her courage. The grit. She saw herself stumble: the self doubt, the way she threw her heart to Jack as if he could have saved her, the alcohol, the shackle-like limitations with which she dressed her life. Rachel saw every shortcoming, every error, the whole balance of the woman's development, and the lack thereof, and she felt empathy. The woman had endured so much.

Rachel also felt pride. She was proud of the woman for what she had overcome, for who she had become.

Then she realized that she was proud of herself.

What she once thought of as failure, she now saw for what it really was—survival. How could it have been any different? It was a miracle, given all that she had survived, given all the contempt her mother had taught her, that Rachel found the wherewithal to care for herself.

Seeing her life this way—in full context—her shame dissolved. There was no place for it. The mistakes, she realized, were necessary. There was no other way forward. No other way to grow.

Neither of them spoke. Regan and Rachel were communicating through thoughts. It was all known. Everything was known. And for all of it, there was grace. She had never felt so safe.

Rachel had thought Billy had been her motivation in life. What she did, she did for him. She kept going for him. In recent years, she knew that he wasn't enough. She saw now that he never was.

This is what Regan wanted her to see. That her life wasn't about Billy. There was more to her than her son. There was more to her than her mother. More to her than Jack. There was Rachel.

And she was enough in herself.

There was something else. Regan wanted her to understand something more.

But she did not want to. She did not want to because she knew that if she did, she would have to go back. Which seemed inconceivable now.

Until she remembered Billy out there in the storm.

Once she consented to return, Regan told her: You are the most spirited woman I have ever known.

Rachel had seen her life as completely as he saw it and felt no embarrassment over the compliment.

Then Regan told her: Your love for your son is remarkable. Love yourself as much.

JACK WAS NO LONGER SHIVERING. THAT FACT, COUPLED WITH THE EUPHORIA spreading through his torso, told him that he was hypothermic. Not far behind Rachel. As a consequence, his limbs were no longer his own. He willed his legs to move, but nothing happened. He couldn't get his quadriceps to contract. Jack believed, as he was taught, that physical limitations were housed in the mind, but he was beyond that now. He tried again to make his quadriceps fire. Nothing happened. The muscles in his legs weren't receiving the chemicals they needed to function. If he had something to drink maybe, but he didn't. It was a physiological reality. He couldn't take another step. For the first time in his life, he could not will more from his body.

That the exhaustion came on so suddenly meant that he hadn't been paying attention. Which meant that he had known: somewhere inside himself he had known that this was his final act. He had summoned his entire reserve to complete it.

JACK COULD SEE RACHEL IN HIS ARM. HE COULD SEE HIS SON OVER THE SIGHT of the gun. And most importantly, he could see himself. He knew who he was.

Jack had felt tormented by his own memories during his decent from the cave. Without context, the recollection of so much killing convinced him that he had lost his way. He realized now that he hadn't. The babies he remembered hanging in the acacia tree, he didn't kill them. He came back to cut them down, to bury them. He came back because he didn't want seven eviscerated babies to be plucked from the branches by the beaks of the birds. He didn't want those seven souls to pass from this world without notice.

The woman he remembered running with her burning child: Jack brought her to the ground. He extinguished the flames.

And the boy soldiers that reminded him of Billy: he would lead the youngest of them by the hand away from the calloused men. He remembered telling them stories while they fell asleep.

Jack had seen the consequence of a world out of balance, and he was here to set things right. He finally understood the full purpose of his calling. Who else could have done it? He had the training. He was accustomed to sacrifice. His whole life had led to this moment.

He was the keeper.

NOT ONLY DID JACK UNDERSTAND HIMSELF, HE COULD SEE RACHEL. HE LOVED her. She was a good woman. It hurt, what he had done to her. He had only wanted to love her, to protect her. But the path he was on led to a different outcome.

He wished he could have accomplished his purpose at some other time, at a time of his own choosing–after Rachel had lived a full life. If that life could not be with him, then with Regan. He wished that she could be happy.

That it wasn't so was another loss. He let it go.

THE COLONEL WAS DEAD. HE HAD SHOT THE HORSE. UNTIL THAT MOMENT it seemed as if he, himself, might survive. But there was no hope for that now, not without the horse.

It was better this way.

For Billy's sake, he wished the Colonel was still alive. By the time Jack saw the threat, it was too late. The soldier who shot the Colonel in the back of the head was only doing what he was ordered to do. Jack understood that. In turn, Jack had killed him. It was what he had to do. He killed the man because he needed more time. A few more seconds to finish the upload and to release the software. Without a direct interface, the program might take months to actualize. Jack had planned for a quicker execution, but this would have to be enough.

The rest of the blue team would be here soon. He knew that, too. But it didn't matter. It was almost over.

TIME HAD DILATED IN THE GUNFIGHT, JUST LIKE ANY OTHER. THE DIFFERENCE was that Jack wasn't focused on that front sight. He wasn't even looking at his sights. Jack was looking at Billy, who was standing in the snow alone.

He was proud of the man Billy had become. Ten years had been lost. Ten years of having a son, of being his father. Gone. That was bitter, and he grieved it.

He could see the conflict in Billy's heart. Regan had been more of a father than he had been. In that sense, Billy's father was already dead.

That hurt.

Jack could also see that Billy thought he was a threat to Rachel. That misperception left Billy with a choice: to kill his father or to risk losing his mother. Jack felt the pain in his own chest—the choice his son had to make. He wished it were easier for his boy. That there was another way to accomplish this. But there wasn't. There were not even seconds left.

Jack couldn't have known that he would meet his son out here. He wouldn't have come if he had known it would end like this. He wouldn't have been strong enough to go through with it.

But Billy was here, and there was a reason for that.

Jack could not ease the boy's burden. He could not make him understand. Billy had his own road to walk. Jack hoped that on that road Billy would find a guide, an old man.

He knew Billy wouldn't be able to kill him, not without his help.

Jack took a final inventory of his broken body. He still had his gross motor skills in his arms and torso, and he had his muscle memory: hundreds of thousands of repetitions firing a handgun.

He looked over the slide. He couldn't see Billy's eyes through the falling snow, but he imagined them. He saw Billy in two forms: the little boy he had carried and the man who would face the new world his father had created.

It was the last lesson he would teach his son. Billy's heart would need it to survive what was to come.

In a moment from now, he'd be gone. What would happen to them? He had to let it go. His wife. His son. He had to let them go.

THE SHOT PLACEMENT MATTERED. HE CHOSE BILLY'S SHOULDER AND BEGAN to squeeze the trigger. What he felt now was confidence. More confidence than he had ever known. He could see Billy. He could see Rachel. And he could see himself.

THE WORLD HAD SHRUNK TO THE LITTLE CIRCLE OF TREES THAT SURROUNDED his family, and apart from the leeward side of those trunks, the world had also gone white: branches, pine needles, the forest floor, and sky. His dad's leather jacket was black, and enough of it still showed through the snow and ice accumulating on it that Billy had a sight picture.

It was a struggle not to look at his mom. He had to focus on what he wanted to hit, not on what he wanted to preserve. It didn't come naturally.

Billy saw the muzzle flash. And, this time, felt the pain of the bullet's impact.

IT HURT, BUT IT WASN'T SO BAD. THE WORST OF IT WOULD BE HIS MOTHER watching him die. It occurred to him that he'd miss it. All of it. The white world was beautiful, and the absence of color helped him to focus.

Then there it was, as clear as anything he had ever seen—magnified—the front sight of his revolver. It gleamed wet. He could make out the tool marks from the machining. His front sight was centered on his dad's black jacket.

Billy heard men shouting. He still thought he was dying. It didn't matter. There was no more time. He squeezed the trigger.

BILLY KEPT THE REVOLVER SIGHTED ON HIS DAD AS HE CROSSED THROUGH THE trees. He moved more slowly when he got close enough to see the death spasms.

For some reason, he was thinking about the sheriff. He felt cold. He thought about Regan and walked closer. Although he knew it made no sense, the guilt made him feel like he had killed the sheriff himself. He stood motionless when his dad caught his eye. Billy was still thinking about Regan. He could finally see his face.

When his dad opened his mouth to speak, Billy dropped the revolver in the snow and watched him die.

BILLY'S MOM FOUND HIS CALF WITH HER HAND AND CRIED HIS NAME. HE knelt down and helped her up. When his mom touched his face with her cold fingers, something inside Billy broke. He squeezed her as tightly as he could and sobbed.

Rachel kept saying his name. She held her boy. She held him while he sobbed.

THE MEDIC TOLD BILLY THAT HIS MOM HAD PROGRESSED INTO A STATE OF profound hypothermia. That she had lost consciousness.

They put her in a harness, then lifted her into the helicopter hovering above the trees.

"Can I ride with her?"

"It'll only slow 'em down." They were huddled in the rotor wash, shouting over the noise.

The helicopter banked then vanished into the snowfall.

"Keep pressure on that wound."

Billy returned his hand to his left shoulder.

The dead were being lined up a few feet away for extraction. One of the soldiers pulled a device from his dad's leather jacket.

"That it?"

"If it is, it comes with a .44 caliber hole." The soldier bent down and dug his dad's gun from the snow. "Can you believe that? The only kit he carried was a fuckin' 1911."

"They don't make spooks like him anymore."

The two men dragged his dad by the arms over the snow and laid him beside the Colonel. His eyes were open.

"Let's just hope the kid shut it down in time."

The two of them looked at Billy.

"He's in shock."

Billy sat barefoot on the porch and looked out over the empty pasture at all the melting snow. The men who had occupied the property were gone. They dressed his shoulder, cleaned the shrapnel out of his back and leg, and gave him a bottle of pills, which he had no intention to take.

From where he sat he could see the Patriarch Run, his entire driveway, and most of the road down to the highway. He watched the traffic, which at his elevation was silent, and thought about all that road had carried. He thought about the old man in the basement of the hotel, the world in the old man's dream.

When he stood up, he saw the flag on the pole in the yard. He had raised it the morning he and Maiden went out to find Moses. No one had taken it down. It was frayed from the storm and no longer a fitting emblem for display.

Billy stood solemnly in the snow before he lowered the flag. He folded it and removed it from the halyard the way one would undress and bathe a deceased lover.

He found his essay about Noah on the desk in the living room and remembered that he would graduate high school next week. Billy took the matches from the desk and built a fire. He stoked the flames with his breath until he could feel the suck of the air.

He watched the embers of the flag float up the chimney and thought about what the Colonel had told him. He tried to figure it out, to at least understand what it was his dad was trying to accomplish.

Billy thought about the sheriff and squeezed his eyes. His face tightened. The remaining fabric hovered, blackened, in the flames.

When the flag was consumed, Billy pulled the letter his dad had written out of his pocket and fed it to the fire.

He walked back to the porch. The sheriff had died protecting him. He had killed his own father. Billy held the porch rail in his hands and tried to comprehend that. To make some sort of peace with it.

RACHEL RODE YOUNG SAM THROUGH THE ASPENS. THE LEAVES WERE orange, some of them already drifting to the earth. In the evening light, the mountain looked as if it were on fire. She climbed up through the ponderosas and came to the same junction she arrived at nearly a decade ago. She hadn't ridden the trail to the right since the afternoon she invited Regan to supper.

She took it again.

The horse climbed over the mountain's shoulder, stepped out of the spruce forest and onto the packed scree. As Young Sam walked the cliff, Rachel watched a turkey vulture circling on a thermal below.

She hadn't slept since May. Most nights she rocked in Regan's chair, painted, or, until he left for college, stood in the bedroom doorway listening to Billy's sleep.

She stopped the horse at the same bristlecone pine tree. Dismounted and unpacked Regan's eleven hundred dollar boots and an oil painting.

The canvas was in a wooden frame. The two of them were holding hands, falling. A wall of granite behind them. Neither of them were clothed. Her hair was pulled upward by the wind. Regan's eyes were closed.

Rachel walked now with crutches. She untied them from the horse. Then she took out a length of parachute chord and tied one end of the rope around the tree. She made a noose out of the other end.

The vulture circled upward, the tip of its banked wing less than a dozen yards from the gnarled branches. It looked Rachel in the eye then banked away.

She hobbled to the edge with the help of her crutches and felt the warm air rising through her blouse.

She told Regan that Billy left the day she hung the painting on the wall. She told him about Charlie. That he was doing okay as the new sheriff. She told him that she'd finally gotten around to mending the fence.

Then she told Regan that without him, life was hard.

"The truth of it is, if I'm not Billy's mother, if I'm not your lover, I don't know who I am anymore."

She began to shake. She felt the wind tugging on the canvas in her hands. She was unstable.

"But I'd like to find out." Her voice was strained, and she struggled to control it. "When you told me to love myself, I'm not sure you were in a position to realize how difficult that would be. It's different where you are, Regan. It just is."

Rachel looked down at the highway. Her elevation was too great to make out the flowers, but she could see the place where Regan died.

"I know what you were trying to tell me. That that's been the motivation all along. Maybe so. Maybe in my case it's just sheer willfulness."

She didn't have anything else to say. She slipped the noose around the painting's frame, stood in the wind for a minute then told him, "I best be gettin' along."

Rachel opened her hands and let it go.

PATRIARCH RUN

A Reader's Guide

A Note from the Author

I wanted to take a moment to thank you for finding me. Making a connection with you is the highlight of my work. If you enjoyed the story, I'd really appreciate it if you'd take a moment to write a review of *Patriarch Run* at your favorite online retailer. Such an act of kindness would go a long way in helping me connect to other readers.

You can find the interviews I conducted with Jack before he died and with Rachel and Billy at the back of this book.

I'm also including a discussion guide. It's probably come to your attention, by now, that I write about themes that matter a great deal to me. For example, the plot of this book is premised on two under-reported, existential threats we face as a species: overpopulation and a civilization absolutely dependent on a vulnerable power grid. There are three types of events that could trigger the scenario outlined in this book: a cyberattack, an electromagnetic pulse (EMP) attack, and a coronal mass ejection. That last event is naturally occurring and does not require any human malice or intent.

A theme, perhaps, even more pertinent to the fate of the human species is our relationship with ourselves. At its core, *Patriarch Run* is a coming-of-age story. It's about two types of fathers, one who sacrifices himself for his son and one who sacrifices his son for his mission. Rachel teaches us that we need to learn to love ourselves if we're going to have anything to offer any one else. In that sense, the story is about making choices, about the type of father, the type of mother we aspire to be.

If these subjects are interesting to you, I'd be happy to engage you more in the discussion guide.

Please remember to write that review. It would mean a lot to me.

Benjamin Dancer

Interview with Jack Erikson
Spring 2010

Benjamin: Jack, it's hard not to think of you as the bad guy. Your intent seems to be mass murder on a scale never seen before in human history.

Jack: I don't know how I can be seen in any other light. If I'm successful, there will be several billion deaths following my own.

Benjamin: I'm having a hard time with that statement. You don't seem like a malicious person. You obviously care deeply about your family. You've spent your life helping those without power to help themselves. I just can't make sense of what you're saying.

Jack: If I'm right in my calculations, the catastrophe I intend to inflict is the only way to save us from a much larger catastrophe in the future.

Benjamin: I'm sorry, but that sounds like crazy talk.

Jack: Do the math. At a growth rate of just one percent, which seems quite low, the human population will double every seventy years. How many people will be suffering from hunger seventy years from now? And if you manage to feed them, how much bigger can the population get before the whole ecosystem comes crashing down? We are in the midst of the Holocene extinction, the Sixth extinction. To do nothing is to doom us and all we know and love to Earth's long and storied fossil record.

Benjamin: Let's assume, for the sake of argument, that your math is right. Isn't there another way? Can't we reach sustainability humanely?

Jack: Obviously, I've come to a different conclusion.

Benjamin: I don't understand. You seem like a good guy. How could you . . . ?

Jack: There is a lot working against a humane solution, namely our own biology. We are wired to reproduce. We are wired for growth, for colonization. It's what we do as a species. We're aggressive. We're territorial. Listen, you're never going to get the elk to stop breeding. They need a wolf to be kept in balance, as do we.

Benjamin: But birth rates are falling in developed nations.

Jack: Yes, they are. And the global population continues to grow. There's not enough planet to pamper us all the way we pamper the West. The timeline for action is finite.

Benjamin: What about your wife, your son?

Jack: We have to share the sacrifice.

Benjamin: You know you sound like a madman, right?

Jack: We've evolved for self-preservation, the preservation of the family, the tribe. Which means we will reproduce. That's our evolutionary programing. We did not evolve to consider the whole planet in our quest for security. Our instincts are more short-sighted, self-centered, more primal.

Benjamin: That sounds so cynical. You make it sound like we're animals.

Jack: And you make it sound like we're not.

Benjamin: If you're right, if you get everything you want, if you reduce the number, all you're buying is time. It'll happen again.

Jack: That's someone else's problem.

Benjamin: Listen, I don't want to talk about the math. I know there's a heart beating in your chest. I've seen it. Your son, Jack. What about your son?

Jack slowly shook his head. His eyes grew red and filled with tears. Then he ended the interview.

INTERVIEW WITH RACHEL ERIKSON
Fall 2010

Benjamin: You might be my favorite person. I don't know anybody else like you.

Rachel: You're kind to me.

Benjamin: I'm serious, Rachel. What you did, what you endured. How is it you never gave up?

Rachel: You might be giving me a little too much credit on that account. If you'll recall, I did give up. It was too much for me.

Benjamin: You're referring to your grief, to your death?

Rachel: Yes.

Benjamin: That's not the way I see it. I think Billy's alive today because of you, because of your fierce love.

Rachel: I don't know what to say about that.

Benjamin: It seems to me that your relationship with Billy has changed. That when he left for college there was some sort of tension between the two of you.

Rachel: Yes. Billy killed his father. He hasn't been the same since.

Benjamin: That must be hard for you.

Rachel: He is in a place right now where I can't reach him.

Benjamin: You mean emotionally?

Rachel: Yes.

Benjamin: I just want you to know that I think you're a great mom. Billy is lucky to have you.

Rachel: That's kind of you to say. But there's an open wound in this family.

Benjamin: I can see that this is a painful subject. I think we can move to another. What do you make of the Blackout?

Rachel: I hope they get it figured out. Winter's coming. I donated my bison herd to help feed the town of Patriarch, as we haven't seen a delivery truck in this county for several weeks.

INTERVIEW WITH BILLY ERIKSON
Fall 2010

Benjamin: I see they've closed the campus.

Billy: Yes. They're trying to send us home. But there's no transportation.

Benjamin: The fuel shortage?

Billy: Yes.

Benjamin: When was the last time you talked to your mom?

Billy: A couple days before I left to come here.

Benjamin: You miss her?

Billy: I guess.

Benjamin: What are your plans?

Billy: I don't know.

Benjamin: I could help you get home.

Billy: That's a kind offer, Mister, but I've got to do some things first.

Benjamin: Like what?

Billy: I don't know.

Benjamin: If I can help you in any way . . .

Billy: Thank you.

Billy stood up. He looked around the room. Then he shook my hand and left.

Discussion Guide

If we can look at being a parent, for the moment, as a spectrum of choices between sacrificing yourself for your children (Regan) on one end and sacrificing your children for your mission (Jack) on the other end, where is it you'd like to be on that spectrum?

Is Jack the good guy or the bad guy?

The way I see it, Rachel saved Regan's life on that cliff's edge. What is it she did? Why do you think he didn't jump?

Billy killed his dad. Would you have pulled the trigger? How do you think one recovers from that?

Rachel survives a lot in order to learn to love herself, to offer grace and compassion to herself. What does her journey mean to you?

If you could take one of the characters in Patriarch Run out to lunch, who would it be?

The story is written from three points of view (Rachel's, Billy's, and Jack's). All three characters are limited in their understanding of the events that take place. And all three of them have misconceptions about those events. That being said, the reader is aware of the big picture through all their perspectives. How does that structure enhance the tension of the narrative?

Imagine a world in which the power went out for an extended period of time. Let's say for months. How would you eat? Drink? What do you think would happen to your community as the weeks went by? Remember, fuel production is as vulnerable as the grid.

Below are a few resources you can explore if you want to learn more about the vulnerability of our critical infrastructure to cyberattack, EMP attack, or to a coronal mass ejection.

EMP Commission Report:
- http://www.empcommission.org/docs/A2473-EMP_Commission-7MB.pdf

Coronal Mass Ejection:
- http://www.npr.org/sections/13.7/2016/04/06/473238503/when-the-sun-brings-darkness-and-chaos

Advocacy groups:
- securethegrid.com

- empactamerica.org
- eiscouncil.com

What effect does an increasing population have on the ecosystem which sustains us?

There are over seven billion humans alive today. We all need to eat. We all need clothes. We all need shelter. Most of us will secure means of transportation, comfort, entertainment. All these things require energy to produce. And all these things are being provided by the finite resources of our planet. What do you think is a sustainable number for our population?

When I interviewed Jack, he was unapologetic about his intention. If it were up to you to talk him out of it, what would you offer as a humane solution?

Below are a few organizations with a range of philosophies that I've partnered with in order to provide some resources to learn more about the sustainability of the human population.

- populationmedia.org
- populationinstitute.org
- growthbusters.org
- populationmatters.org
- populationinstitutecanada.ca
- biologicaldiversity.org
- populationconnection.org
- footprintnetwork.org
- worldwatch.org

National security is viewed as an issue on the right, politically, and sustainability as an issue on the left. It seems to me that renewable energy (wind, solar, geothermal, etc.) could contribute a lot to the interests of both parties. What role might renewables have in making a more secure and more sustainable civilization?

I'd be very interested in having a conversation with you. You can meet me at my website to explore these ideas further. BenjaminDancer.com.

The Western Lonesome Society

A Debut Novel by Robert Garner McBrearty

978-1-942280-12-5

In this hilarious, poignant Western, Jim O'Brien writes the quixotic saga of his ancestors who grew up with a tribe of Comanches. As his grip on reality loosens, O'Brien weaves into the tale modern day stalkers, drug dealers, secret agents, strippers, a mad linguist, an imaginary therapist, Ernest Hemingway, and an RV trip through the soul of the West. Having been displaced, each of the characters must embark on the Great American Quest for a place to truly call home.

MORE GREAT BOOKS FROM CONUNDRUM PRESS

Glassmusic

A novel by Rebecca Snow

978-1-942280-01-9

In the serene fjordlands of Norway in the early twentieth century, Ingrid has led a blissful childhood until she becomes holder of her family's secrets. Her father, a blind preacher who ministers through sacred music played on glassware, increasingly relies on Ingrid to see for him even as it threatens to tear apart his marriage. And after she witnesses an assault against her sister, Ingrid must decide when to speak and when to remain silent. *Glassmusic* explores the sometimes devastating realities of loyalty and jealousy, with philosophy, music, and love serving as guides.

Thin Blue Smoke

A Novel about Music, Food and Love
by Doug Worgul

978-1-942280-11-8

LaVerne Williams is a ruined ex-big league ballplayer and ex-felon with an attitude problem and a barbecue joint to run. Ferguson Glen is an Episcopal priest and fading literary star with a drinking problem and past he's running from. A.B. Clayton and Sammy Merzeti are two lost souls in need of love, understanding and another cigarette. *Thin Blue Smoke* is an epic American redemption tale. It is a story of love and loss, hope and despair, God and whiskey, barbecue and the blues. Hilarious and heart-rending, sacred and profane, this book marks the emergence of a vital new voice in American fiction.

Cinematic States

Stories We Tell,
the American Dreamlife,
and How to Understand Everything*
by Gareth Higgins

978-1-938633-17-1

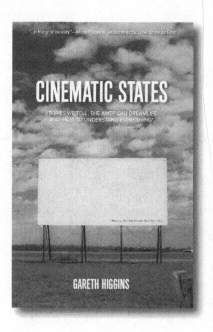

Northern Irish writer Gareth Higgins explores American myths in one of their most powerful forms. This irreverent yet moving journey through each of the 50 states of his adopted homeland asks what do the stories we tell reveal about ourselves, and how can we reimagine who we are? Scott Teems says *Cinematic States* is "thoughtful and unique and insightful and funny. It's unlike anything I've ever read."